MIRACLE
in a
DRY SEASON

MIRACLE

in a

DRY SEASON

SARAH LOUDIN
THOMAS

BETHANYHOUSE
a division of Baker Publishing Group
Minneapolis, Minnesota

Published by Bethany House Publishers
11400 Hampshire Avenue South
Bloomington, Minnesota 55438
www.bethanyhouse.com

Bethany House Publishers is a division of
Baker Publishing Group, Grand Rapids, Michigan

Printed in the United States of America

Library of Congress Cataloging-in-Publication Data
Thomas, Sarah Loudin.
Miracle in a dry season / Sarah Loudin Thomas.
pages cm
Summary: "In small town West Virginia, 1954, one newcomer's special gift with food produces both gratitude and censure. Will Perla Long and her daughter find a home there?"— Provided by publisher.
ISBN 978-0-7642-1225-3 (pbk.)
1. Single mothers—Fiction. 2. Bachelors—Fiction. 3. Women cooks—Fiction. 4. Public opinion—Ficiton. 5. West Virginia—Fiction. I. Title.
PS3620.H64226M57 2014
813'.6—dc23 2014003681

Song lyrics quoted: "Shall We Gather at the River," Robert Lowry, 1864; "Are You Washed in the Blood?", Elisha Hoffman, 1878; "I'll Fly Away," Albert Brumley, 1932, "In the Sweet By and By," Sanford F. Bennett, 1868.

Scripture quotations are from the King James Version of the Bible.

This is a work of fiction. Names, characters, incidents, and dialogues are products of the author's imagination and are not to be construed as real. Any resemblance to actual events or persons, living or dead, is entirely coincidental.

Cover design by Kathleen Lynch
Cover photography by ©Debra Lill/Trevillion Images

Author is represented by Books & Such Literary Agency

14 15 16 17 18 19 20 7 6 5 4 3 2 1

For Jim,
who sees the best in me and encourages me
to live up to it.

1

Wise, West Virginia
1954

CASEWELL'S STOMACH GRUMBLED. He hoped no one in the surrounding pews could hear it. He'd thought to eat some warmed-over biscuits this morning, but the barn cat had slipped into the house and found the bread wrapped in a dish-cloth on the back of the stove. Even though most of a biscuit remained, Casewell knew better than to eat after a cat.

His stomach growled a little louder, and he wondered what he could rustle up for dinner. Normally, he'd have Sunday dinner with his parents, but they were visiting his aunt, who had lost her son—his cousin Harold—in the Korean War a good two years ago. She had yet to get her feet back under her, as his mother put it, so they visited when they could. In the meantime, Casewell would fend for himself.

He could scramble an egg and fry a potato, but he'd burned more than one pot of beans, and his attempts at biscuits and corn bread never browned right. He'd always assumed he'd leave his parents' house for a home with a wife in it, but at the advanced age of thirty-five, he lived alone in a house he'd built with his own two hands.

Pastor Longbourne invited the congregation to bow their heads for the closing prayer. Casewell sighed and did as asked. The pastor could get windy at the close of service, and Casewell thought to pray for a short prayer but decided it wasn't proper. He shifted his six-foot-four frame on the hard pew to find a better position and scratched his jaw where his red beard covered a scar that ran from his ear to the corner of his mouth. The wound had healed decades ago but still itched from time to time. A reminder of . . . Casewell forced his attention to the prayer. He didn't need any reminders.

The prayer was indeed long, and toward the end, Casewell's belly growled loud enough for the dearly departed in the cemetery outside to hear. He heard a giggle from the pew behind him. He dared to peek over his shoulder. A child—a little girl of perhaps five or six—covered her mouth as her mother placed a quieting hand on her shoulder. The girl stilled, but she grinned at Casewell so he forgave her giggles. He was grateful his parents weren't there to hear. His father would not hesitate to offer criticism.

"Amen," intoned Pastor Longbourne, and the congregation echoed him.

The pastor walked to the door of the church, and his flock began filing out past him, shaking his hand and offering compliments on the sermon. Waiting his turn, Casewell got a better look at the little girl and her mother—at least he assumed this was her mother. They were new to the church. The pair appeared to be accompanying Robert and Delilah Thornton, who lived in the heart of the little community of Wise—such as it was. Robert kept the one small store that served the immediate area. Locals had to drive eighteen miles to reach a chain grocery store, and no one there would know the local gossip, so the Thorntons did well enough. Perhaps the woman and child were family come to visit.

The woman stopped to speak to the pastor, offering her hand and ducking her head. A little thing, she had cornsilk hair under a scrap of a hat, rosy cheeks, and pink lips. She was pretty enough, but Casewell knew pretty didn't guarantee pleasant.

The little girl peeped out at Casewell from behind her mother's skirt and giggled. He grinned back without even meaning to. And there was little point in considering how pretty her mama was—nice or not—since there was almost certainly a papa in the picture.

Casewell's turn to clasp Pastor Longbourne's hand finally came, and then he stepped out into the soft spring air of the churchyard, eager to make his way through the crowd so he could head home and find something to eat. He could always resort to a jelly sandwich, though it would be a far cry from his mother's Sunday fried chicken.

As he walked through the crowd, Casewell caught snatches of conversation.

"... young when she had the child ..."

"... what kind of husband would ..."

"... too pretty for her own good ..."

Casewell fought the urge to plug his ears. As he neared the gate to the churchyard, Delilah Thornton intercepted him and grasped his arm. "Casewell, allow me to introduce my niece, Perla. She's staying with us ... for a time. You might remember her family—they moved from here back in '45."

Casewell wondered at the slight hesitation, but then Perla

stood before him, and her clear, blue eyes completed the pretty picture he'd been noticing inside. She smiled, though there was something solemn lingering around her eyes.

"Pleasure to meet you," he said, dredging up a vague memory of a girl with blond curls. "And is this your daughter?"

The little girl smiled up at him as she clung to her mother's leg. "This is Sadie," Perla said, placing a hand on the child's strawberry-blond curls. "She has little to say but finds a great deal to laugh at." Sadie giggled again, as if to prove her mother right.

At that moment Casewell's belly rumbled so long and loud that there was no question of pretending otherwise. Casewell felt his ears grow warm and scuffed a boot in the dirt.

"I'm afraid I missed my breakfast this morning," he said. "And I had best be getting home to my dinner."

He gave the group a nod and started toward the gate when Delilah said, "But your family is off visiting. I'm guessing there's not much in your cupboard. Please come eat with us."

"Right, Casewell," Robert said. "Put your boots under our table. There's a mighty fine pork roast in the oven at home, and Perla here has a knack for gathering spring greens. I know you won't get a better meal in all the county."

Casewell opened his mouth to decline, but after one look into Perla's china eyes, he heard himself agreeing to go along. He blamed his moment of weakness on the promised pork roast. The group walked toward the Thorntons' 1949 Chevy sedan. Casewell admired how good it still looked after several years of use—certainly better than his beat-up '38 truck with the paint peeling off the fenders. Sadie left her mother's side and slipped a little hand into Casewell's large, rough one. She looked up at him with huge brown eyes, and he felt his heart squeeze. Whether or not the mother charmed him, the daughter certainly did.

The pork roast sat succulent under a crisp, roasted layer of fat. Casewell cut his portion carefully so he got a little fat with each bite. He also ate turnips boiled and mashed with butter and cream, fresh-baked light bread, and the promised greens wilted in bacon grease. Casewell was beside himself.

After eating his fill, he sighed and pushed his chair back a little. "That might've been the best meal I've ever eaten," he said. "I thank you."

"Perla did most of this," Delilah said, smiling at the younger woman. "She claims she needs to work for her keep, but of course she doesn't."

Perla ducked her head and scrubbed at Sadie's chin, as though the speck of grease from the greens couldn't wait another minute.

"And you'd best take home a mess of these leftovers," Robert said. "It's the darnedest thing—anytime Perla cooks we seem to have leftovers for a week."

Casewell protested but not very long or loud.

"Come see my dolly," Sadie said, breaking into the adult conversation.

Perla shushed her daughter. "Don't be silly, sweetheart. Casewell is a grown man and men don't take much interest in dolls."

"I make it a habit not to contradict pretty ladies," Casewell said, feeling expansive. "But I'd be pleased to see Miss Sadie's dolly."

Sadie jumped up; then she plopped back down. "May I be excused?" she asked.

"Yes, you may, but don't keep Mr. Casewell long. We'll have some dessert out on the porch directly."

These were quite possibly the only words that could add to Casewell's feeling of satisfaction with his current lot in life. He stood and allowed the little girl to lead him into what Delilah referred to as the parlor. Casewell sat on the Victorian sofa with its high back and lumpy cushions. It sloped in such a way that Casewell felt the need to dig his heels into the carpet to keep from sliding onto the floor.

Sadie made a beeline for the corner, where a doll sat on a block of wood with a small board propped up behind it to form a simple chair.

"This is Amy," she said, retrieving the doll. "She knows my secrets."

"It's important to have someone you can trust with your secrets," Casewell said. "But then, you probably don't have too many yet."

"Only the one about not having a daddy," Sadie said with a sigh. "Everyone else has a daddy, but Mommy says it's our lot in life to get along without one."

Casewell raised his eyebrows. A widow, then. Or she was . . . well, surely she was a widow. He started to ask and then caught himself. What a question to ask a child.

"Well, it's good you have Amy," he said. Then his eyes fell on the makeshift chair. "But is this all the furniture she has?"

"Yes," Sadie said. "Mommy says I mustn't leave Amy on the big people furniture, so she made me this chair. I wish Amy could have a bed, too, but she sleeps with Mommy and me for now. Mommy says that's okay, since it's just us."

Casewell smiled to himself, thinking that he knew how he could thank Perla for the fine meal she'd prepared that day.

Delilah called them to the porch for dessert—huge slices of angel cake with sliced and sugared strawberries.

"The chickens have taken a laying fit," Delilah said as she handed Casewell a slice big enough for two men. "Got to use all them eggs up somehow."

Although the slice was large, it was so light and airy Casewell made short work of it. He declined a second slice for fear he might appear a glutton.

"Too bad you don't have your mandolin with you," Robert said. "A sweet piece of music would be just the tonic to settle that meal."

Casewell grinned. He would play a piece of music anywhere, anytime, for anyone. Music was the only thing he liked better than a good meal cooked by a pretty woman.

"You're a musician?" Perla asked.

"Oh, some would call me that, but I mostly just fool around with the mandolin my granddaddy gave me. I guess it wouldn't hurt your ears."

Robert laughed. "Casewell is one of the finest musicians in Hartwell County. He's being modest. We'll have to get up a dance here before too long—maybe after the spring planting gets in. You put Casewell on the mandolin, George Brower on the banjo, Steve Cutright on the fiddle, and sometimes I pitch in with the harmonica or some spoons, and you've got something you can shake a leg to. 'Course, Casewell here likes them solemn tunes that wail. But he'll save them till everybody's too tired to dance. Yes sir, mighty fine, mighty fine."

"Oh, that would be fun," Delilah said. "We haven't had a dance in ever so long. I'll start putting a bug in the ears of all the ladies as they come by the store." She smiled at Perla. "It's always up to the women to organize something like this. The men just come when we tell them and eat up all the food."

Perla's smile seemed a little uncertain. She bit her lower lip. "I'm not sure I ought to be dancing," she said.

"Whyever not?" Delilah asked.

"Well, with Sadie and all . . ."

"Nonsense. And anyway, if you don't want to dance, you can sit and listen. There's plenty of ladies who prefer to sit out the dancing and visit."

"The old ladies," Robert said with a snort. "And it would serve them better to exercise their feet and let their tongues rest a minute."

Delilah frowned and Casewell tried to hide his smile.

"Oh, do have a little dignity," Delilah said. "Perla can help with the food. She has such a knack for cooking, and we always seem to have too much for just us. What she needs is a crowd to feed."

Casewell stood. "Well, I, for one, would be happy to play and to eat anything Perla cares to cook. Count me in. But for now, I'll be heading home to tidy up my place before Ma gets back and has a fit over how I've let things go."

"Bachelors," Delilah said in a way that sounded scornful and affectionate all at once.

Sadie scampered inside to bring Casewell his Sunday hat. He dropped to one knee so she could help settle it on his head. Casewell felt self-conscious and awkward until he looked up and caught Perla watching him. The look in her eyes made him hope, against his better judgment, that she was a widow.

After helping Delilah tidy the kitchen, Perla went to the room she now occupied at her aunt and uncle's house. Her gaze drifted from object to object. The quilt her grandmother made lay folded across the foot of the bed, the Bible her mother gave her when she turned eighteen sat on the bedside table, her brush and comb on the dressing table. It was the sort of room she'd always dreamed of calling her own.

Her eyes came to rest on the child napping peacefully on top of the coverlet. Here was something she had not dreamed of. She adored her ginger-haired Sadie, just turned five, but some days being a mother was simply too hard. And now this.

Perla's mother had agreed that it was probably for the best when Perla suggested going to Wise to stay with her aunt and uncle. "Robert and Delilah have a real nice place. Least it was last time I went out there," her mother had said, as if that would make leaving easier. "You probably remember the store well enough from when we lived there. You can be a help in the store. Won't nobody know . . ."

Perla thought back to her mother's final words before her father drove her—in silence—the six hours from Comstock to Wise. "You hold your head up," her mother said. "If it weren't for all that food, I think folks would overlook . . . the child. But take the two together, and it makes everyone uneasy." Perla remembered her mother stepping forward to take her hand, squeezing it hard. "Daughter, God doesn't make mistakes, and I say that child and your way with cooking are both miracles straight from heaven. It's just miracles don't always feel like it at the time."

Perla hadn't wanted to come. She might have even whined about it a little. She'd certainly carried on more than a grown woman of twenty-four should. When her mother released her hand, Perla missed the pressure and the warmth. She'd felt oddly bereft standing there in her parents' house. She'd tried to tell herself she could always come back.

2

At home, it took Casewell all of twenty minutes to move his boots from the chair by the fireplace to the rug by the door, hang up some clothes lying around his bedroom, and sweep the living room and kitchen. Thanks to the Thorntons and the cat, there weren't any dishes to wash and he decided to leave the dusting. His mother would be sorry if she didn't have something to do when she came to check on him.

Not that she would ever criticize him one way or the other. No, that was his father's job. Casewell had been trying to please his father for decades. It wasn't that his father was unkind; it was more a matter of not knowing what he was thinking—good or bad. Casewell tended to suspect it was bad.

Chores done, Casewell walked across the backyard to a stout little outbuilding that he had designed and built. It had a wide ramp leading up to the door so he could drive his tractor in and out. Heavy beams above were open so he could slide boards up there for storage—he could even put together a makeshift second floor that would hold boxes or cast-off tools he wasn't ready to part with. One side of the building held the tractor and tools he needed for farmwork. The far side held his woodworking tools—his treasures.

Casewell stepped up to his worktable and handled several scraps of lumber stacked underneath. There were a couple of nice pieces of maple that he thought would be perfect. He set to work on his thank-you gift for Perla and Sadie.

The next morning, Casewell needed to put aside work on his gift to visit Elizabeth and Evangeline Talbot. Before church, the twin sisters, nearing their seventies, had asked Casewell to stop by Monday morning so they could discuss a project with him. Casewell was curious what they might want him to do—likely something around the old homeplace they'd inherited when their parents died within days of each other. Although the Talbot sisters had sold off the farm equipment and a fifty-two-acre parcel of rich bottomland, they'd kept the rambling farmhouse they'd lived in since birth. Probably the banister needed repair or a doorsill was rotting.

Casewell pulled up under a large oak with leaves just starting to unfurl. He was admiring the tree when a voice came from the porch.

"Once they're the size of squirrels' ears, it's time to plant corn."

Casewell turned and saw Angie—no, Liza—standing on the top step, smiling at him.

Strangers often had a hard time telling the twins apart, but those who knew them had no such difficulty. Both were a whisper over five feet tall, with silvery hair braided and twisted into a bun at the nape of the neck. But somehow, Angie's hair remained perfectly in place, while Liza's tended to fray and fall in wisps around her face. And while they both had blue eyes, Angie's had a hint of ice, while Liza's looked like faded cornflowers.

Liza had been engaged once, but her fiancé, Frank Post, ran off with Buffalo Bill's Wild West Show on a tour of Europe in 1902. By the time he came home some thirty years later, everyone had given him up for dead, and Liza was running the farm alongside her sister and father. Once old man Talbot was too feeble to work the fields, the twins did most of the farming themselves.

"Howdy, Casewell. Come on in. Sister and I have a special order for you." Liza clapped her hands, looking like a child on Christmas morning.

Inside, the more staid Angie showed Casewell the large kitchen and the wall where she wanted a cupboard.

"We'd like to display Mama's china and a few other things," she explained.

"Oh, and a pie safe," Liza said. "And a potato bin—the kind that tilts out."

"But nothing fancy," Angie said. "This is for practical use. No need for fancy."

"It's our seventieth birthday." Liza's faded eyes sparkled. "And this will be our present."

"No need to tell our age, sister. And we need a cupboard, birthday or no." Angie turned sharp eyes on Casewell. "But the price has to be right. We must be good stewards of what Mama and Papa left us."

Casewell pulled a piece of paper and a stub of pencil out of his breast pocket. He made a rough sketch of what he had in mind, the sisters looking over his shoulder and nodding along. When it was done to their satisfaction, Casewell penciled a number in the corner. Angie pursed her lips and then gave a brief nod.

Back in his workshop that evening, Casewell began the actual construction based on his pencil drawing. He often gave thanks for his ability to earn a living doing something he loved so dearly. Smoothing his rough hands over the sawn lumber, he could feel the shape of the furniture rising up to meet him. The smell of sawdust and the rhythm of the plane sliding along the grain soothed him in a deep, soul-satisfying way. He could lose himself for hours in his workshop, missing meals and working until he became aware of the time only after losing light with the setting sun.

He had pieced together the shell of the cabinet and was settling in to address some of the finer details when he heard a light scuffling at the door. Turning, he smelled the cigarette smoke even before he saw his father leaning against the frame. John Phillips was a tall, lanky man with a shock of white hair that had once been coal-black. Dad's narrow face, lined from days spent working the farm, stood out starkly tan against his white hair. Although not traditionally handsome, he was striking with an unbending air. Casewell rarely saw him without a hand-rolled cigarette, squinting against the smoke rising past his eyes.

As his father moved into the workshop, Casewell noted that his limp seemed more pronounced. He'd worked briefly in the mines, but a cave-in took his only brother's life and left him with a hitch to his gait that served as a constant reminder of what he'd lost. John swore he would never mine again, and he'd held to that promise, even in years when the farm lost steadily and the income from a few months of mining would have been welcome.

Casewell saw the limp but knew better than to mention it. His father didn't leave much room for weakness in himself or in others. He would not have appreciated his son noticing his discomfort.

"Your mother is over at the house fussing about," Dad said, drawing smoke deep into his lungs. He exhaled. "I told her you're a grown man able to take care of yourself, but she never could leave well enough alone."

Casewell nodded, smiling to himself. If Emily Phillips were content to leave well enough alone, his father probably wouldn't have lived this long. She'd insisted Dad do the exercises that helped him regain the use of his foot. She'd made the garden stretch in the years when income from the farm was thin. And she'd traded her needlework—embroidered pillow slips, handkerchiefs, and baby gowns—for staples like sugar and coffee when the Thorntons had extended as much credit as they could. Casewell doubted his father knew what lengths his mother had gone to in order to keep the family going and knew no one would dare tell him.

"What's that you're working on?" he asked.

"A cupboard for the Talbot sisters. I plan to have it done before their birthday. It's their gift to each other."

"Don't know what two old ladies need with new furniture." He pinched the ember from his cigarette and dropped the stub in his breast pocket. "They've made do this long."

"They have," agreed Casewell, knowing better than to get into a drawn-out discussion about the advantages of improved storage for two women approaching seventy.

"Got anything an old man can do?"

This was a new development in their father-son relationship. While his father approved of Casewell being a carpenter, he'd not shown much interest in the work itself. In the past few months, he'd begun stopping by to lend a hand. Casewell didn't mind. His dad didn't have much to say, and he enjoyed the quiet companionship with a man whose love he'd never been sure of.

"You can sand down that door front," Casewell said, pointing with his chin. "I pulled the pieces with the nicest grain."

"So I see," he said.

They worked in silence for a time. Dad cleared his throat.

"Before I forget, your mother wants you to come to dinner this evening. She heard you ate Sunday dinner with the Thorntons, and I reckon she wants to know all about that niece of theirs staying with them."

Casewell smiled. "Sounds good."

"Reckon Emily will be about done messing in your business," he said. "Good work on that cupboard, son."

"Thank you, sir." Casewell supposed that was about as close as he'd ever come to hearing his father say he loved him.

That evening Casewell joined his parents for a meal of beans and corn bread. The beans had been cooking all day with ham hocks, and the cornmeal was ground from the Phillipses' own corn. His petite, dark-haired mother with the smiling gray-green eyes called this a poor man's supper. It didn't take her long to broach the subject she was most interested in.

"So tell me about Delilah's niece," she said to Casewell.

"Well, she sure can cook," he said and helped himself to another wedge of corn bread.

"That's a fine thing in a woman, to be sure," Mom said. "But what is she like?"

"She's pretty—yellow hair and blue eyes, I think. She didn't have a whole lot to say, but she seemed pleasant enough."

His mother sighed. "Like pulling teeth. Doesn't she have a child?"

"Yup, a funny little sprite. I think maybe I talked to her—Sadie, it is—more than her mother. She showed me her doll." Casewell racked his brain to think of something that would be of interest.

"And the father?" she urged.

"Don't rightly know," Casewell said. "The child said something . . ." he trailed off, fearing he was wandering into something too much like gossip.

"Said what?"

"Well, she's just a child. There's plenty of reasons for a woman to be visiting family without her husband." Casewell folded his napkin and shoved back from the table a notch.

His mother was not so easily dissuaded. "And how long are they staying? There's a rumor . . ."

"Enough, woman," Dad said. "You'll have to run down the other hens if you want to gossip about this new girl. Come out on the porch with me, son."

Casewell obediently followed his father while his mother began tidying the kitchen. Once outside, Dad fished the makings for a cigarette out of his breast pocket. He held a paper in one hand and shook out the tobacco from a tin with the other. He rolled the cigarette in a single motion, with the practice of years. He licked the edge to seal it and gave one end a twist. He struck a wooden kitchen match on a post and began puffing. His gnarled fingers were yellowed where he'd held a thousand cigarettes.

Casewell, like most of his peers, had experimented with smoking as a boy. He'd tried corn silks and grapevine and finally tried the real thing when his friend Carl stole the makings from an older cousin. Casewell wanted to smoke like his father, his grandfather, and his dead uncle, but he never could get the hang of it. Smoking didn't impress your friends when you were hacking and choking. He finally gave up trying and now was grateful a love for tobacco didn't drive him out on the porch all through the day and in all kinds of weather. His mother didn't allow smoking in the house, and Dad respected her in that.

"So this girl is good lookin', is she?" he asked.

"I suppose so," Casewell said. "But there's likely a husband somewhere, and even if she's a widow, there's sure enough a child. That's a whole other kettle of fish."

"True enough. Still, you're about the right age to think of settling down, and seems like no one around here has caught your eye. Though I've seen more than one try it." He slanted a look at Casewell. "It's a man's duty to find a good woman who can raise his children in the fear of God. And your ma probably wouldn't mind a grand-young'un or two."

This was quite possibly the longest speech Casewell had ever heard his father make. And he was surprised the man seemed to advocate for him to get involved with a woman he barely knew.

Casewell wanted to marry and have children. He thought of it often. But no woman had quite come up to his standards. He was looking for a God-fearing woman who would keep the house and raise well-behaved children. She needed to be smart enough to carry on a good conversation with him and to teach the children until they were old enough for school.

He'd taken notice of a young lady or two over the years. Even now he recognized that Melody Simmons probably wouldn't mind if he came calling, but pretty as she was, she was kin to the worst moonshining clan in the county. He aimed to stay clear of that bunch. And he certainly didn't want a woman with notions about working outside the home. Lately it seemed like all the women his age either married young or were "liberated."

The country was changing rapidly. While the Korean War had ended, Joseph McCarthy had the whole country on alert for Communists, and that Marilyn Monroe was setting a terrible example for women everywhere. Such things seemed very far away to Casewell. There were places back in the hills where folks still didn't have electricity or running water. Casewell didn't have a television set, though his parents had one, and he'd watched a few programs with them. He liked the westerns—*The Lone Ranger* and *Dragnet*—where the good guys won out in the end.

Casewell leaned against the side of the house and fished out a toothpick. "You're right, Dad, it is time I settled down, but even if this Perla is available, there's more to it than that."

"Right enough. Just thinking out loud."

After that the two men stood in silence and watched the light fade from the pasture and the woods. A deer walked into the far edge of the field and grazed her way down toward a pond. Casewell would have been willing to bet she had a fawn stashed somewhere nearby. But you'd never see it. He'd walked right up on fawns that he didn't see until he almost stepped on them. Nature knew how to protect her young.

At home that night Casewell found himself replaying the afternoon he'd spent with Perla and Sadie. There wasn't much to it, but what he did remember agreed with him. Perla behaved like Casewell tended to think a woman ought. She'd been mostly quiet, tending to her daughter and the meal. And as he'd noticed before, she was easy on the eyes. Now that he was beginning to think of Perla as perhaps more than just a guest passing through, he realized that he'd done very little to engage her in conversation. He and little Sadie had talked more than he and Perla did. Well, if Perla's visit lasted long enough, he'd have to remedy that.

3

THE FOLLOWING SUNDAY, Pastor Longbourne invited Casewell to play along with George and Steve during the service. They struck up a rousing version of "I'll Fly Away" that had even the staid Presbyterians tapping their toes. He saw Sadie stand up and dance a little before her mother coaxed her back into the pew. After church, the musicians were swamped by well-wishers, and Casewell watched Perla climb into the Thorntons' car as townsfolk blocked his path to the door.

That afternoon he went to see the Talbot sisters so that he could get their opinions on a few finishing touches for their cupboard. After giving him the information he needed, Liza and Angie insisted he stay and visit with them. They produced a pot of tea, and Casewell found himself sitting on a sprung sofa, trying to balance a teacup on his knee. With his mother's Sunday dinner in his belly and the twins' prattle in his ears, he had a hard time staying awake.

Casewell tried to pay attention as Liza turned her blue flannel eyes on him.

"We're not fond of gossip," she said. "But since you're a single man, you probably ought to know about that Perla Long."

Casewell jolted awake.

"Now, Liza," cautioned Angie, "we oughtn't to say anything until we know for sure that she's a harlot. It could just be mean talk over a pretty woman."

"I suppose you're right," Liza said. "Just because Melanie Saunders says she's never been married doesn't make it true."

"And the Bible is clear about carrying tales," Angie said.

Casewell felt as if the sisters were playing a game of badminton as they gently batted their bit of gossip back and forth in front of him. Angie turned to Casewell and gave him a tight smile.

"Pay no attention to us," she said. "Scandalous stories travel faster than plain ones, and we have no business telling you anything we're not sure of. Perla is probably a lovely young woman and Melanie Saunders is jealous."

Casewell had a dozen questions but didn't see his way clear to ask any of them. Liza apologized and turned the conversation to peonies and whether the ants they attracted were necessary to make them bloom, or if it was safe to knock the little pests off. As soon as he could do so politely, Casewell told Liza and Angie he'd have their cupboard for them by Thursday and took his leave.

He pondered what the sisters had to say about Perla. He was strongly opposed to gossip, but he couldn't very well unhear what the Talbots had said. He also couldn't think of a way to determine if what they had hinted at was true, short of asking Perla herself, and that he would not do. Casewell toyed with the idea of dropping some hints around his mother so that she might be inspired to do a little digging, but that felt wrong, too. Regardless, he found Perla Long somewhat less attractive at bedtime than he had when he'd awoken.

Casewell worked hard to finish the Talbot sisters' cupboard that week. The unfinished thank-you project for Perla and Sadie sat on the corner of his workbench. He worked around it for a couple of days and then packed it into a crate and pushed it under the bench. He'd get to it once the paid work was out of the way.

On Thursday Casewell loaded the finished piece of furniture into the back of his truck with the help of his father and carefully cushioned it with old quilts. He drove slowly over to the Talbots', smiling to himself. It was a fine piece of work, and he was glad the twins would have it. He charged them less than he could get elsewhere, but the Talbots weren't up on the current cost of handcrafted furniture, and he suspected they might faint if he charged what it was worth.

Liza and Angie were waiting for Casewell on their front porch, hands clasped and faces eager. Liza leaned out to see better as Casewell and his father began unloading the base of the cabinet. Angie frowned at her sister and stood up a little straighter.

As he lifted the furniture free of the tailgate, Dad stumbled slightly and Casewell had to lunge to take the bulk of the weight. Dad grunted and seemed to recover himself, so Casewell shrugged it off, supposing that neither of them were getting any younger. It was nothing.

"That's the bottom part, isn't it?" Liza asked.

"Of course it is," Angie said. "The top is still in the truck. Open the door for them."

The sisters got in the way only a little as they tried to help the men bring both pieces of the cupboard into the kitchen.

The two men settled the base into place and then centered the top against the wall. It fit perfectly and Casewell stood back, a twin on either side, to admire his work.

Liza sighed. "It's perfect."

"Well, nothing is perfect, but it's mighty close," Angie said. "Now let's see how it works."

The two women began placing rose-strewn china plates on the open shelves. A teacup in its saucer went in front of each plate. Then a teapot with sugar and creamer found a home on a doily on the far right side of the serving board. Once everything had been placed, the twins stepped back to check the overall effect. Liza sighed again but apparently did not feel the need to speak.

"Now," Angie said, rubbing her hands together, "let's check the workings."

She sent Casewell to fetch a sack of potatoes from the cellar, and he poured them into the potato bin while Angie tried all the doors and made sure the latch on the pie safe was to her satisfaction. She stepped back to stand beside Liza again and nodded once.

"We are quite pleased," she said. "Liza, fetch our purse."

Liza disappeared upstairs and soon returned with a well-worn black leather purse. Angie took it and unsnapped the clasp. She withdrew cash and carefully counted out the correct amount onto the kitchen table. She paused, looking torn, and then pulled out an additional five-dollar bill.

"This is for you and John for your trouble in delivering the cupboard," she said.

"Why, thank you, Angie, but that isn't necessary," Casewell said.

"I insist," Angie said, tapping the stack of bills. "Your work is solid and you delivered on time. John, you raised a good boy."

Dad grunted and nodded at Casewell. "Take it. You surely earned it," he said.

The sisters offered coffee and molasses cookies, which the men accepted. Casewell's father wasn't one for socializing, but the twins' cookies were legendary. They sat around the kitchen table while the women chattered on about how handsome the cabinet was, how it dressed up the room, and how nice it was not to have to go to the cellar for potatoes so often.

The talk eventually turned to the barn dance Delilah was getting up. The sisters were trying to decide what they would bring.

"Can't go wrong with a batch of them cookies," Dad said, making his first real contribution to the conversation.

"Oh, I know," Liza said. "But sometimes I get the urge to try something different. I just ordered the new *Better Homes and Gardens* cookbook, and oh my, there are some lovely things in there. So fancy." She looked wistful.

"Plain and good is better than fancy any day," Angie said, brushing imaginary crumbs from the tablecloth. "A basket of fried chicken and a plate of cookies always get eaten up."

"I suppose so," Liza said, looking disappointed.

"I hear that Perla Long is a mighty good cook," Angie said. "You've had her cooking, haven't you, Casewell?"

"Yes, I guess I have," he said. "And it was right tasty."

"What did she make?" Liza asked, leaning forward.

"Well, now, she made a fine mess of greens along with roast pork. Oh, and an angel cake for dessert."

Angie sniffed. "Angel cake only uses egg whites. It's a waste of yolks. Extravagant."

"It was good, though," Casewell said. "She sent some home with me, and I ate on it all week."

"Someone told me she always makes way more than is needed when she does the cooking," Liza said. "They have more leftovers than they know what to do with over there at the Thorntons'."

"No gossiping, sister," Angie said, then made a *tsk-tsk* sound. "Wasteful, wasteful."

"Time to go, son."

Casewell was surprised his father had tolerated sitting and visiting with the Talbot sisters this long. He was probably itching for a cigarette. Dad stood slowly, pushing himself upright from the edge of the table. It seemed to take him a moment to straighten his back.

Once outside, Casewell said, "Hope that heavy furniture wasn't too much for you, Dad. I'd hate to see you get down in the back."

He shot him a pointed look. "That'll be the day when I can't help my son deliver a few sticks of furniture." He pulled out his makings and built a cigarette, blowing smoke out the truck window in lieu of conversation.

Casewell pulled into his parents' driveway and watched his father climb out, waving a hand in his son's direction as he trudged toward the door. Casewell slid out of the truck and followed him in. Dad looked a little surprised but didn't comment.

"Thought I'd say hey to Mom," Casewell explained.

Once inside, Dad headed straight for the living room and settled onto the sofa with the newspaper. Emily was in the kitchen baking her homemade white bread.

"I'm so glad you came in," she said with a smile. "Let me get you something to eat."

Casewell laughed and stopped his mother from raiding the Frigidaire. "I had molasses cookies with the Talbot sisters," he said. "I'm fine."

"Well, you can take one of these loaves home with you as soon as they come out of the oven," she said, settling for feeding him later.

"So, Ma," Casewell said, hoping to sound casual, "everything all right with Dad? He seemed a little tired today."

"Did he?" Emily turned away to finish wiping down the counter where she'd kneaded her bread.

"Yeah. I figure it's nothing, but I wanted to check with you."

"Oh, I'm sure you're right," she said. "Probably didn't sleep well last night, and he's not as young as he once was. Scoot in there and read the paper with him. This bread will be out in ten minutes."

Casewell stuck his head in the living room and saw that his father was snoring softly with the paper open across his chest. Casewell stepped back into the kitchen.

"He's napping. Don't worry about the bread. I'll get some next time."

"Napping?" Casewell thought he heard a note of alarm in his mother's voice, but she quickly smoothed it over. "Well, then, I'm sure he just had a restless night." She nodded emphatically and Casewell wondered which of them she hoped to convince.

❧

Perla was grateful Sadie was such an easy child. The little girl rarely fussed and fit in with adults better than most children. She had an easygoing, cheerful way about her that somehow put grown-ups at ease. Perla noticed that people talked to Sadie without resorting to a high-pitched voice or silly questions. Sometimes Perla caught herself talking to Sadie about things the child had no business knowing—things about her father and their situation. Perla tried to remember that Sadie was five and needed protecting, but she had no one else to talk to. Sadie was a comfort, and Perla hoped that coming to Wise and removing them both from everything they knew hadn't been a mistake.

Robert and Delilah were lovely. They hadn't asked a lot of questions when Perla wrote to ask if she and Sadie could come stay for a while. Delilah just called and said of course they should come and stay as long as they liked. Perla had offered to pay a little rent or help out in some way, but the Thorntons refused adamantly. Perla missed her mother, but the looks and the whispers had gotten to the point that Perla knew the only thing to do was to go where no one, except Robert and Delilah, knew her story. Perla's mother, Charlotte, had protested but not very much. She came around much too quickly to the idea of her daughter and granddaughter leaving, and Perla thought maybe she sensed a certain level of relief.

The sisters had always been close. Just thirteen months apart in age, they had been mistaken for twins a time or two, and it was a comfort for Perla to have someone so like her mother fussing over her and Sadie. And then again, there were times Aunt Delilah reminded her so much of her mother that Perla would have to find a quiet corner to cry over missing her mother and regretting what she had done to shame her. Mother always said the shame wasn't on Perla, but the way the folks in Comstock acted, there was no doubt where they laid the blame.

The one thing the Thorntons had allowed Perla to do was to take over almost all of the cooking. With Robert and Delilah at the store most days, it helped to have Perla bringing them lunch around noon and having supper ready when they came home in the evening. Delilah used to come home an hour early to start dinner, but now she could take her time and help Robert close up each evening. Perla hoped that she was truly a help to her aunt and uncle. And she did have a knack with food.

Sometimes Perla's way with food unnerved her a little. She would take a chicken or some potatoes into her hands, and it seemed as if she didn't decide what to do with them—they decided for her. Almost before she knew what she planned, she'd have enough chicken and dumplings to feed half the county, or so many potatoes au gratin she couldn't find a pan big enough. And the food was good. People often told Perla she should write her recipes down, but she wasn't sure she could even remember what she put in them half the time. When she cooked, it was almost like she went into a trance and the rest of the world didn't matter; just transforming raw ingredients into something delicious and life sustaining was the closest Perla got to being happy.

No, Perla realized, not happy. She was happy when Sadie laughed or cuddled close. What she felt when she cooked was a deep, abiding peace. She might have preferred to cook all the time just to retain that feeling, but sometimes when she put a meal on the table, she realized that she had lost a chunk of time. She knew she'd been in the kitchen preparing food, but she could no more recount her movements than she could fly. Serving dinner was like waking up from a deep and restful sleep. And Perla worried that she neglected Sadie at those times.

4

AT CHURCH THAT SUNDAY it soon became obvious that Delilah had succeeded in stirring up interest in a barn dance. Within a week or so farmers would have their spring planting done, and barns were mostly empty with the past winter's hay having been fed out by now. After some lively discussion, it was decided that George Brower's barn would be the best spot. His barn had a large open room with the cowshed on the upper side where the hill behind offered some protection. Well into his fifties and never married, George kept the barn neater than his house. His being the banjo player clinched the deal, although there had been some muttering that George kept his place a little too "dry" for some of the men who liked a nip now and again.

They set the next Saturday as the date. The way the ladies buzzed around the churchyard after the service sent most of the men scurrying to bring cars around in hopes of getting Sunday dinner sooner rather than later. Even so, quite a few meals were late that day.

Casewell made arrangements with George and Steve to

hold practice that week so they'd be up to snuff for the dance. Robert caught wind and said he'd join them with his harmonica but not to count on him to play the whole time.

"Got to dance with my wife and that pretty niece of mine," he said with a wink.

The week flew by for Casewell. He wouldn't admit it, but he got lost in his music, and nothing satisfied his soul so much as sharing the sweet sounds he could draw from his mandolin with anyone inclined to listen. He not only played with the other members of their impromptu band that week, but also found himself pulling out his mandolin each evening and thinking over all the music he wanted to play on Saturday.

When Casewell rehearsed with the rest of the group, they mostly played lively dance tunes, but left to his own devices Casewell tended toward sweet, sorrowful music. He played "The Long Black Veil" almost every evening that week. Something about that song resonated deep in his soul. Sad, sinful song that it was, about a woman committing adultery with her husband's best friend, she deserved to walk those hills crying. Even so, Casewell's heart went out to the adulteress. He couldn't explain it and didn't care to try; he just lived in the music while he played.

By Saturday evening, the community was in an uproar. Women baked all day or fussed over what they would wear. The men hurried through farmwork or chores—more often at the behest of the women in their lives than of their own accord. By six that evening George's barn glowed from manger to hayloft. The main floor was clear for dancing, with plywood laid over some bales at the far end of the room to make a stage for the musicians. Two long trestle tables were set up to the side and filled with hams, biscuits, loaf bread, sliced beef, deviled eggs, pickles, cakes, pies, and cookies. Icy pitchers filled with sweet tea, lemonade, and punch sat at one end. Some of the men would almost certainly have a little something stronger in the trunks of their cars, but it was early yet, and the only thing anyone was drunk on was anticipation.

Casewell, George, and Steve had the crowd flat-footing across the floor in no time. Most folks had grown up doing the traditional Appalachian dance that was a cross between Irish step and tap dancing. The cacophony created by all those feet tapping and shuffling in time to mountain tunes made a music of its own, and an hour passed before Casewell knew it. Steve called a break for refreshments with a waggle of his eyebrows, which meant he had a little something stashed out back to perk him up. Casewell set his mandolin aside with the care a mother would use placing a baby in its cradle. He stretched and headed for the refreshment table.

"You boys are in fine form," Robert said, shaking Casewell's hand.

"Thought you were going to join us," Casewell said, grinning.

"Oh, I may yet—once I've wore myself out with eating and dancing," the older man said with a wink. "Now step right up here and fill you a plate. That's Delilah's hummingbird cake over there, but you'd better have a ham biscuit or two first. Perla brought that basket of biscuits over there, and although I've seen at least a dozen people reach into it, seems like they've hardly made a dent. Better fall to so you can keep your strength up. This crowd looks like it could dance all night."

Casewell let Robert talk on while he filled a plate with food. He made his way down the length of the table to where the drinks left wet rings on the tablecloth. Perla stood behind the table with a cup in her hand.

"Can I pour you a drink?" she asked.

"Sure," he said. "How about some of that sweet tea?"

Perla poured and Casewell had to confess that she looked like an angel standing there. A straw hat that was little more than a headband held her honey-wheat hair back from her brow and sent it cascading down her back. Her pink dress was cinched in at her waist, with a full skirt falling to below her knees. There was nothing suggestive about her clothes, but somehow she looked more womanly than any other female in the room. Casewell swallowed hard.

"Have you been enjoying the dance?" he asked.

"I've enjoyed watching it," Perla said. "I don't really know these dances. I guess I haven't had much of a chance to learn." She ducked her head and smoothed the cloth at the edge of the table with gloved hands.

"We'll do some square dancing here before long. It's easy to jump in on that. George will call the steps, and even if you don't understand, all you have to do is watch the other folks in your square."

"Maybe I'll try," Perla said, still pressing the tablecloth with her fingers.

Casewell felt the urge to protect her—from what he wasn't sure. "If I didn't have to play, I'd show you," he said, sounding like an eager schoolboy. He blushed and saw that Perla did, too. "Guess I'd better eat this." He rushed to fill the space between them with words. "They'll want to dance some more before long." He nodded once and went to sit on a corner of the stage to eat, wondering what in the world had just come over him.

Steve sauntered over, breath slightly boozy. "Fine-lookin' woman, that," he said, nodding toward Perla. "And from what I hear, might be she's easy to get on with."

"What do you mean by that?" Casewell asked, spine stiffening.

"Well, she's got that young'un and no man to speak of. Ain't but one way for a woman to get a child of her own." Steve winked and leered across the barn at an oblivious Perla.

Casewell felt a surge of anger, although he'd made some of the same sorts of assumptions without speaking them aloud. He wanted to defend Perla, but he couldn't think what to say. He really didn't know the woman, and Steve might be right. Casewell looked across the room, where Perla was helping some of the children to slices of cake. No, he didn't know how Perla came to be in Wise with a child and no husband, but he would do his best to give her the benefit of the doubt.

"I wouldn't know about that," Casewell said, "since I don't go around gossiping with the women much."

Steve flushed, then grinned and slapped Casewell on the back. "Reckon you don't," he said. "Now eat up so we can get these folks back to dancin' afore they get bored and go home."

The band did several square dance sets and then started taking requests for favorites, which had folks stomping up and down the barn floor. Certain members of the group were definitely better lubricated than they had been at the beginning of the evening. Limbs were looser, attitudes more relaxed, and the dancing was spectacular. Soon some of the older folks and the families with children began drifting home.

Casewell's parents were long gone, and he saw Robert and Delilah headed out carrying a sleeping Sadie. He'd lost track of Perla some time back and assumed she'd left as well. As the party wound down, George and Steve laid down their instruments so they could eat, drink, and visit with friends—some of whom were good-looking women, including Melody

Simmons, who kept sending smiles Casewell's way. He could easily have joined them, but as long as folks would listen, he was happy to keep playing. Anyway, this was when he could play the songs he liked best—melancholy ballads and old songs from Ireland and Scotland. He was enjoying himself so much that he didn't notice Perla until she spoke as he finished a mournful tune.

"That was lovely," she said.

Casewell turned and saw her standing near the stage, hands clasped in front of her. "I thought you were gone," he said.

"I stayed to help clean up the food. There's still plenty and it'd be a shame to waste it. As a matter of fact, Delilah suggested I send some home with you."

"That'd be fine," Casewell said, still caught in the mood of the music. "You look pretty tonight," he said, before he even knew his mouth had shaped the words.

Perla blushed. "Thank you," she said. "I wasn't too sure about coming, but I guess I'm glad I did. I even square danced once." Her blush deepened. "Well, I don't mean to talk your ear off. Let me get you a basket of food for when you go."

"I appreciate it," Casewell said, looking around at the crowd that had dwindled to almost nothing. "Reckon I'll be heading out now. Looks like this party has run out of steam."

Perla smiled and went to fetch the food while Casewell said his good-byes. He met her near the door and took the heavier-than-expected basket.

"This'll hold me," he said, then opened his mouth as if to say more but didn't know what.

"It was nice seeing you," Perla said. "I'll be getting on back myself now."

"Who's seeing you home?" he blurted.

"Why, I thought I'd walk. It's not far and it's such a pretty night. And somehow I feel safe around here."

"I'll drive you," Casewell said. "It's on my way."

Perla hesitated then nodded her agreement. She picked up her empty basket, and they started out in the cool of the evening. At first they rode in silence. Casewell wanted to know so much about Perla, but the questions that ran through his head weren't the kind he could put to her directly. Finally, Perla broke the quiet.

"How long has your family lived around here?"

"Oh, about six generations or so," Casewell said. "The Phillips brothers came down from Massachusetts when this was still part of Virginia. There were three of them, and they all settled within a day's travel of each other. John Phillips is the brother I came down from. Guess I'm the last of his particular line for now. I know my parents would sure like it if I married and had a son to carry on the name, but, well . . ." Casewell trailed off.

"Never met the right girl?"

"Reckon I'm somehow related to most girls around here, but yes, you're right. No one's ever caught my eye that way."

"You might have to look further afield," Perla said.

"Maybe, maybe not." Casewell felt a little clumsy with this gentle banter, but he realized he was enjoying himself.

"Guess there are plenty of rumors about me and how I'm not married," Perla said.

Casewell had an impulse to stomp on the brake, but he controlled himself as he struggled for a response. "I don't pay much attention to gossip," he said at last.

"But you've heard some things." It was a statement, and Casewell didn't deny it. Perla continued. "I don't know you that well, but from what I've seen and heard of your family, I tend to think you're good people. I'd like to tell you the truth. I don't know exactly what folks are saying, but I see the way women stop talking when I step up to them and how men look at me like . . . well, it's an uneasy way to be looked at. Do you mind to know?"

"If you want to tell, I can listen," Casewell said, feeling a mixture of anticipation and dread.

"All right then. I'm not married, nor have I ever been. Nobody knows who Sadie's father is, and that's something I won't tell. But he's not to blame. I am. And although it's been hard raising that child on my own, I wouldn't trade her for anything." Perla's chin rose in the air, and she looked out the side window into the dark. "She's the single best thing in my life, and I thank God for her every day—no matter how I got her. I had the idea that if I came here, I might leave the gossip and mean talk behind, but I see that it's followed me. I'm not expecting you to stand up for me, but you seem kind, and I wanted you to know that while I am what they say, I'm not ashamed of having Sadie."

Casewell's mind filled with warring emotions. He admired Perla's spunk, and as she became more animated and determined, he thought she was probably the most beautiful woman he'd ever seen. But how could she talk of her sin so lightly? How could she say she wasn't ashamed? He compared her in his mind to some of the other women he knew—Delilah, his own mother, and even Melody from the dance. None of them would ever do such a thing. He felt certain of it.

Casewell let his silence stretch too long. A single tear slid down Perla's cheek.

"You judge me, too," she said. "I can't ask you not to, but somehow I hoped . . ."

"I'm sorry," Casewell said. "It's a lot to take in."

"I know," Perla said. "Sometimes I can't take it in myself."

"I appreciate your honesty, but how can you not regret sinning against God?"

Casewell had to navigate a curve before he could look at Perla. He thought she swiped at her face, though he couldn't be sure.

"I am a sinner. But God used my sin to bring me the most wonderful love I've ever known. How could I regret that?"

Casewell had no answer. He was relieved to see the glow of the Thorntons' porch light.

"Thank you for carrying me home," Perla said. "It was kind of you."

Casewell thought maybe she wanted him to thank her for sharing her secret with him, but he couldn't do that. He wished that he didn't know and that he'd never laid eyes on Perla Long.

"Good night, then," he said and, after watching her safely to the porch, drove away.

Perla tiptoed into the house, hoping everyone was in bed so she wouldn't have to explain her teary eyes. She slipped into her room and saw Sadie curled on the bed, fast asleep. She drew the door shut, removed her gloves, and began unfastening her hat. She heard a tap at the door.

"Perla, I tucked Sadie in. Robert and I are about wore out. You need anything?" It was Delilah.

Perla leaned against the door and whispered back. "I'm fine." She hoped her voice didn't sound shaky.

"'Night, then."

Perla put a hand against the door and whispered, "Good

night." Then she slid to the floor and cried in earnest. The first time she'd laid eyes on Casewell Phillips, she thought he was quite possibly the finest-looking man she'd ever seen. Oh, she'd liked the looks of Sadie's father well enough, but Casewell seemed more . . . complete. More self-contained and whole.

But he also seemed like a righteous man, and Perla knew she needed to confess her situation to him before she let him touch her heart. She had hoped he might be the forgiving sort—the kind of man who could let the past be past. When he offered her a ride, she decided to tell him everything—well, nearly everything. Then, if he judged her like everyone else, she could rid herself of any romantic notions. And if he didn't? Well, no need to think about that—he did judge her. And it seemed like her foolish heart had jumped the gun.

5

Casewell looked for Perla at church the following morning. He had no intention of speaking to her or approaching her, but somehow he wanted to see her—to know that his inability to take her story in stride had done no harm. Robert and Delilah were already in their seats, and he wondered if she had stayed away. That idea weighed heavy on Casewell, although he couldn't say why. Maybe her sin kept her away.

He turned to the hymnal to find the first song and then caught movement out of the corner of his eye. He saw Perla slide into a back pew with Sadie in tow. She seemed pale, her mouth set in a straight line. In spite of that, she looked lovely in a blue dress that made her eyes shine, sad and knowing.

The whole congregation seemed a bit sluggish that morning, as though the revelry of the night before had used up all of their enthusiasm. Pastor Longbourne took his usual fiery sermonizing up a notch, probably to make up for any sinning that had gone on the night before.

After the service, Casewell hung back so that Perla would have plenty of time to wind her way out of the churchyard.

He shook the preacher's hand last and stood for a moment on the top step of the church. He spotted Perla immediately. She stood near the gate in the churchyard, alone except for little Sadie. Casewell saw women shoot her a glance, but no one approached. He felt as though he had spread the rumors about Perla himself, seeing her gently ostracized. She didn't linger long but soon turned and went to sit in Robert's car until he and Delilah were ready to go.

Casewell felt anger burn in his chest at the way the women turned their backs on Perla. They didn't know her story. They were only guessing and repeating the tales that had followed Perla from her hometown. No one had the facts.

Casewell felt his chest deflate. He had more facts than anyone and had turned his back on Perla as surely as those who were only guessing. But honestly, what else could he have done? He couldn't condone such behavior, especially when Perla didn't seem to feel the least remorse. God might forgive such things, but there had to be human standards. They would all be in a fix if everyone could go around committing such sins with no judgment visited upon them. Casewell didn't like it, but he had to have standards. There had to be standards.

That afternoon Casewell determined to finish the set of doll furniture he had started for Sadie. He told himself it would be a shame not to finish it, and there was no reason to visit the sins of the mother on the child. Casewell told himself it had nothing to do with wanting to somehow make amends, to get back in Perla's good graces after he felt he had somehow fallen short the night before. Maybe even to console her for the rejection she faced—no, certainly not that.

He buried himself in the work, lost himself in finely crafting a miniature chair, bed, and table. As he labored, Casewell found himself enjoying the close work. He added small details, carved flourishes, and stained the wood a deep mahogany. When he finished late that evening, he realized that he'd eaten no dinner. He set the furniture out on his workbench so the stain could dry and considered his stomach. He wished he could walk into the house and find a woman setting supper out on his table—a woman other than his mother.

Casewell laughed at himself and stretched muscles cramped from the detailed work. He'd raid the basket Perla sent home with him the night before—that was the ticket. In a way, he felt he'd earned food from her hands.

Inside the house, Casewell lifted the basket from the floor beside the stove where he'd placed it when he'd arrived home. The basket felt even heavier, but Casewell supposed he was just tired. He turned the gingham tea towel back and began lifting food out. There were biscuits, thick slices of ham, canned peaches, slices of cake and pie, and a jar of chowchow. He split the biscuits on a plate and forked the ham on top, then spooned the chowchow alongside. He thought he'd manage in spite of the food sitting out for most of a day. After one bite, though, he marveled at how fresh everything tasted. The bread wasn't stale and the ham wasn't dried out. He finished his meal off with a slice of dried-apple pie and a square of gingerbread, both as delicious as they must have been when they came from the oven.

Casewell packed the remainder of the food, which still seemed plentiful, into the Frigidaire and supposed he'd eat on it for most of the week. It was a shame that Perla Long had to go and have a child out of wedlock. If it wasn't for that, she was just the sort of woman he'd been waiting for.

That night Casewell slept fitfully. Dreams woke him, but he

couldn't remember what they were about. He woke early the next morning and toasted some buttered biscuits in the oven for his breakfast. Then, even though it was early, he headed for the Thorntons' store to pick up some finishing nails for one of his projects. He stepped up onto the stoop in front of the store and peered in the window to see if Robert or Delilah was about yet. Robert spied him and came to open the door.

"Come on in here. I'm not open yet, but you can keep me company."

Casewell stepped inside and drifted toward the boxes of nails.

"Lordy," Robert said, obviously in the mood for conversation. "Those women are about to run me ragged."

"Oh, yeah?" Casewell scanned the shelf.

"Delilah says it's obvious that the rumors folks are spreading about Perla are upsetting the girl, but I haven't heard anything, and this place is where all the news gets spread. I don't know what Delilah is talking about, and Perla seems fine to me." He looked thoughtful for a moment. "Of course, all she does is cook, clean, and take care of Sadie. She hardly ever goes anywhere. It was all we could do to get her to go to the dance the other night, and she came home from that all hangdog. Delilah says something happened to upset her, but I can't imagine what. Folks around here wouldn't treat her bad."

Casewell realized he'd been standing with his hand in the box of finishing nails while Robert rattled on. He pulled out a handful and dropped them in one of the little paper sacks.

"I'll take these," he said.

Robert moved around behind the cash register. "You haven't heard anything, have you?" he asked.

"About what?"

"Perla. Haven't you been listening?"

"Oh, well, you know how it is. Folks talk just to fill up the quiet."

"Then you have heard something," Robert said. "Is it bad, what folks are saying?"

Casewell blushed. It was no worse than the truth, but what could he say to his friend and Perla's uncle? "Folks are just guessing at her . . . situation," he said. "Folks like to assume the worst." He blushed deeper.

"That they do." Robert sighed. "Wish there was some way to set 'em straight."

Casewell looked up, surprised. "But she said . . ." he trailed off.

Now Robert looked surprised. "She told you about herself?" he asked. "Well, now, I'm glad she found someone trustworthy to confide in. Maybe that'll cheer her up a mite."

"But you said you'd set them straight," Casewell persisted. "Seems like maybe folks are guessing pretty close to the truth."

"Why, I'd tell 'em how Perla is a fine Christian girl who made a mistake but has taken responsibility for it and is raising her child to know the Lord and respect her elders. I'd say how my niece hasn't done anything worse than most folks, only the result of her choice is more obvious. I'd tell 'em God's forgiven that girl and ask who are they to hold anything against her. I'd say whichever one of them was without sin could go ahead and throw the first stone."

Robert banged the flat of his hand against the counter. "Yessir, maybe I ought to call a town meeting and say just that."

Casewell noticed that his mouth hung open. He closed it with a snap.

"Anyhow, I'm glad she's found you for a friend. You're one of the good ones. That'll be fifty-eight cents."

Casewell paid, said his good-byes, and walked home, wishing that Robert truly had something to be glad of and wondering if he was one of the good ones or not.

Casewell meant to take the doll furniture to Sadie that afternoon, but after talking to Robert, he felt torn. Would Perla mind seeing him? Would she regret having confided in him and send him away? But so what if she did? Robert talked big, but he was a married man with no children of his own. The shame of this thing wasn't on him. Casewell had imagined courting Perla, if only briefly. How could he love a woman who'd given herself to a man not her husband? God might forgive, but there was no forgetting, and it wouldn't take long for rumors to start once Casewell gave a present to this woman's child.

Casewell's mind was finally made up by the sweet little pieces he had so carefully crafted. It might be vanity, but he couldn't stand the thought of boxing up the furniture and shoving it on a shelf. He'd only stay a minute, and he'd be polite and distant with Perla so that anyone watching would know he only meant to be kind.

Casewell tucked the little pieces into the basket Perla had sent him home with Saturday night. He needed to return it, anyway. He felt a little silly carrying a basket as he approached the Thorntons' house, but he didn't see anyone watching. Sadie sat in the porch swing, deep in conversation with her doll. Casewell was glad. Maybe he could just give the toys to Sadie and be on his way without having to see Perla at all. He cleared his throat so Sadie would notice him. She looked up.

"Hello," she said, her shyness seeming to have faded now that she knew Casewell a little.

"Hey, there, I've got something for you," Casewell said. "Or rather, for Amy." He surprised himself by remembering the doll's name.

"Oh, we both like presents," Sadie said. "Maybe we can share."

Casewell sat on the top porch step and placed the basket beside him. "Well, you'd better come see what's in this basket, then."

Sadie scurried over and pushed aside the dish towel Casewell had placed over the furniture. She gasped and then crouched down, using both hands to hold Amy as if letting the doll look into the basket.

"You can take them out," Casewell said, enjoying the child's wonder more than he expected.

Sadie reached in and removed the chair, then the table, and finally the little bed. She placed them in a semicircle in front of her and then just gazed at them. Casewell grinned.

"Maybe Amy would like to try them out," he said. "You know, to see if they're the right size."

Sadie glanced at him as though to make sure he meant it, then carefully sat her doll in the chair. It was an excellent fit. Casewell had given the chair arms, and they held the doll upright. He reached over to pull the table up in front of Amy. Sadie giggled and clapped her hands.

"We can make her some dishes out of bark and acorn caps. I've seen girls around here do that."

"We can?" Sadie looked at him with eyes wide. "And can we keep these? Or will you take them back home with you?"

"Oh, they're for you to keep." Casewell colored. "I knew

it was hard on Amy not having a proper chair or a place to sleep."

A sound caught Casewell's attention and he looked toward the door. Perla stood behind the screen, watching. Casewell leapt to his feet.

"Oh, hey there," he said, rubbing his hands on his pants. "I, well, I had some leftover bits of lumber and took a notion to try my hand at some doll furniture. Never tried that before, and well, since it's my first attempt, I thought I'd just give it to Sadie." He stopped talking and looked at Perla, hoping she wouldn't take this wrong. Perla stepped out onto the porch but held the door behind her with one hand.

"They're lovely," she said. "Probably the nicest toys Sadie has. Thank you."

"Oh, well, like I say, it's nothing much, just fiddling about with wood."

Perla turned to her daughter. "Sadie, did you thank Mr. Phillips?"

Sadie stood and flung her arms around Casewell's legs, squeezing as tight as her little arms would let her. "Oh, thank you, Mr. Phillips, thank you!"

Casewell felt an inexplicable lump rise in his throat. He lifted his hand and held it over the child's head for a moment, hovering there like a hummingbird taking the measure of a flower. Then he patted Sadie awkwardly. "You're welcome, Sadie," he said. "Glad you like them."

He turned back to Perla. "I'd best be getting on. I brought your basket back." He nodded toward it. "Sure have been enjoying that good food."

"I'm glad," Perla said. "And thank you, again." She stepped back inside and let the screen door shut with a small bang.

Casewell stepped backward onto the top step and stumbled slightly. He turned and hurried away, throwing a hand up over his shoulder in farewell.

Perla moved back inside the house, far enough to be out of sight while still having a view of the road and Casewell's broad back as he strode away. She had been foolish to confide in him. She knew that now. He was a good man—too good, apparently, to make room for a woman who had such an obvious sin hanging around her like a five-year-old shadow.

Once Casewell disappeared and Perla could see that her daughter would play with her new toys for a while, Perla drifted toward the kitchen. Robert and Delilah would be home from the store soon enough, and she'd have a fine meal waiting for them. One of Robert's customers had traded a leg of lamb for some supplies, and a bushel of spring peas waited to be shelled. Perla pulled the basket over to a kitchen chair and sat with a metal bowl in her lap. She began stripping the shells, soothing herself with the music of peas chiming against the bowl.

When the Thorntons arrived home that evening, Perla stood beside the table spread with a banquet. The roasted leg of lamb sat in the center of the table, herbs dark against the glistening browned flesh. Creamed peas cooked with torn lettuce sat alongside a bowl of roasted parsnips browned in butter. A basket of yeast rolls completed the feast.

"Perla, you're the best thing that's ever happened to us," Robert said almost reverently.

Delilah eyed the table and then Perla, squinting a little into her face. "Perla," she said, laying a hand on her arm. "Perla, are you all right?"

Perla gave herself a shake and smiled. "Oh," she said, "you're home. I thought I'd better do something with that leg of lamb and the peas. They won't keep forever, you know." She looked confused for a moment. "Did you bring Sadie in with you?"

"I did," Delilah said. "She was asleep on the front porch with the most cunning little set of doll furniture scattered about her. Where did that come from?"

"Casewell brought it by. For Sadie," Perla explained. "It's for Sadie."

"Of course it is." Delilah smiled. "Casewell is so thoughtful."

"Yes," Perla agreed. "Now, let's eat this food before it gets cold."

6

CASEWELL KEPT TO HIMSELF THAT WEEK. He didn't feel like talking to anyone, and considering some of the things folks were talking about lately, he didn't care to listen, either. He worked in his shop during the day and spent his evenings reading the Bible or playing his mandolin. He could pick up his instrument, start strumming, and suddenly find that the day was gone and it was long past bedtime. Company was good, but sometimes being alone was better. And then the phone rang on Friday night.

Casewell was on a party line with several housewives. They'd learned they could pick up the phone and talk to each other without even dialing. Most afternoons there was a steady conversation going on, with women jumping in and dropping out as families and chores allowed. As a result, Casewell didn't much use the phone. Its ringing took him by surprise.

"Hello?" he answered after the third ring.

"Casewell, it's your father." His mother's voice was tense and urgent.

"What's the matter?" Casewell hoped it was nothing, but knew his mother would only call in an emergency.

"I'm not sure. He seems to be in terrible pain, but he keeps telling me it's nothing. I want to take him to the hospital, but he says he won't go. I don't know what to do—"

"I'm on my way."

Casewell ran out into the yard and cranked his old truck. It wasn't entirely reliable, but it would usually take him where he needed to go. Normally, he'd walk to his parents' house, but tonight he wanted to get there as fast as possible. His father never admitted pain, and his mother never panicked. Something was wrong.

At the Phillipses' farm, Casewell found his father doubled over in his recliner, moaning softly. Mom stood beside him, a hand on his back, tears slipping down her cheeks.

"C'mon, Dad, we need to get you to the hospital," Casewell said.

"I won't go," his father gritted out, not raising his head or moving.

"Pa, either you're getting into that truck, or I'm carrying you. Now, what'll it be?"

His father shuddered and seemed to slump even lower. "Help me, son," he said. And Casewell did—half supporting, half carrying his father, who seemed not to weigh nearly as much as he should.

The three of them jammed onto the bench seat of Casewell's truck. Dad sat in the middle, grunting softly each time they hit a pothole or rough patch of road. Casewell drove, trying to focus on the road and the hour-long trip to the nearest hospital. He thought if he stared at the center line of the winding two-lane road hard enough, he might keep the fear at bay.

St. Joseph's was a Catholic hospital, and a nun met them at the door. She ushered them in as Casewell helped his father hobble toward a chair. A nurse in a crisp white uniform with a perfect white cap perched on her perfect brown hair came to them and asked some questions. Dad was taken into an examination room, and Casewell helped his mother fill out forms.

Sitting on a weirdly modern chair in the waiting room, Casewell felt like he'd just woken up from a terrible dream, only to discover that it wasn't a dream at all. His mother leaned hard into his right arm and seemed to be breathing heavily—as if she'd been running.

"You okay, Ma?" he asked.

"Oh, I don't know." She looked surprised by the question. "He's all right, isn't he? They would have told us if he weren't all right?"

"Yes," Casewell said, not at all certain that they would. "Probably something he ate. They'll have him right as rain in no time."

"Yes, of course." Mom straightened a little. "Right as rain."

❧

"Cancer," said the kind-faced doctor with shaggy gray hair and faded blue eyes. Casewell thought there were tears in the doctor's eyes, but maybe it was just the effects of age and long hours. There were definitely tears in his mother's eyes, though. Tears that spilled over and streaked her cheeks.

"We'll need to do some more testing, but I'd say he's pretty far advanced. Has he been complaining about pain? Feeling tired?"

Mom said no immediately, but Casewell thought about the times his dad had seemed tired or weak and the day he fell asleep after helping him move furniture. He started to contradict his mother, but instead he caught the doctor's eye and nodded his head once.

"I'm betting John's not a complainer," the doctor said. He'd introduced himself, but Casewell had immediately lost his name. Now he saw it embroidered on his white jacket—Dr. McNeil.

"No," agreed Casewell. "He pretty much keeps his feelings to himself."

Casewell thought he should be asking some questions, learning what the prognosis was, but he couldn't formulate the words. He was impressed that he'd thought of the word *prognosis*. He turned pleading eyes on Dr. McNeil, hoping he would somehow understand.

The doctor must have, because he began speaking. "I know the two of you have some questions and want to know about the treatment and possible outcomes, but I'd like to wait to get into all of that. When those other tests come back, I'll be able to give you better answers. I don't want to scare you unnecessarily," he paused. "Or give you false hope."

"Can we see him?" Mom asked in a small but steady voice.

"Absolutely," the doctor said. "Follow Sister Agatha. She'll show you his room. We'll want to keep him at least until the tests are back, and then we'll plan accordingly. I gave him something for the pain, so he may be a little groggy."

"To be in so much pain," Casewell started, "that means . . ."

"We'll figure out what that means," Dr. McNeil said. "Just go on in there and see him."

They turned and followed a plump nun through the stark halls to room 218.

⁂

"Get me outta here," Dad growled as soon as he saw Casewell. "I've had enough of this nonsense. Take me home."

He struggled to swing his legs over the side of the bed and began tugging at the IV in his arm. Sister Agatha swooped in to push him back.

"Get this penguin off of me. I feel fine," Dad yelled as he pushed at Agatha. The nun kept her hold with a tenacity that surprised and impressed Casewell. Or maybe his father really was weakening. Casewell stepped forward to help, placing a soothing hand on his father's shoulder.

"Dad, just settle back there and let's talk for a minute. We can sort all this out."

"You'd better believe we can. You've got five minutes to get me situated and on my way out of here."

Casewell took a deep breath and waited for his dad to settle back against his pillow. Maybe he was imagining it, but Casewell could have sworn his father was relieved to rest for a moment. "You feel better because the doctor gave you something for the pain. If the medication wears off, I doubt you'll feel so spry."

"Don't need drugs. No one asked me if I wanted 'em. I could probably have that fraud's license for slipping me something without asking if I wanted it." John crossed his arms across his chest, batting at the IV as he did so.

"Dad, looks like you may be sick, after all," Casewell said, wondering how much the doctor had told him and hating the idea of being the one to speak the word.

"Cancer," snorted Dad, relieving his son of that responsibility, at least. "What's that fool know about me having cancer? Pokes at me, asks a few questions, hooks this contraption up to me." John tugged at the IV line again. Sister Agatha grabbed the stand and then checked the connections. "Don't make no difference to me. Just get me on home."

Casewell had no idea what to say to convince his father to stay in the hospital. Reason, threats, pleading—none of them seemed the way to go. Then Mom stepped forward.

"John," she said, her eyes soft and her hand gentle on her husband's arm. "I'm asking you to do what the doctor says. You're a strong man, and I don't have a doubt that if you do have cancer, you'll get over it. But until we know just what it is we're dealing with, I'd be grateful to you if you'd stay right here where the doctor can get at you."

The fire seemed to go right out of Dad, and he sagged back against his pillow. He laid one hand over his wife's and closed his eyes, squeezing them shut for just a moment. "All right," he said. "But just until tomorrow."

"Yes," Mom agreed. "Until tomorrow."

Three days later Dr. McNeil informed Casewell and his mother that John Phillips had lung cancer as well as black lung. The cancer was likely caused by cigarettes, and the black lung was from coal mining. Mom protested that John had given up mining years ago and that he didn't smoke that much, not really.

"Black lung can only be caused by inhaling coal dust," the doctor explained. "There are various causes of lung cancer, but smoking is the likeliest culprit." Dr. McNeil rubbed his hands on his pant legs. "Unfortunately, the cancer has spread to John's bones—that's what caused the extreme pain he was experiencing."

Mom stuffed a knuckle between her teeth and seemed to gnaw at it. Casewell opened his mouth, trying to find his voice, but the doctor understood his question before he found it.

"I'm afraid the prognosis isn't good. Actually, there's not a whole lot we can do other than keep him comfortable. Surgery isn't an option at this point. We can try chemical therapy—what they call chemotherapy—but I don't want to get your hopes up." The doctor looked from Casewell to his mother and back. "I'm terribly sorry."

Casewell was surprised to hear himself speak. "How long?"

"No one but God knows that, son. But I've not seen anyone last much more than"—he hesitated—"than six months."

Mom gasped and gulped as if she couldn't get any air into her lungs. Casewell put his arms around his mother and held her steady until she began breathing normally. Her gasps turned to pants and then to a soft crying that seemed to bore into Casewell's skull. It was impossible. He wouldn't accept it. Not now, not today. His father could not be dying of cancer. No.

"Does Dad know?" he whispered.

"He knows he has cancer," Dr. McNeil said. "I'm not sure he understands what that means."

His mother's hand tightened around Casewell's wrist, the nails digging into his flesh. "Go to him," she said. "I'll be along."

Casewell started to protest.

"Go," she said. "Now."

Casewell walked into his father's room. Dad sat up in bed smoking a cigarette.

"Dad, you aren't supposed to have that," Casewell said, feeling weariness well up in him like a black tumor, pressing against his stomach, his lungs, even his heart.

"What the devil does it matter?" Dad snapped. Casewell had rarely heard his father speak so harshly. He supposed if there was a time to do it, this was that time.

"Right," he said, waving smoke away as he sat on a chair next to the bed. "So you've talked to Dr. McNeil."

"That quack told Walt Farmer he was dying eight years ago, and Walt feels better today than he ever did. Bunch of crap." Dad coughed so hard tears came to his eyes. When he got his breath back he inhaled deeply on his cigarette, burning it down to his fingertips. He ground out the butt in a kidney-shaped pan on his bedside table.

Casewell watched his father's yellowed fingers and thought about how rarely his father had touched him. He'd gotten a few good-boy pats as a child and slaps on the back once his father deemed him an adult. There had been spankings, of course, but even then his father was more likely to use a switch than his bare hand. He racked his brain trying to remember a hug—something his mother handed out daily—but the best he could come up with was the time his dad had put an arm around his shoulders after he graduated from high school. He also remembered that Dad had quickly removed the arm, as if afraid someone would see.

"When are you taking me home?" he growled. His now empty hand lay on top of the cover, and he kept pinching the sheet between his thumb and forefinger and then smoothing it down again.

"They want to try a treatment out on you—some kind of chemical therapy. Dr. McNeil thinks it might help," Casewell said. "I figure—"

His father cut him off. "You can figure all day long if you want to. They're not trying some sort of experimental whatever on me. Let someone else be their guinea pig. Now get out there and find somebody to unhook me from this contraption." He shook his arm so violently, he nearly dislodged the IV on his own. "Now."

Casewell went out into the hall and leaned against the wall, trying to breathe deeply in and out, trying to find a pocket of calm in the midst of the whirlwind. Neither of his parents seemed to be taking this news well. He wasn't taking the news well, either, but that could be because he hadn't been given even a moment to take it all in.

My father is dying, he thought. He felt he barely knew the man, but he loved him fiercely and unreasonably. He had no better reason for loving his father than that he was his father. It shouldn't have been enough, but it was. Casewell didn't mean to slide down the wall, but he found himself sitting, his knees at eye level. He placed one hand on each knee and waited for the tears running down his face to subside.

Casewell didn't see Sister Agatha approach, but he felt her settle next to him like a pigeon fluttering to the ground. She handed Casewell a plain white handkerchief. "I thought I'd come pray with you," she said. "Would you prefer I did so aloud or silently?"

"Silently." Casewell knew there were no words for this situation, but as long as Agatha prayed silently, he could imagine that there were. She bowed her head, and he felt peace radiating out from her. But like a kerosene lamp on an icy morning, it could not reach his core.

After a few minutes, he placed his hands on the floor and pushed himself to standing. He reached down and helped Sister Agatha to her feet. She kissed the rosary around her neck and made the sign of the cross. Casewell thanked her. He looked into her eyes and thought maybe she understood that while she had not reached him with her prayers, she had been a sort of help after all. He went back into his father's room.

His mother had slipped into the room while Casewell was

in the hall. She had to have seen him hunkered there, but she didn't mention it. She barely looked at him at all. Her focus was entirely upon her husband, who was holding her hand and staring at the ceiling.

Casewell cleared his throat. "I think you should stay and try this treatment," he said. He thought he saw his mother squeeze his father's hand harder. He knew she closed her eyes and bowed her head.

His father took a deep breath that sent him into a brief coughing fit. When he had composed himself again, he looked his son in the eye. "I appreciate that you want me to fight this thing. And I've always been one to fight for what I want." His face convulsed slightly and he cupped his empty left hand over his wife's and his own. "But what I'm after now is the right to go home and . . ." He coughed again. "To go home and let be what will be. You don't have to understand it, son. Just go along with it."

"Mom?" Casewell said the single word, and it was a question, a command, and a plea. "Mom, what do you think?"

"We're going home," she said, looking at her husband with a depth and a rawness that somehow embarrassed Caswell, as if he had walked in on his parents being intimate. He ducked his head.

"Well, then," he said.

"Well, then go find that old fraud who's trying to tell me how to die."

Casewell went.

The old fraud was more than reluctant to let his patient go, but he'd been doctoring the Phillips family for several generations, and he said he guessed stubborn was a genetic predisposition. He made Casewell and his mother promise to bring John in for a check-up every two weeks, although Dad indicated that he'd be less than cooperative. Still, he was too eager to leave the hospital under his own power to fuss too long and loud about Dr. McNeil's requirements. He agreed grudgingly and the doctor threatened to come to the house if necessary.

"Come around dinnertime," Dad growled. "Least that way it'll be worth your time."

By the end of the day Casewell was driving back the way they had come just three days earlier. The world looked different. His mother sat in the center of the truck's bench seat this time, clutching a bag with prescription painkillers that Dad swore he would never take. Casewell found himself hoping that his father's stubborn streak could somehow ward off cancer, could somehow change the rapid division of cells. That stubbornness could keep his body from turning against him—from turning against them. Casewell prayed and watched the familiar, unfamiliar landscape roll by.

⁂

The family made an effort to return to normal. Casewell went home to catch up on his carpentry projects, his mother spent her days working in her kitchen garden, and Dad continued to walk the fields, tending to the spring calving. He walked more slowly and rested more often, but he refused to give up his work.

When Casewell came to supper about a week after his father's return from the hospital, his mother called him into the kitchen to help her. "He's taking them pills," she said. "Not many and not often, but he's taking them."

Casewell nodded. "I guess that's good."

His mother gave him a sharp look. "I wouldn't say that. He must be in a world of pain to take help from a pill bottle."

"But at least he's taking help," Casewell said.

Emily made a *tsking* sound and began dishing up the meal. After they ate—mostly in silence—Dad scooted his chair back and pushed himself to his feet. "Come on out here on the porch with me, son." He began fishing makings out of his breast pocket. Emily opened her mouth as though she would speak, then pressed her lips together in a tight line.

On the porch, Dad rolled his cigarette and then stood looking at it. "Reckon it's too late to quit now," he said. But he didn't raise the cigarette to his lips. "We need a good year, son," he said, squinting across the pasture. "Even if I die quick, it's gonna cost money."

The frank statement hit Casewell hard. He knew his father's prognosis, but to hear him speak of it so calmly, so matter-of-factly, took Caswell's breath away.

"I've got some pretty calves coming on this spring. All we need is a summer with good grass and plenty of hay to put up for winter. Come fall, we can sell off some of the cows for good breeders and keep some younger ones for stock. By spring the yearlings will be ready to go to market, and you can turn a nice profit that'll keep your mother. Beyond that, I leave the running of the cattle to you. Sell 'em or keep the line going. All I ask is that you always take care of your mother."

His dad seemed to have shrunk a notch by the time he finished his speech. Casewell was too choked by emotion to speak for several minutes. Finally, he said, "Dad, you know I'll always take care of Mom. You don't even need to think of that. And we'll handle the cattle however you want. I just wish . . ." Casewell knew without finishing his thought that his father had little use for wishes.

"Wish all you want, son. You can even pray. Probably most

of the old women around here dropped to their knees as soon as word got out that I'm dying. They'll pray for me, but I don't hold out hope for it working. I don't expect half of 'em to even mean what they pray." Dad looked at the cigarette he still held in his hand and tucked it into his pocket next to his tobacco tin. "I ain't afraid to die, boy. I just hate to leave . . ." He shot a look over his shoulder into the house, and Casewell saw him swipe at his face. "I hate to leave your mother."

Casewell was ashamed that instead of being touched that his father loved his mother so much, he was disappointed that Dad hadn't said that he'd hate to leave anyone else—like his son.

7

CASEWELL TRIED TO FORGET that his father was dying. There wasn't much point in remembering. His parents behaved as though the days spent in the hospital had been a disappointing vacation they'd just as soon forget. So Casewell did the same, as best as he could. He kept up with his woodwork, played his mandolin of an evening, and tried not to think about death or Perla Long. And then, Angie and Liza called about their garden.

"Casewell, we need your help," Angie hollered into the telephone.

"Oh, we do, we do," Liza echoed. Casewell assumed she was on the extension.

"That Williams boy has left us high and dry," Angie said. "He promised to come hoe the garden once a week and to carry water from the creek if need be, and we haven't seen hide nor hair of him since the beginning of the month."

"Oh, the garden is terrible weedy," Liza said. "We've done what we can, but it's not like when we were girls."

"We'll pay the same we offered that Williams boy," Angie said, steel in her voice.

"Oh yes, we'll pay," Liza sighed.

Casewell wished with all his might that he hadn't answered the telephone. "I'll come over after supper," he said.

"Why don't you come have supper with us, and that can be part of your pay," Angie said with a bounce to her voice that let Casewell know she thought she'd hit on a good idea.

"Do come," Liza said. "We're having beans and corn bread."

"All right," Casewell agreed. Why not? He had no other plans.

At the Talbots' house the sisters already had supper laid. Casewell took his seat—"In Papa's chair," commented Liza with a look of affection—and waited for the other two to settle in their places. Once alight in her chair, Angie turned cool eyes on Casewell and asked him to pray. He had never been entirely comfortable praying aloud, but Casewell made his way through a simple prayer and then dished out the food.

"It's so nice to have a man at the head of the table," Liza said. "Angie usually serves, but it's really a man's place."

"Women serve just fine," Angie said, then softened as she watched Casewell begin to eat. "But it takes a working man to do food justice."

Throughout the meal the sisters talked about the recent dance, how their chickens were laying, the fact that it hadn't rained in a while, and finally came around to what Casewell supposed had been on their minds all along.

"I hear your father had a short stay in the hospital," Angie said as she sliced a pound cake sitting on the cupboard Casewell had built. "Is he well?"

Casewell shouldn't have been surprised by this line of questioning, but he hadn't thought what he would say. He took a big bite of cake and chewed slowly.

"Well, he has cancer," Casewell said at last. "But he seems to be doing okay, and he's determined to keep up with the farm."

"As it should be," Angie nodded. "We have an uncle who was supposed to have died of cancer three years ago, and he still works his farm without one sign of being puny."

Liza looked like she was going to say something, but Angie shot her a look, and Liza began clearing dishes instead.

"Doctors do the best they can, but they don't know what they're talking about half the time," Angie said. "Dr. McNeil told me I had a ticky heart five years ago, but here I am, strong as ever. Was it McNeil what said John has the cancer?"

"It was." Casewell knew Angie meant to boost his spirits, and he also knew she was a long way from an authority on anything medical, but he soaked up her words like gospel, nonetheless.

"There you go," Angie said, softly slapping the table. "Tell John we'll be praying for him."

"I will," Casewell said. "Now what can I do to help in the garden?"

"Hoe's in the shed," Angie said. "And there's a bucket out there. We need the weeds knocked back and water carried from the creek. Seems like it hasn't rained in a month."

Casewell nodded and headed out to the shed to collect the tools. The sisters had a small garden patch with corn, sweet peas, tomatoes, potatoes, green beans, squash, spring onions, and some lettuces that had already been hit pretty hard by the rabbits. He hoed for about an hour. He knew he wasn't being as thorough as his father would have demanded in the family plot, but he didn't want to stay all night. After the weeds were somewhat in check, he took the bucket and stepped down to the creek.

Casewell pushed rhododendron branches aside in the gathering dusk. The music of the water spilling over stones immediately soothed him. He felt the coolness and the smell of damp earth rising to meet him. There was a swimming hole just a little further down where he had spent many a pleasant summer afternoon. The icy water flowed over rocks that looked almost black in this coal-rich part of the country. He stopped to breathe it all in.

After a moment, he crouched down to dip the bucket and realized with a start just how low the water was. He knew it had been dry for a while, but this creek usually ran steady no matter the weather. It still flowed, but he had to move further into the streambed to find a pool deep enough to fill the bucket. This would take longer than he expected.

On Casewell's fifth or sixth trip back to the creek, he stopped a moment to rest on a cool, dark rock. He sat with his booted foot on a barely submerged stone in the center of the creek. He could feel the coolness of the water slowly making its way through to the sole of his foot.

"I like to sit here, too," came a soft voice. Casewell turned and saw Liza standing on the bank. "It's a good spot to think or sometimes not to think."

"I suppose it would be," Casewell agreed, rising to fill his bucket again.

"Oh no. I didn't mean to hurry you," Liza said, beginning to pick her way across the rocks toward Casewell. He stepped closer to give her his hand. She perched on a stone near Casewell's, so he sat down once more.

"Frank and I did some of our sparking here." Liza looked wistful. Casewell hadn't been born yet when Frank ran off to be an animal wrangler for Wild Bill's Wild West in 1902. He was twelve or so when Liza's fiancé returned. Either Frank had taken to the bottle when he was in Europe or he took to it soon after he got home. He was rarely seen in polite company, and when he did come to town, he was almost always drunk. Casewell found Frank's behavior shameful.

"Once I took off my shoes and waded in this creek with Frank. Oh, I thought I was bold then. Maybe I was bold." Liza paused and leaned forward to dip her hand in the water. "I don't think I've felt bold even once since I gave up on Frank."

Casewell got the feeling that Liza might have forgotten he was there.

"Angie gave up on him long before I did, but she was always the sensible one. Mother said I was a dreamer." Liza sat gazing into the water so long that Casewell began to feel uncomfortable. Frank Post wasn't fit to clean Liza's boots. He cleared his throat and stood.

"Reckon I better finish watering the garden."

"Oh, I did interrupt your work, didn't I? Don't tell Angie. She'll fuss." Liza looked around as if finally seeing the creek with its canopy of trees and rhododendron almost enclosing it. "My, I think this may be the lowest I've ever seen the water."

"It is mighty low," agreed Casewell. "Guess it hasn't rained upstream, either."

"Help me to the bank, if you would." Liza held out her hand in a gesture that made Casewell see her as she must have been—a slender young woman with kind eyes and a gentleness that likely charmed Frank. He felt a flash of pity for the old drunk. Liza wasn't the only one who'd missed out.

Casewell finished carrying water and went in to tell the Talbot sisters good-bye. Angie quizzed him about how low the water in the creek was. He wondered that she didn't go down there herself to look. If Liza could make it, Angie would surely have no problem. The sisters finally bid Casewell good-night, and he headed for home.

The garden work was something Casewell wasn't used to anymore, and he could feel his tired muscles stiffening as he prepared for bed. He lay down and waited for sleep to come, which it almost always did quickly. But this night he lay awake, picturing a young woman wading in cold creek water while a young man looked on. Poor Frank. Poor Liza. Would they have been happy together? Would they still be married today? Would Liza have stayed "bold" if she'd had the love of a good man to encourage her? Would Frank have stayed sober?

His ponderings led him to think of Perla Long. Perhaps Sadie's father had made Perla feel bold and alive. Casewell felt anger burning in him at a man who would refuse to take responsibility for his child. And how could a man let a woman like Perla slip through his fingers? She had exercised poor judgment, certainly, but she didn't act alone.

Casewell realized he'd tangled his sheets around his legs. He felt trapped, caught up like a fly in a web. He kicked and pulled at the covers, almost panicking over the constricted feeling of the sheets wound about him. He got loose and sat on the side of the bed, panting a little. He pulled on his clothes and went out to the workshop to do some sanding. Sleep seemed elusive at the moment.

Casewell finally crawled into bed in the small hours of the morning. He woke far too early when the telephone jangled. He staggered into the kitchen and answered it.

"Casewell, I think you should come see your father today." His mother spoke without preamble.

"Is everything okay?" Casewell asked, still groggy with sleep.

"Fine, fine. I just think you should come today."

"All right. When?"

"Come on over now, and I'll feed you breakfast," she said and hung up the phone.

Casewell replaced the earpiece over the rotary dial on his wall phone. He scratched behind his ear in an absent kind of way, and it occurred to him to find the phone call a little strange. He walked back to his bedroom to get dressed.

At his parents' house, Casewell entered without knocking. He could smell sausage frying and his stomach rumbled. It had been a long time since the Talbot sisters' beans and corn bread hit bottom.

"Smells good, Mom," he said, pulling out a chair at the kitchen table and sitting. His father sat in his place, hunched over a cup of coffee, scowling. "Hey, Dad, how're you feeling this morning?"

His father let fly a curse that made Casewell flinch. "If one more person asks how I am, I'm gonna cut 'em."

Casewell glanced at his mother standing at the stove. She cast a worried look over her shoulder. She turned back and began cracking eggs into the sausage grease.

"How many, John?" she asked.

"None," he grunted. "Why should I eat if I'm gonna die anyway?"

Casewell began to see why his mother had called. "I'll take three, Mom," he said. She smiled gratefully.

"So, Dad, how're the calves coming?" he asked.

His father blew heavily, as if trying to disperse a cloud of mosquitoes. "They're coming. Can't say the same for the grass. No rain makes for poor feed."

"I was at the Talbot sisters' last evening. Creek's mighty low. Liza said it was the lowest she'd seen it."

"Drought," Dad intoned, as if he were about to launch into a great speech. His eyes were a little glassy. "Gonna be a terrible drought. I can feel it in my bones. Could be the end of us all." He turned crazy eyes on Casewell. "Not just me—all of us."

"Well, now, you never know." Mom slid a plate with three eggs, sausage, and biscuits in front of Casewell. She set a plate with just one egg in front of Dad, as if she were trying not to draw attention. Then she fetched her own plate and joined the men at the table.

Casewell began to eat. He hoped his father would follow the example, and he did for three bites. Then he pushed his plate away and stood to look out the window. "A great drought. Like when Joseph predicted seven years of lean. A biblical drought."

Casewell felt a chill crawl down his spine. His father spoke like some kind of prophet, though Casewell assumed it was the cancer eating at his mind and his well-being. Something like that would make anyone go dark and gloomy.

"We'll be all right, I reckon," Casewell said. "The creek has never gone completely dry, and the wells around here are plenty deep. It's just a dry spell. We have 'em most every year."

His father returned to the table and finished his egg and biscuit. Then he got up and went to sit on the porch and smoke.

"At least he ate," Emily said. "I haven't been able to get him to eat anything for two days. And when he talks like that, it's all I can do to stay in the room."

"It's all right, Mom." Casewell put his large, calloused hand over his mother's. "If you didn't get a little out of sorts, I'd wonder about you."

"That's just it." Emily turned frightened eyes on her son. "The dying I can stand. It's this crazy talk that's wearing me out. I try to talk sense to him and he gets angry. So angry. But leaving him alone isn't enough, either. He somehow wants me to be with him in his crazy talk. He wants me to talk back, and I have no idea what to say."

"Maybe you should just listen and agree. Maybe he just wants someone to hear him."

"Don't we all," Emily sighed. "Don't we all."

THE JOY AND FELLOWSHIP the people of Wise felt the night of the barn dance began to fade as day after day of cloudless skies brought worries of drought. Summer seemed too much too soon as temperatures climbed and the sun beat down without mercy. Casewell had been to the Talbots' to carry water three times, and he hauled barrels of water to his parents' house to try to keep their garden going. Each time he pulled up to the edge of the garden with his sloshing cargo, his father watched from the porch.

"I'd help you, son," he said, "but it won't do no good." Then he laughed and slapped his thigh. He'd never been one for jokes, and his laughter sounded eerie to Casewell.

By the middle of June, the creek at the Talbots' dwindled to a trickle. Dead fish stank initially, but soon they were so desiccated hardly any smell remained. The pond Casewell dipped from to water his parents' garden was little more than sludge and dying frogs. Gardens withered and folks were uneasy.

Talk at the Thorntons' store grew gloomy. Locals quoted the book of Revelation and talked about end times. The farm community suffered, and as a result, fewer folks shopped at the store. No one ordered Casewell's handiwork, and a general feeling of doom hung around like dust over a dirt road on a still day.

That Sunday the congregation murmured and shifted, uneasy in the hard pews. Casewell couldn't get comfortable, and Pastor Longbourne's voice seemed to drone in a way that made it hard to understand the words. Then, near the end of the service, Pastor Longbourne mentioned the dry spell.

"We are facing a drought," the pastor said, gripping the sides of the pulpit. "Gardens are dying, crops are failing, cattle will soon be hungry. We must pray. But it isn't enough that we pray individually. We must pray collectively. The church will be open every day this week, and I expect to see every one of you here to pray that God will rain His blessings down upon us.

"And not only must we pray, we must also repent. In Deuteronomy chapter eleven, verses sixteen and seventeen, you will find the words, 'Take heed to yourselves, that your heart be not deceived, and ye turn aside, and serve other gods, and worship them; and then the Lord's wrath be kindled against you, and he shut up the heaven, that there be no rain, and that the land yield not her fruit; and lest ye perish quickly from off the good land which the Lord giveth you.'"

Pastor Longbourne's voice softened as he finished reciting the Scripture. He suddenly released the pulpit and brought both fists down on the Bible that always lay open there. The crack of the impact reverberated through the now-hushed church.

"There are sinners among us," he said. "There are those among us who have turned aside from the Lord our God, and His wrath has been kindled against us. Repent. Repent and pray. It is our only hope."

Normally the congregation would sing a closing song and

receive a benediction before moving into the churchyard to visit with one another. But on this Sunday, Pastor Longbourne made a slashing motion through the air in front of his face. "Go," he said. "Eat your Sunday dinner, spread your gossip, and watch your future wither and die on the vine. As for me, I will pray." The pastor moved to the side of the pulpit and carefully lowered himself to his knees. Those in the front pews could hear the crack and pop of his joints. He clasped his hands and began to pray softly, under his breath, his voice rising and falling like the humming of a hive.

At first the congregation sat slightly stunned, as if afraid to move. Then a few eased to the front of the church or out into the aisles to kneel and pray. Even the children sensed the need to remain quiet and still. Longbourne's individual hum soon doubled, then tripled, with the occasional punctuation of "Amen" or "Yes, Lord."

Casewell had never seen anything like this. His mother leaned forward next to him, her forehead resting on her folded hands on the back of the pew in front of her. Some cried, some begged, and some raised their hands in the air. One even lay down in the aisle. Casewell bowed his head and tried to pray for rain, tried to pray for forgiveness of his sins, although he had a hard time saying exactly what his sins were. He felt his father stir beside him and looked up.

Dad stood and made his way to the front of the church. He looked down at Pastor Longbourne and then turned his gaze across the congregation. "Fools," he bellowed. "You are fools to believe that God will hear and forgive. God does not forgive. God punishes—He weakens and shames and taunts you with your shortcomings. There will be no rain. God does not care for any of you."

He limped down the aisle to the door. As he passed, Casewell thought he heard his father mumble, "Nor does He care for me."

⁂

Even after Dad's outburst, many in the church stayed to fast and pray. Others took the opportunity to slip out and go home. Mom looked torn, so Casewell told her he thought they should find his father and go to the house. She nodded and they found Dad smoking a cigarette in back of the church. He remained quiet the rest of the afternoon, as if he had used up any energy he had spreading despair.

That evening in his own home, Casewell fell to his knees and prayed that God would forgive his sins, whatever they might be, and stop punishing the people he loved. He prayed that his father would find that the cancer had been a mistake, that his mother would have the security of a healthy husband, and that the community would have rain. Casewell begged God to bring relief to the people around him. "Not for my sake, Lord," Casewell breathed, "but for theirs."

That night Casewell dreamed that his father was cured and, as a result, became cruel and miserable. He dreamed that his mother cried at the news of his father's good health. He dreamed that rain came and floods washed all the crops away. The people he loved most turned on him, called him names, and said that their problems were his fault. Perla appeared carrying a casserole dish that she placed in front of Casewell. She handed him a spoon. "Eat it," she said. "This is for your sake."

Casewell woke in a cold sweat and thought for a moment he might be sick. The nausea passed, though, and he lay for a long time staring at the ceiling, trying to think of what he wanted to say to God. He finally fell asleep again, still trying to form the words of a prayer.

A few days later, Casewell stopped by the Thorntons' store to pick up a few groceries. His mother kept him well stocked, but he needed coffee and sugar. Robert and Delilah were talking quietly in the back when he came in. Delilah moved toward the front counter.

"What can I get you?" she asked.

"Coffee, sugar, and how about a wedge of that hoop cheese, there. Oh, and a box of saltines."

Delilah gathered the few things and began ringing them up. "Guess you've heard that some folks have yet to leave the church after Sunday's service," she said.

"No, I hadn't heard. But the preacher said he'd keep the church open all week. Guess some folks took him serious."

Robert drifted forward while Casewell and Delilah spoke. "Some folks say it's like when the disciples tried to cast out a demon and couldn't do it," he said. "Jesus told them it couldn't be done but by fasting and prayer. I, for one, don't understand how that'll help, but who knows? Seen any clouds this morning?"

Casewell stepped to the door and scanned the sky. "Clear," he said.

"Those poor people must be half-starved by now," Delilah said. "Fasting is one thing, but starving yourself is just foolish. I feel like I ought to take some food over there, but, well," she looked uneasily from Robert to Casewell.

"What my wife is trying to say is that business has been mighty slow lately. Crops aren't looking so good and folks have started cutting back. We're barely selling the necessities, much less anything that could be called a luxury. Shoot, even coffee sales are down." Robert slapped the sack of beans on the counter in front of Casewell. "We don't have as much to spare as we once did, and from the looks of things, I'm not feeling too confident about the future."

Just then Perla stepped through the door with Sadie trailing along behind her. She carried a large pot that looked heavy. "Delilah, I hope it's all right that I made a pot of beans to run over to the church," she said. "And I've got a couple of cakes of corn bread back at the house if one of you would run get it. I figured to take it over so those that want to eat can do it."

Delilah blushed. "I'm so glad you thought to do that, Perla. I'll get the corn bread, but what will people eat from?"

Casewell gave a start. "Business has been slow," he said. "I've taken to making wooden bowls from scraps. I must have twenty or so stacked up in the workshop."

"Well, fetch 'em and meet us at the church," Delilah said. "We'll see about feeding the hungry masses."

Not long after, Casewell found himself handing bowls of creamy beans and hunks of corn bread out to his neighbors and friends at the church. A few refused, saying they would continue to fast, but most accepted the food gratefully and ate it with relish. Soon, folks who hadn't been at the church got word the Thorntons were hosting a bean supper and began drifting in—some bringing their own bowls. Casewell sighed when he saw the crowd swelling. They would run out soon and people would be disappointed.

But Perla kept dishing up beans and breaking off pieces of bread until the fifty or so who had come had been fed. Those who finished first rinsed their bowls in a tub Robert had hauled over and handed them to the next in line.

As the crowd dwindled, Casewell looked up to see Frank

Post drift in the door. It was probably the first time he'd set foot inside the church since coming home in 1930. His thick, wavy hair had gone entirely white and stood at odd angles from his head. Casewell saw the old man glance around and try to smooth his wild hair into place. His face wore creases and lines that suggested he'd spent much of his life laughing in the sun—though he wasn't laughing now. He was almost painfully thin, and his blue-gray eyes were soft and tired like faded flowers.

Frank approached the table and shifted uneasily from one foot to the other. The smell of stale liquor seemed to ooze from his pores. He licked his lips and looked like he might speak. Before he could, Perla took the old man's hand and pressed a bowl into it.

"There's plenty," she said. "Let me know if you'd like more."

Frank gave a stuttery nod and went to stand by an open window to eat. Casewell felt scorn rise as he watched Frank scoop beans into his mouth with his fingers. He turned back to his work and tried to forget about the old drunk. It was a good thing Jesus loved Frank Post, because Casewell didn't much care for him.

After the last person had accepted his meal, Casewell turned to Perla, certain he would have to find his own lunch. She handed him a bowl, which he accepted with raised eyebrows.

"And look," Delilah said, wonder in her voice, "there's still a little left." She held up the pot with several spoonfuls of beans still in the bottom and waved her hand at half a cake of corn bread.

Perla laughed softly. "Oh well, it always seems to work out."

Casewell lifted a spoonful of beans to his mouth and was immediately distracted from the mystery of how they had fed so many. The beans, simple beans, melted in his mouth. Perla must have used a ham hock to give them their slightly smoky, savory flavor. He could sense the shape of each individual bean in his mouth just before they dissolved into a deliciously creamy mass. And the corn bread was moist with a wonderfully crisp crust. He would have expected it to be cold and maybe even a little dried out by now, but it was quite possibly the best thing he'd ever put into his mouth. There were actual pieces of corn in the bread, and it had a slight tang that vibrated across his tongue—buttermilk probably. Normally he would wish for butter or some jelly on his corn bread, but he couldn't imagine anything improving this food. He finished, and just as he thought to ask for a little more, he realized that he was perfectly full and perfectly content. He did not desire another bite.

Casewell looked across the church to where Frank helped Perla collect bowls and stack them in a large basket. He had thought her beautiful before, but now he was sure she was the most breathtaking woman he had ever laid eyes on. He hated that Frank was so near her.

Perla saw him walking toward her. "Casewell, thank you for the bowls. I'm amazed we got all those people fed, but things usually work out. Have you ever noticed that?"

Casewell shook his head and tried to give Frank a stern look without Perla seeing.

"Well, they do. Not always the way you think they will, but they turn out." Perla dropped her head and didn't move for a moment. "Of course, with your father sick, that probably sounds like nonsense," she said. "I'm praying for him and the rest of your family. I'll try not to be trite when you're dealing with something so difficult."

Casewell finally found his voice. "Thank you," he said as he handed her his empty bowl. It wasn't what he wanted to say at all. And he could have sworn he saw Frank grin at his discomfort.

By Saturday most folks had given up on the prayer vigil, although a few were still praying. Casewell had dropped in a couple of times to join the praying, but somehow his heart wasn't in it. He felt like they were asking God for something that God had already decided about. Like Abraham trying to bargain for Sodom and Gomorrah. The cities were destroyed, and of the few who escaped, one became a pillar of salt just for looking back. Casewell knew God was not to be trifled with. He had a plan and there was a fair chance none of them would like it. Casewell had prayed for many things that he did not receive. He knew better than to expect God to go soft now. The safest thing was to pray "Thy will be done" and then grit his teeth for what would come.

Saturday evening he walked home from the church. Only two old-timers had stayed, saying they would pray through the night. Casewell felt torn between admiration for their stamina and scorn for the waste of time and energy. As he walked, he noticed the grass had withered and the leaves that had unfurled soft and green on the trees just a few weeks before were now curled and brittle looking. A fine layer of dust had settled on everything, and Casewell felt as if a fine grit coated his teeth.

Word got out that some wells had gone dry, and those families now carried water from neighbors. Farmers fed what remained of their winter hay stores to the cattle. It was time for the first cutting of the year, but there simply wasn't anything to cut. His father had turned his cattle out into the hayfields, letting them graze what little could be found. Not only would there be no feed stored up for winter, but it was doubtful there would be enough to get through summer.

As Casewell trudged along, getting his boots dusty and trying to breathe through his nose, a truck pulled up beside him. It was his father.

"Hop in," Dad said, stopping in a cloud of dust. Casewell opened the passenger door and slid onto the cracked seat.

"I'm rethinking my plan, son." He shoved the truck into gear and eased forward so as not to stir up any more dirt than necessary. "Them cows I planned to sell this fall may not live that long without rain. We need to sell the calves now and hope the cows can tough it out until next year."

"Prices are bound to be low," Casewell said. "Maybe it will rain. Maybe we should just wait it out."

Dad cast him a sidelong glance and then turned his head and rolled the window down to spit. As he rolled it back up, he said, "And maybe wishing will cure me of cancer. Your mother is trying to make me well by pretending I ain't sick. I can tell by the feeling in my bones that it sure ain't working." He massaged his right thigh as he spoke.

"Are you in pain, Dad?"

"That's about the stupidest question I ever heard. I haven't felt good for the last fifteen years, and now every morning when I get out of bed, I hurt a little bit worse. Don't ask me ever again about pain, son."

Casewell felt tears rising and hated himself for it. His father, never a gentle man, was turning cruel with his illness. *It's just the cancer,* Casewell told himself. *He can't help it.*

"Come to the house Monday," Dad said, pulling up in front of Casewell's house. "The sooner we get those calves to market, the better. This drought will only get worse. Prices may be poor now, but they'll drop to nothing soon enough."

Casewell felt impatience and frustration rise in him. "How do you know?" he asked, speaking more sharply to his father than he had ever dared. "What makes you so sure?"

Dad sighed, air whooshing out of his lungs. "The devil told me. Don't expect to see me in church tomorrow. Comfort your mother the best you can." He shoved the truck back into gear and waited for Casewell to get out. Casewell slammed the door harder than he needed to and didn't look back as his father drove away.

Sunday morning dawned with an uneasy feeling in the air. Children whimpered, old folks mumbled prayers, and everyone shifted in the pews as if they couldn't get comfortable. Frank Post sat in the back right corner, his hair somewhat tamed. Maybe the old drunk was making folks uneasy, or maybe it was the week of praying and the drought putting them on edge. But Casewell noticed as Perla and Sadie trailed Robert and Delilah to their usual pew, a disturbance seemed to follow in their wake—a murmur that wasn't altogether pleasant.

Pastor Longbourne got up and said that instead of their usual service, they would pray throughout the morning, along with some Scripture readings. "There are rumors that this drought is not natural," he said. "That someone among us has brought it on us as punishment for our sins. Or perhaps for the sins of someone in particular. It is not for me to say, but if you have sinned, I call on you to repent as though your life depended upon it. Repent as though all of our lives depended upon it."

Casewell could have sworn that the pastor looked at Perla as he spoke, but surely not. There was sin aplenty to go around.

The service seemed to drag on forever. Old man Peterson took a fit and began speaking gibberish. The old folks called out that he was speaking in tongues and listened attentively, as if they could decipher what he was saying. As he ranted on, an old woman cried out, "Repent, harlot! He calls on you to repent."

Casewell didn't know how much more he could stand, but finally Pastor Longbourne called for a closing prayer that went on for a good ten minutes. Following his "Amen," Casewell rose to his feet and hoped others would accompany him out the door. He had always considered himself a stalwart member of the congregation, an upright pillar of the community, setting a good example for others. But somehow on this morning, it was all he could do not to run as far as possible from the church and the people who seemed to fill the building with fear.

Stepping into the churchyard, Casewell stood off to the side, watching others make their way out. They gathered in clumps and talked quietly among themselves. It had the feeling of a funeral.

George Brower eased over to where Casewell stood and shoved his hands deep into his pockets. "Ever seen the like?" he asked.

"I reckon not," Casewell said. "And I hope not to see it again anytime soon."

"The drought is bad enough, but this witchcraft talk is getting folks too riled up for their own good."

"What are you talking about?" Casewell asked, stunned by his friend's words.

"That Perla Long feeding a hundred people out of one pot

of beans and half a cake of corn bread ain't natural." George shuffled his feet in the dust. "Folks figure there's no explanation for it other than witchery."

"It was a big pot of beans, and there were at least four cakes of corn bread," Casewell said. "I was there to help hand it out. And there weren't any hundred people. What kind of nonsense is that, anyway?"

"Old man Peterson says that folks what ate from Perla's hand lost the will to pray and went home. He says she must be a witch to make food last like that and to make people so contented that they'd give up doing the work of God after eating it."

Casewell was having a hard time following George's explanation. "Wait a minute. You're saying that folks suspect Perla is a witch because she fed them?"

"I guess it was the way she fed them. Never running out of food, like magic."

"Shootfire, man, I was there handing out the bowls. Does that make me a witch, too?"

"I think the term is *warlock*, but no, I haven't heard that anyone thinks that. They just think she's, well, enchanted you a little or some such." George seemed to be trying to drive his hands right through the bottoms of his pockets. "It's foolish, I guess, but you know how people are, making judgments and deciding things on their own."

Casewell felt the anger begin to drain out of him. He did know how people were. He knew how he was and the kinds of judgments he'd made about people. The kind of judgment he'd made about Perla with her illegitimate child. Anger began to give way to shame, and he looked around the churchyard for Perla. He didn't have any idea what he would do once he found her, but the need to know where she was and what she was doing rose in him like sap in the spring. He could no more fight it back than he could stop the sun from rising. But Perla and the Thorntons were gone.

"Where is Perla?" he asked.

"I think maybe Delilah got a whiff of what was going around and bundled her and the child on back to the house." George squinted into the distance. "Probably for the best."

Perla went straight to the room she shared with Sadie when they arrived home from church. Her aunt, uncle, and daughter were in the kitchen pulling out leftovers for lunch, but Perla excused herself, saying she wanted to change her clothes. She stripped off her gloves, tossed her hat on the bed, and loosened the fabric belt that matched her periwinkle dress. She reached back for the zipper, then dropped onto the edge of the bed. She had been moving mechanically, but suddenly the will to keep putting one foot in front of the other left her. All she could do was sit, hands braced against the bed to either side.

She had heard the whispers. She had seen the looks. And it was worse than being a scarlet woman. It was worse than being known as the woman who gave in to the lust of the flesh and now had to carry her sin with her in the form of an innocent child. They thought she was evil. Not just sinful—that, she could stand—but to believe that her ability to feed people, to give them love in the form of nourishment, was witchcraft? How could they?

"I'll have to stop cooking," she whispered to herself. "It always happens, so I'll just have to stop."

But it was the only thing she had to give to Robert and

Delilah. It was how she repaid them for their kindness and for giving her a place to stay. Perla knew business was slow at the store, and if the drought continued, it would get worse. Her aunt and uncle would never ask her to leave, but if she stayed and gave them two extra mouths to feed, the least she could do was cook food that somehow multiplied in the preparation.

"God," she said in a low voice, "why would you curse me this way? Why would you give me a gift that appears to others as evil?"

Perla eased down onto the bed as if she ached, as if a sudden movement would be disastrous. Once her head touched the pillow, despair washed over her, and she fell asleep. As if sleep would absolve her of the agony of her abilities.

And in sleeping, Perla dreamed. She dreamed of a man in a robe with sandals on his feet. It looked like he was praying over baskets of food. And then people came and began taking food from the baskets, and no matter how many came, there was still more for them to eat. And they were satisfied.

9

CASEWELL WENT TO HIS WORKSHOP as soon as he got home. He sat and looked around. The space was clean. All the shavings and bits of wood had been swept away. He had stacked leftover pieces of lumber under his bench, and the larger lengths were securely stowed in the rafters. Everything was in its place. The only thing missing, thought Casewell, was a work in progress. He had finished all his commissions, and he was tired of making bowls. With the drought putting a strain on nearly everyone's finances, he knew there would be no orders for kitchen stools or new shelves or front-porch repairs. He was bored, and with everything on his mind, boredom was eating away at him.

He thought to go to the house and get out his mandolin, but he couldn't seem to put the thought into action. He stared at his tools and the pieces of wood until something began to take form in his mind.

A bed. Casewell had always wanted to make a really beautiful bed. Not just a serviceable piece of furniture, but a grand, magnificent piece that would be a source of delight and wonder to its owner. So often his work required him to build practical items for daily use. Even when he made something more challenging, like the Talbots' cupboard, the furniture was simple and straightforward. There was little demand for intricate carving or fancy work. But now he had the time and the materials lying about idle. He would make a bed with a high, elaborate headboard and a footboard too beautiful to ever drape a pair of dungarees across. He would make something more wonderful than he ever had before.

Casewell slapped his knees and stood up to take stock of his lumber. He had a plan and he was excited about it. He knew he should be worried about the drought and how he and his neighbors would make it through the year. He knew his father was in trouble and his mother was suffering by his side, but he still found himself feeling like a kid headed off to the fair. Wonderful things were right around the corner.

A thought hit Casewell. What would he do with this bed once he made it? He could always keep it, but what did he need a fancy bed for? His parents—of course. He would make a Christmas gift of the bed to his parents. Assuming his dad was still around. Casewell shook that thought off. He'd be around. Christmas wasn't so far away, and his father was still as active and ornery as ever. Well, almost. Casewell began to pull out lumber so that he could see his fancy bed take form in it.

That evening Casewell sat on the front porch, feeling contented in spite of worrying about his father, the weather, and Perla Long. The bed was taking shape as though his hands knew what to do without his head telling them. It had been a long time since Casewell made something bigger than a bowl just for the pleasure of it. He felt good.

It was one of those soft summer evenings when the days

were hot, but the nights were still cool. The air had an almost mossy quality to it—even the color of the dusk settling across the pasture and the trees beyond seemed green. Casewell sighed and laced his hands behind his head, tilted his chair back on two legs, and braced his feet against a porch post the way his mother always told him not to. He smiled.

Across the pasture, Casewell thought he saw movement—probably a deer browsing in the edge of the woods. He kept watching until he could make out a figure walking slowly across the dying field. Eventually he could see that it was a woman, and soon he recognized Perla. It was clear she had no intention of walking close enough for him to speak. She followed an arcing path through the field that would soon begin carrying her further away. Without giving it much thought, Casewell stood and walked out to meet her.

"Mind if I walk with you?" he asked.

"No," she said without looking at him.

"Sure is a pretty evening," he said.

Perla looked up and around, as if checking to make sure he was telling the truth. "Yes." She had been walking slowly with her hands clasped behind her back, but now she released her hold and began to move with more purpose.

"Where are you headed?"

"Back to the house. I hate to leave Sadie for long."

"I'm so used to being alone, I guess I forget how some folks relish a few minutes to themselves." Casewell matched his long stride to Perla's shorter one. "And here I am, interrupting your solitude."

Perla looked surprised. "I don't mind," she said. "Pretty much everyone else is leaving me alone right now." She made the statement without any hint of bitterness or anger. "I'm afraid the rumors are even bothering Robert and Delilah. I may have to find somewhere else to go soon."

"But you can't leave," Casewell blurted.

Perla laughed a little. "You're probably right—I can't. But I may have to just the same."

"Where would you go? Back home?"

"No," Perla answered slowly. "There are stories there, too—probably the same stories. No, I guess I'd have to find someplace new. Someplace where I can pretend I don't have . . ." She hesitated, then thrust her chin out. "This misbegotten child and this strange way with food."

Casewell tried to hide his shock and quickly asked, "What's strange about your food? It's mighty good and I guess you always make plenty, but I haven't noticed anything else."

"Haven't you?" Perla gave him a bemused look. "Usually the women notice first. Delilah realized I had a . . . well . . . a knack, right away. But I think she loves me too much to say anything or even to think it's odd. Robert's like you—he's still not sure what people are talking about."

"So what is it, then?"

Perla stopped and turned to face Casewell. "I guess if I can tell you about Sadie, I can tell you about my cooking. I seem to have a gift for plenty—for making lots of food out of almost nothing."

"Well, I guess there are quite a few ladies around here who can do that." Casewell felt relieved. "Mom can take just a few potatoes and turn them into a meal fit for a king. Surely that's not so strange."

"No, Casewell. It's not just using ingredients to their best advantage. When I cook, whatever I cook doesn't run out. Not for a long time. Like those beans at the church. I made enough for maybe twenty people, but we didn't run out until everyone was fed."

"Oh, now, I was there and you made food aplenty. Why, there were the four cakes of corn bread and—"

Perla cut him off. "I made two cakes, Casewell. Folks ate at least nine—probably more. I just went back to the basket for the same pans over and over again. I hoped no one would notice."

Casewell stood unmoving, a look of confusion on his face. "But how is that possible?"

Perla stamped a foot, crossed her arms across her chest, and gripped her upper arms as if she were cold. Tears came to her eyes. "I don't know," she whispered. "I've prayed and prayed that God would take this thing from me, but He just won't do it. I try not to make so much food, and it's almost as if the less I make, the more there is. How can abundance be a bad thing?" Her eyes pleaded with Casewell to explain.

"It's not," he said. He reached out and placed one hand awkwardly on her shoulder. A Scripture popped into his head—*I am come that they might have life—and that they might have it more abundantly*. "I think it's a gift," he said. "And sometimes the gifts God gives us feel like burdens, but we have to trust that He knows what He's doing. How have you used your gift?"

Perla relaxed her grip on her arms. "To feed people—mostly people I love."

"There you go. Folks just don't understand. Shoot, I don't understand, but from what I know of you, I'd say you're closer to an angel than a witch." He reddened as soon as he realized what he'd said and dropped his hand back to his side.

Perla smiled and began to walk again.

"That I am not." She laughed softly. "But if you can see your way clear to accept me as I am, maybe others will, too." She glanced at him, a faint twinkle in her eyes. "When I first arrived here, I heard you described as a pillar of the community."

Casewell felt his face burn hotter. But this time what he felt was more shame than anything. When she'd first arrived, he would have agreed with her, but now . . .

"No more than you're really an angel, I guess. Folks are mighty quick to slap labels on people around here."

"I think it makes them feel safer." Perla glanced up at the stars beginning to show. "People like to know where they fit, and it's easier to find your own place if everyone else is safely in theirs."

They walked the rest of the way to the Thorntons' in silence. Casewell stopped at the bottom of the steps and watched Perla make her way up onto the porch. She turned at the top to wish Casewell a good-night. The light from inside the house cast a halo around Perla's hair, and Casewell had to smile. She might not be an angel, but she couldn't help looking like one.

She seemed to hesitate, then spoke. "Thank you, Casewell. I felt like maybe you judged me harshly after I told you about Sadie. Somehow, after this evening, I feel, well, I guess I feel like you've forgiven me. Like you're not going to hold my sins against me anymore. I appreciate that."

Before Casewell could reply, she turned and disappeared inside the house.

Why did she continue to bare her heart and soul to Casewell Phillips? Perla berated herself. She hadn't felt the condemnation radiating from him the way she had on the night she told him about Sadie. But still, what was it about the man that seemed to pull the truth from her?

She tried to remember the Scripture about the truth setting you free, but it wouldn't come. And she surely didn't feel free just then. She felt laid bare—stripped to her core with little left to hide behind. And she wanted to hide more than anything. She wanted to hide from the stares at church, from the whispers she couldn't help but overhear, from the choices she'd made, and the repercussions that continued to unfold.

Alone in her room while Sadie listened to the radio with Robert and Delilah, Perla sat at the dressing table and unfastened her hair where she had rolled it at the nape of her neck. She closed her eyes and remembered how it had felt when Sadie's father unfastened her hair and let it fall soft against her shoulders. Her eyes flew open and she reached for a brush. She must banish such thoughts from her mind. She had no business giving in to her longings. And remembering was the last thing she needed now.

Perla drew the brush through her hair, jerking at knots. She slowed and thought about Casewell's hand on her shoulder. It was obvious he'd been uncertain about touching her, which made it all the more tender. His big heart had overcome his sensibilities. She bowed her head. She might have loved a man like Casewell if she hadn't thrown herself away on a man she'd known she could never have.

Folding her arms on the table, Perla laid her head down. She meant to cry, but the tears didn't come. She felt as dry and barren as the world around them. Walking with Casewell, hearing him call her ability with food a gift from God, she was beginning to understand just how far reaching her choice would be.

That night Casewell knelt beside his bed to pray. He'd given up this affectation a long time ago, but somehow it seemed the thing to do. The floor was hard beneath knees that weren't quite as flexible as they'd once been. He clasped his hands and squeezed his eyes shut, but nothing came. Casewell usually found that prayer came easily. He could close his eyes, think of his Lord, and just let the thoughts roll through his mind as naturally as the sunrise. But on this night, when he stilled his mind to tap into his connection with God, he found himself at a loss. Nothing came. The flow had stopped.

Casewell's eyes flew open and he shifted on his knees. There was a bit of dirt or a tiny stone under his right knee, but he did not move to brush it away. He gritted his teeth and closed his eyes again. The presence that he so often felt seemed absent. "Oh, God," he whispered, dropping his head forward onto the edge of the mattress. Where could God be? He had always been so sure of his faith, of where he stood with God. But on this night he felt lost, alone, like he was wandering in a wilderness.

A dry, arid wilderness, thought Casewell, *where crops are dying and people are so desperate for answers, they lash out at one another. They're looking for someone to blame, someone to take responsibility.* Casewell had been a child during the Depression, but he could remember enough. He remembered saving his too-large and eventually too-small shoes just for church. He remembered those times when the bounty of their cellar waned while they waited for the spring planting season to wax. He remembered having little more than corn bread and milk for dinner and seeing the hard looks on his parents' faces.

Casewell tried to focus, to remember what it was he wanted to say to God. Usually the names of those in need paraded across his mind in a never-ending array, and he would call God's help down for them. Casewell had prayed for the church and the farms and the local businesses. He had prayed for the sick, the confused, the outcast. But on this night, all that would come to mind was that he needed to pray for his own soul. He needed to pray that his heart would soften and he would come to know his fellowman and love him. But that seemed like nonsense. Casewell clasped his head between his hands and wrinkled his brow with the effort to keep his eyes closed and his mind focused on God.

It was no use. Nothing came. Casewell pushed himself to his feet and made his way to the bathroom to clean his teeth and wash his face. He felt that God had abandoned him. And then, without warning, he thought, *Judge not, that ye be not judged.* He actually spun around as if someone had spoken the words from the hall. Of course no one was there. He shook his head and finished readying himself for bed.

10

Caswell headed for his workshop as soon as he'd swallowed some coffee the next morning. His father had changed his mind about selling the cattle, so he had the whole day ahead of him. He hadn't felt this eager to get to work in years. It was invigorating, and it was an escape from the desolation he'd felt the night before. He was completely absorbed in his work when Frank Post knocked on his open door.

"Howdy, neighbor," Frank said. "Mind if I sit and visit a spell?"

Casewell did mind but said he'd be glad of the company and stood to stretch out his neck and shoulders. He couldn't imagine why Frank had come to see him. The man had no friends to speak of and until recently was rarely seen anywhere other than his own home or the Simmonses' back porch, where just about everyone knew moonshine was stored under the third step from the bottom.

"Whatcha making there?" Frank asked.

"A bed."

"Well, now, that's a tall order."

"Actually, it's not an order. I've just always wanted to make one." Casewell ran his hand over the piece of wood he was shaping. "Most likely I'll give it to Mom and Dad for Christmas."

"I was real sorry to hear about how sick your father is," Frank said, staring at a point between his booted feet. "I never got to know him real well, but he always seemed like a good 'un."

"He is that." Casewell turned back to his work, hoping Frank would take the hint and leave.

"Reckon you could find time for a commission?" Frank asked.

Casewell stopped what he was doing and turned back to Frank, curious. "I could. Paying work is mighty thin right now."

"I need a tea table. The finest, most delicate, prettiest little tea table you can conjure. From the looks of that carving you've sketched out over there"—he pointed at the unfinished footboard with his chin—"I'm thinking you're the man for the job."

"That's the kind of work that takes time. I've got plenty of time, but I'll have to charge more than I would for a plain table," Casewell said, tugging his beard.

"I've got time and I've got money. So far I haven't had near as much use for either one as I would have thought when I was your age. But now, well, it's time to set some things right."

Casewell couldn't help wondering if Frank thought to make amends with Liza. He was still trying to figure women out, but he was skeptical that a table, no matter how nice, was really the way to say you were sorry for abandoning your fiancée. Even so, it was paying work, and it would help him pace himself on the bed.

"All right then, I'll make some drawings to show you what I'm thinking and bring them over to the house tomorrow," Casewell said.

"Nope. I'd rather come on by here. I don't have near enough reasons to get out and about. How's four o'clock sound?"

"Fine. Now as to the payment—"

"We'll talk about that tomorrow," Frank cut in. "I'll be more than fair. I've been unlucky in life in a lot of ways, but money's not been a worry for a long time. Wish it could do anybody any good."

Frank stood and flexed his knees. "I still get around pretty good, but these old joints seize up on me if I stay still too long. See you tomorrow." He walked out the door as silently as he had come.

Casewell considered that if he were the sort to spread gossip, he'd have plenty of grist for the mill. Who was the table for? Where did Frank get his money? Was he sober for once? The old man seemed to be sober—how long would that last? Casewell stood thinking for a moment; then the unfinished bed caught his eye, and within moments he was once again completely absorbed in his work. He'd start the tea-table drawing after supper.

The next afternoon Frank arrived at four on the dot. Casewell showed him a sketch of a dainty little piecrust table with a top that could be removed and used as a tray. Instead of carving, he thought he'd try his hand at a little inlay. He laid out a geometric design based on one of his mother's quilt patterns. He could use cherry and maple to create the starburst in the center of the table. He planned to use walnut for the base. Casewell was pretty pleased with himself, and Frank agreed to the design right away. Before Casewell could name a price, Frank offered an amount almost twice what Casewell had been thinking. He agreed and accepted a down payment but said he would only accept the rest once the table was done.

"Sounds right," Frank agreed. "Guess you've come a long way from the troublemaker I knew back in the day."

Casewell looked at the older man in confusion. "Troublemaker?"

"Lordy, son, I know you were drunker than a skunk, but surely you remember?"

Casewell felt heat rise up his neck and a roaring start in his ears. "How do you—"

Frank quirked an eyebrow. "I was there. Come to think of it, I guess you wouldn't remember that part." The older man leaned back against the doorframe, as though settling in for a long story.

"I'd come out to the still to shoot the breeze and get my weekly allotment, but the Simmons boys were in high dudgeon when I got there. Seems somebody'd robbed the still and fouled up the copper tubing. Not only did they lose a run of liquor, but it was going to take some serious money and time to get the still working again."

Casewell closed his eyes and sank onto a stool. He thought no one knew. He'd been so sure no one ever knew.

Frank continued, seeming to enjoy the tale. "If those boys had been hornets, I would have guessed some fool had stuck a stick in their nest and stirred. I thought to leave, but they kind of pulled me in to help look for the culprit. Seems the feller what done it had left a trail a blind man could follow. We didn't have to go far before we come across you laid out under an old pine, snoring away. By the time I saw it was you, Clint already had his knife out and looked like he aimed to skin your face off."

Casewell's hand rose to find the scar along his jawline. His beard hid it, but his fingers knew how to read the raised flesh under the whiskers. "He might have killed me," Casewell whispered.

"Oh, he planned to. I reckon he cut on you to wake you up so he could kill you proper. Only you didn't much wake up, and I suggested an alternative. I paid 'em for what you took, along with enough to fix the still, and they agreed to let it be."

"How much was it?" Casewell couldn't hide his shock. It was bad enough that Frank knew he'd stolen moonshine and gotten drunk. To find out after all this time that his life had been saved by the town drunk was too much.

Frank looked Casewell straight in the eye. "I don't remember," he said. "And likely wouldn't say if I did. The past is past. Looks to me like you smartened up and turned out just fine. Let's speak no more of it."

"I can't charge you for that table. Take your money back."

Frank turned away and walked toward the door, leaving Casewell sitting on his stool, cash clutched in his hand. "There is no debt. If there was, it's been long forgiven. I'll be seeing you." And with that he was gone.

Casewell spent the rest of the week working on his two projects. Shaping the bed eased his mind, while the table plunged him into turmoil. Could forgiveness be that easy? Would his father have forgiven him for being a thief and a drunkard? Casewell felt pretty certain he would not. And the town drunk handed out forgiveness like it was the easiest thing in the world. Casewell hadn't even asked for it. He hadn't even known to ask for it. Casewell owed Frank more than he'd ever imagined, and Frank wouldn't let him pay the debt. All he could think to do was to make the most beautiful tea table the world had ever seen. It wasn't enough, but it was something.

The days flew by and Casewell hardly left the workshop except to eat and sleep. On Saturday his father rolled into the yard in his pickup in the middle of the afternoon, bringing the now ubiquitous dust cloud with him.

"Your ma done sent me to fetch you home to supper," he said when Casewell walked toward the truck. "She called, but you ain't been answering your phone."

Casewell had noticed that not only did his father curse occasionally now, but that his way of speaking was less careful. His father prided himself on not sounding like a country bumpkin and had always insisted Casewell avoid slang and poor grammar. Was this a symptom of cancer? he wondered.

"I've been working pretty hard lately, but I'm glad you're here. I could use a break, and I haven't been around to your place enough lately. I haven't even carried water to the garden this week."

"No need," Dad said. "Waste of time trying to fight this drought. I was hoping you'd give up. If you haven't, I'd recommend it."

Casewell thought he'd do well not to answer that. "Let me wash up and put on a clean shirt."

"I ain't going nowhere," Dad said, slouching in the driver's seat.

Casewell looked at his father a moment, but he just sat there, hat pulled low over his eyes. Casewell waited, not knowing for what, and when nothing else was forthcoming he went into the house. What had he been waiting for? He thought a moment. Ah, he had expected to see his dad pull out some tobacco and roll a cigarette. He couldn't remember the last time he'd seen him waiting for even two minutes without a cigarette between his lips.

After changing, Casewell walked out and swung into the truck beside his father. The pervasive smell of cigarette smoke was missing. Maybe he'd forgotten his makings at the house. He opened his mouth to ask about it and then decided not to. *Let it lie,* he thought. *Let it lie.*

When they pulled into the side yard, Casewell felt a little shocked to see how wilted the garden was. The corn was stubby; the bush beans were a sickly yellow and drooped to the ground; the squash leaves that should have been huge and shading delicate blossoms were small and sagged heavily over just a few clenched yellow flowers. He stood and stared.

Dad walked past Casewell. "Come on, son. All that water you hauled was a waste of time. Roots are shallow and plants are stunted. No need to waste any more time with that."

"But it hasn't been that long since I was here last. I thought the garden would hold up at least until today," Casewell said.

"Even a truckload of water won't save some of that stuff." Dad patted his pocket and seemed surprised to find it empty. "If it started raining tonight and rained good the rest of the summer, most of the garden would still be shot." He turned and let his eyes follow the fence line across the road where cattle grazed the parched field. "Can't make up the missed cuttings of hay. Can't make dead plants come back to life. Cattle gotta eat and so do we." He turned cool eyes on his son. "Hard times are coming. Makes dying seem a little easier."

Casewell felt frustration rise in the back of his throat like bile. He wanted to tell his father he was wrong. It would rain. The crops would be saved. The cattle would thrive and he would not die. But Casewell knew words wouldn't change anything. He knew his father was most likely right.

Supper that night was a solemn meal. Mom tried to make conversation and act cheerful, but even she had run out of sunlight by the time she dished up last summer's canned peaches for dessert.

"Not many of these left," she said, spearing a golden crescent of fruit. "I was counting on that tree over behind the cellar house making a good harvest. The way it was covered in blossoms this spring was a sight to behold. But the fruit is small and hard—wormy, too. I'm afraid I won't be able to salvage much to put up for winter."

"Mom." Casewell laid down his fork and looked hard at his mother. "Will you be able to get by if you don't have anything to put up this year? No green beans to can, no tomatoes or peaches, no potatoes to put in the root cellar. What will you and Dad have left come January?"

His father snorted. "Don't count on me needing anything to eat come January."

Emily shot her husband a stern look and turned to Casewell. "Well, son, I suppose we'll have enough to get along. I always put up way more than we need, so there's some to tide us over. And I imagine I'll get something out of the garden so long as it rains in the next week or so. No need to worry yet."

"It ain't gonna rain." Dad spoke the words harshly and stood, slamming his chair into the wall behind him. He glared at his wife and son and then went into the living room and slouched in a chair, where he stared at nothing.

Tears welled in Mom's eyes. Casewell couldn't stand to see his mother cry like this. "Mom, it's okay," he said, reaching out to touch her arm.

She placed her hand on top of Casewell's. "No, son, it's not. My orchard is dying, my garden is nearly dead, and my husband is eager to follow them." She looked at Casewell. "He doesn't want to live anymore. Medicine can't fight that." Tears began to run down her cheeks. "Love's the only thing that can fight it, and he's hardened his heart against me."

Casewell drew his mother into his arms and let her cry, fearing at any moment he would break under the weight of her grief. He knew his father's heart had hardened against him a long time ago.

Casewell was so absorbed by his work that he paid little attention to what was happening in the community over the next few weeks. But as the dog days of August approached, the drought became so dire no one could remain oblivious to it. Cattle were chewing on twigs and eating ivy, and there wasn't a farmer in the county with even one bale of hay remaining in his barn. Housewives raided cellar stores as gardens wasted away. Everything was coated in dust, and creeks had been reduced to dry rocks.

On a Tuesday, Casewell stood back to admire the bed he had wrought with his own two hands. The headboard was six-feet high, and both it and the footboard bloomed with roses. The wood had been sanded and polished to a high sheen. He ran his hand across the curve of the footboard and traced a rose with his finger. It was lovely and he felt a swell of pride. Suddenly he wanted to show the bed to Perla more than anything. He wanted her to admire it, touch it, and exclaim over its workmanship. But of course she would never see it. Casewell had made the bed for his parents, and it would be inappropriate to show a bed, of all things, to a single woman.

He shook the feeling and turned his attention to the tea table beside it. He was proud of his work there, too. The tray clicked into the top smoothly, making it easy to lift out and carry from room to room. The inlay was intricate but not gaudy. He thought it would somehow suit Liza Talbot, who managed to be dignified and homey at the same time. Not like her sister, who had always struck Casewell as a little stuck-up—a little too formal with everyone who crossed her path.

Casewell sat and looked at his work. Satisfaction spread through him. This was the kind of thing he had been made to do. Playing music pleased him, and most any work he could do with his hands satisfied, but this shaping of wood into useful and beautiful objects—this was what God intended for him to do. At one time, Casewell had thought God would have a grander plan for his life, but it seemed like woodworking was to be his lot. And that was just fine.

As he walked outside, Casewell felt like he was waking up from a deep sleep. He looked around at what was suddenly an alien landscape. He realized that the grass in the yard was brown, and there were bare spots of nothing but dirt. Some of the trees had lost their leaves, and those that remained looked sad and shriveled. A stand of pines close to the road was coated in a layer of dust, as was the mailbox. And it was hot. The sun beat down on the cracked earth, and Casewell noticed an absence of birdsong. He had emerged from his work into a wasteland. Fear rose in him, a foreboding tide that somehow seemed greater than the drought they were facing.

Casewell walked down to the Thorntons' store. He went with the pretense of buying something for his supper, but he also hoped he would hear the latest news. He wasn't disappointed. He walked into the store and found George, Steve, and some other men gathered around the counter, talking in low voices.

"Hey, fellers," Casewell said, "what's the news?"

"Not good," George said. "Word is some cattle down toward Indian Ridge have died for lack of water. Creeks are dried up, ponds are nothing but bottom muck, and even the springs are giving out. Most of us around here have deep wells, but we're gonna have to use those for our own selves." He shook his head and looked at the toe of his scuffed boot. "It ain't good."

Roger spoke next. "Some folks are getting low on food, too. Not everybody stocks a cellar the way your ma does. Shoot, even Robert here is running short on stuff."

Casewell looked around the store and saw that shelves were thinly stocked. "Why don't you get more stuff in here?" he asked Robert.

"Nobody's got money to buy anything, and my local suppliers are hard up. I've called more than sixty miles around trying to get some fruit or vegetables, and everybody's been hit hard by the drought. I've got some canned stuff, but like I say, nobody's got money for it, and it costs extra to bring things in from so far."

The men shifted uneasily and looked at each other's shoes. "What are we going to do?" Casewell asked.

"Just what we've been discussing," George said. "We were thinking it might be good to pool our resources, bring supplies down here to the store, and feed the whole community that way."

"I've been saying we need to let Perla do the cooking," chimed in Robert. "She's got a way with food, makes it stretch further than you'd think."

The men looked uncomfortable. "I don't know as my wife would eat what Perla cooked," Roger said slowly. "I don't mind myself." His eyes darted from face to face. "But some of the women seem to think there's something strange about that one."

"Are you men?" Casewell asked more loudly than he planned, but he didn't soften his tone. "Are you going to let the women bully you out of letting the best cook in the county stretch what food we've got to feed the whole town? Maybe there is something a little different about Perla Long, but I say we treat it like a gift, not a curse. We're in a fix here and I, for one, aim to do what it takes to get through."

As Casewell spoke, the men seemed to stand a little straighter—to stick their chests out a little further. One of them said, "They're probably just jealous because she can cook and she's easy on the eyes. Can't let that sway us."

There were nods of agreement and soon a general consensus was reached. They would go out and suggest to their neighbors and families that they bring everything they had down to the Thorntons' store and start a community kitchen. Robert said he'd haul his stove and Frigidaire over so they could set up a work area in the back of the store, where there was already a deep sink for cleaning. They made tables out of crates and some old doors Robert had stacked out back, and soon they were ready to put their plan into motion.

11

YOU TALK TO PERLA," Casewell said to Robert. "She may not like this at first, but I'm betting she'll come around."

Robert gave him a thoughtful look. "Know her that well, do you? Well, I suspect you're right. Delilah will get her to go along. Might not hurt if you asked her, too."

"I doubt that'll be necessary," Casewell said.

But the next morning, as Casewell boxed up some dry goods and canned things his mother had left for him to add to the community food stores, the phone rang. It was Robert, saying that Perla refused to cook. "She says she's caused enough trouble and suspicion around here, and she's not inviting more gossip by cooking for the whole community. Neither Delilah nor I can budge her. You'd better come see what you can do."

Casewell heaved the crate of food into the back of his truck and drove to the Thorntons'. He had no idea what to say and seriously doubted that he was the one to convince Perla of anything. Still, he found himself looking forward to talking to her.

She was sitting on the Victorian sofa in the parlor. Sadie sat on the floor, quietly arranging and rearranging the doll furniture Casewell had made for her. The little girl grinned at him. He walked over and sat in a delicate side chair. He thought it might break. Perla sat with legs crossed, seemingly engrossed in watching her right foot as she jiggled it.

"Robert told me you won't cook for folks."

"Why should I? To give them more ammunition? I've hardly left this house in over a month just to avoid adding fuel to the fire. And now you want me to strike the match."

Casewell thought she had a point. "I heard the Snowdens have just about run out of anything to feed their six kids. It'd be good of you to help, if only for the sake of those children." Even as Casewell spoke, he felt that this wasn't the right argument.

"Send the children to me," she said. "I don't owe their parents anything. They can stay home and go hungry." A tear slid down her cheek.

Sadie came to lean on her mother's leg and gazed up into her face. "Did they hurt your feelings, Mama?"

"Yes, sweetheart, but don't you worry about it. I'm okay." She cupped the child's cheek in her hand.

"Aren't you supposed to forgive people when they hurt your feelings?" Sadie asked.

Perla hung her head, and Casewell felt like he'd been hit with an electric shock. Perla had thanked him for forgiving her, but had he? Did he even have a right to? He suddenly wanted to fall to his knees and beg her to forgive him, but he wasn't entirely sure what needed forgiving. *With what judgment ye judge . . .*

"Perla, I . . ." Casewell began to speak. "I need to tell you something." But he still didn't know what it was.

"Yes?"

"I judged you," he blurted. "I had no right to, but I did." He darted a glance at Sadie. "You're a good mother and a good woman, and you have a remarkable gift that I think is from God. You said the other day that you felt like I had forgiven you. There's nothing for me to forgive, but I think I need your forgiveness."

Casewell hung his head and squeezed his eyes shut. He felt Sadie move to his side and lean against his knee. He opened his eyes and looked into the child's.

"I love you, Mr. Casewell," she said.

He looked up at Perla, who was crying softly but also smiling. She reached out to touch his cheek, and he felt peace fall on him softly, like rain.

Perla agreed to cook for the community, but only if Delilah, Robert, and Casewell helped. Casewell couldn't imagine what help he would be, but he agreed. Somehow he thought he owed it to Perla.

Food had already begun arriving at the Thorntons' store when the cooking crew showed up the next morning. Crates, boxes, sacks, and jars were stacked on the front porch, and people stood or sat on the porch and in the yard. It was quiet and there was a general atmosphere of unease.

Perla walked out ahead of her little group, chin up and eyes boring a hole in the front door of the store. She looked neither to the right nor to the left as she waited for Robert to open the door and usher her to the makeshift kitchen he'd set up in back.

"Bring me anything that will spoil first," she said. "We'll start with that."

Not much more than an hour later, Casewell and Robert

began dishing out beef stew to anyone who was hungry. The hush that had met them when they arrived continued to hang in the air. Casewell could have sworn he saw one or two of the older ladies bob a curtsy as he ladled stew into their bowls. He and Robert had helped make beaten biscuits, pounding the dough after Perla's arm gave out. Casewell wished folks would talk and laugh and make some noise, but he couldn't find a way to get them started.

And then Frank showed up.

"I hear the best cook in the whole of West Virginia is dishing out a free supper," he said, striding into the store. The silent, wild-haired drunk had been replaced by a dapper gent with a smile for everyone. "I could eat a bear, as Davy Crockett once said, and I aim to sample the victuals."

People looked up in surprise, and Casewell could have sworn he saw a little fear on a few faces. But then smiles started to spread as Frank made his way to the stewpot and asked if there was an extra bowl lying about. Casewell filled one of his own handcrafted bowls and handed it over. Frank dipped two fingers into the stew and scooped out a bite. He closed his eyes.

"Lordy, manna from heaven wouldn't taste half this good," he said with a sigh. "'Course forty years of beef stew might get old, but I'd be willing to give it a shot." He winked at Perla where she stood stirring a pot at the stove. She pushed strands of golden hair back from her perspiring forehead and gave Frank a tentative smile.

"I've eaten from your hand before, but I don't believe we've been properly introduced," he said.

"This is my niece, Perla." Robert came forward from where he'd been sitting on a keg of nails. "She's spending some time with Delilah and me, and this evening she's been kind enough to tackle feeding this unruly crowd." Robert nodded at the silent group gathered around the store.

Frank leaned in close to Robert and spoke in a stage whisper. "They'd best try and look like they're enjoying this tasty grub, lest Miss Perla take offense and refuse to feed 'em anymore. The gods on Mount Olympus might get tired of ambrosia, but I sure could eat this stew another night or two before givin' it up."

George Brower was sitting not far off, and he quirked a smile. "You ever hear tell about Joe Cutright's old dog Sloomer? The dog what ate a whole bucket of pig slop afore anybody noticed?"

Robert grinned. "Seems like I mighta heard that one, but Frank here probably ain't. Go ahead and tell it."

And with that, the whole lot of them were off and telling stories, eating more stew, raving over the biscuits, and laughing until their sides hurt. Even Perla began to smile as folks came around to thank her for cooking and to compliment her on the food. Casewell felt something ease deep inside him. Maybe it would be all right after all.

But the next morning things were far from all right. In the night someone had slipped up on the porch of the Thorntons' store and painted a pentagram in whitewash across the front door. A cardboard sign hung from the knob. It read, "I am against you," declares the Lord Almighty. "All because of the wanton lust of a harlot, who enslaved you by her witchcraft."

As soon as he got to the store, Robert called Casewell, and the two men did their best to scrub away the evidence before anyone saw it. But news traveled fast, and they were only half-done when a crowd began to gather. Pastor Longbourne soon made his way to the porch steps. He stood with one foot on the ground and one two steps up. He leaned on his knee and considered the work being done.

"Washing it away won't change anything, son," he said to Casewell. "Sin is sin, and it will always come to light."

Casewell ignored him as he worked at the stain.

"These good people"—Longbourne waved an expansive arm at the crowd that had gathered—"don't need the help of an evil idolater to see them through these difficult times. God will see them through."

Casewell suddenly had a vision of himself standing in the crowd behind the preacher. He saw himself nodding along with what Longbourne said, agreeing and condemning without hesitation. He saw himself judging Perla Long to perdition for sins no worse than his own.

Turning, scrub brush still in his hand, Casewell glared at Longbourne. The pastor returned the look for a moment and then stepped back, putting both feet on the ground. Casewell stepped forward. He felt Robert place a hand on his arm, but he shook it off. He had no idea what he meant to do until he stood on the edge of the porch. He looked at the group of people, holding one eye and then another until no one would meet his gaze.

"'Judge not, that ye be not judged. For with what judgment ye judge, ye shall be judged.'" Casewell turned his back and resumed scrubbing.

"Don't you spout Scripture at me, boy," yelled Longbourne. "God has turned His back on Wise just as surely as He did on Sodom or Gomorrah. We must root out the evil if we have any hope of winning God's favor." The pastor stood, chest heaving. Then he raised an arm and pointed a bony finger at Casewell.

"Spellbound, that's what you are. You and anyone who's eaten from that witch's hand."

There were gasps from the people standing about—most of whom had enjoyed Perla's stew the day before. Longbourne turned to those standing behind him. "Repent," he cried. "Go forth and sin no more. Do not partake of this evil again."

People began drifting away, and Casewell knew that within fifteen minutes the entire community would be aware of what had just happened at the Thorntons' store. After the previous day's success, they had invited everyone to come back for a noon meal. Perla was due to arrive and begin cooking in about an hour. Casewell had a bad feeling.

12

Casewell was pacing along the porch when Perla arrived, walked inside, and tied on an apron. She began making pastry, mixing, lightly kneading, and rolling out piecrusts.

"I thought we'd have chicken pie today," she said to Casewell. "There's canned meat and plenty of vegetables. This flour and lard should stretch far enough to feed a crowd."

"There may not be a crowd." Casewell stood back, as though Perla might lash out at him if he got too close.

"Because of the preacher?" she asked. "Because of the hateful things out front this morning?"

"Well, yes. How did you—?"

"Oh, Casewell. There were half a dozen women just itching to tell me what was painted on the door and printed on that sign. I was pretty upset when I heard."

"But you came down here, anyway." Casewell's confusion mounted.

"Yes. You said something to me. You said that I have a remarkable gift from God." Perla stopped rolling out dough and leaned on the table, head down. "For a lot of years I considered this ability a curse. I hid it as much as I could. When people did notice, it usually brought me grief. It never occurred to me that this . . ." She hesitated, searching for the right word and finally giving up. "That this thing I can do with food could be a blessing. There are folks who will scorn me and abuse me, but I think it's my duty—my calling—to feed the hungry. The only thing that would be worse than what happened out front this morning would be my refusing to use my gift to help people."

Casewell took two steps toward Perla, stretching out his hand, not sure what he meant to do with it.

"Come help me," she said. "God will see that it all comes out the way He intends."

Casewell's hand closed over Perla's wrist where she braced herself against the table. He held on to her as though she might run away if he let go. She looked up and into his face, her eyes so clear and wide and blue. Casewell felt something flutter in his chest. It might have been an angel's wings, or maybe it was just his heart. He began opening jars.

Only two women came for food that day. Casewell knew one was a widow with four children under the age of twelve. The other was Liza Talbot.

"Angie had a fit when I told her I was coming, but I came just the same," she said to Perla. "I will confess that your cooking ability makes me a little uneasy, but who am I to question a miracle?"

"You think this is a miracle?" Perla looked at Liza with such hope.

"Well, I know folks have talked about how the devil can do

things that look like miracles to fool people, but your feeding people is such a good thing right now. Isn't there something in the Bible about how the devil can't work against himself?"

"That's in Matthew, chapter twelve," Casewell said.

"Exactly," Liza nodded emphatically, as if that were all the argument she needed. "Whatever's happening here, the Lord will use it for good." She patted Perla on the hand and took a bite of chicken pie. "Oh, my stars, this is good," she exclaimed. "People will cut off their noses to spite their own faces, won't they? Yes, indeed. If you'll make me up another bowl, I'll take it home to Angie, and if she won't eat it, then I surely will."

"Of course!" Casewell cried, startling Perla and Liza. "If folks are too afraid to come get this food, we'll carry it to them." He called for Robert, and the men began planning.

Robert and Delilah would deliver the food. Perla wanted to go, too, but Casewell and Robert agreed that she was a little too polarizing at the moment. So she stayed at the store with Casewell and Sadie in case any customers came by. None did.

Toward evening, Perla asked Casewell to watch Sadie playing on the porch while she disappeared behind the shelves where the makeshift kitchen was set up. Casewell sat in a rocking chair and watched the little girl play with her doll and empty thread spools. Sadie's absorption in her play left Casewell time to think. He didn't often just sit and think. He was almost always working, and while he often found that he didn't need to think about tasks like hoeing or sanding, he didn't use that time for deep contemplation, either.

Rocking and listening to Sadie carry on a soft conversation with her toys, he found himself filled with something like yearning. He wanted something with every fiber of his being—what was it? He felt peaceful and contented, which was completely unexpected. His father was dying, his mother was suffering, the drought had a death grip on the land, and Perla was being ostracized. Things were not going well. And yet, sitting with a child at his feet and a woman in the kitchen at his back, he felt happier than he had in a very long time—maybe ever.

Casewell closed his eyes and lifted a prayer to heaven. He asked that God help him understand the gift of peace and help him hold on to it. He asked that his heart's yearning please God and benefit his fellowman. He asked for wisdom.

Casewell was about to open his eyes when he felt Sadie place a hand on his knee. He looked at her clutching her doll in the crook of her arm and smiled.

"I love you, Mr. Casewell," she said and then returned to her game on the porch floor.

Casewell nearly choked as tears rose in his throat, and he fought to keep from sobbing aloud. This child loved him. Why would she love him? Because he'd made her some toys? Because he'd talked to her a time or two and now sat with her on the porch? There was no real reason for a little girl to love him. But even as he marveled that she did, he realized that he loved her right back. More than he would have ever thought he could love someone not his own flesh and blood.

By sunset Robert and Delilah had carried chicken pie to most of the houses within a five-mile radius of the store. They'd been turned away by some, but most folks were glad to get the food. When they pulled up to the store, Casewell was saved from spending any more time with his suddenly overwhelming emotions. Robert and Delilah climbed out, looking worn but happy.

"We have enough left for our own supper," Delilah said. "I just love how that works out."

"Folks were accepting?" Casewell asked, hoping they didn't hear the catch in his voice.

"More than one hinted they wouldn't mind if no one else knew they took the food, and I think the rest pretended they didn't know who did the cooking," Robert said. "All's well that ends well. Let's eat. I've been smelling this good chicken all afternoon."

Just then Perla stepped out of the store, a smile like a sunrise lighting her face. "Come on in," she called. "I fixed up something special for the delivery crew."

They all trooped inside, Casewell taking Sadie's hand and wondering at how it fit so snugly into his palm. At the rear of the store, a door had been placed across two sawhorses to make a worktable. Perla had found a rose-patterned cloth to drape over it and had dragged the chairs from the potbellied stove over to their makeshift dinner table. She had placed a chicken pie with a fancy crimped crust in the center of the table. Casewell's bowls sat at each chair, with spoons resting on tea towels in place of napkins. Perla had rounded up a few stumps of candles and set them in china teacups on either side of the pie. There was a peach cobbler, still bubbling hot from the oven, sitting on the stovetop. Coffee mugs and a tin pitcher of water finished off the setting.

Casewell breathed in the aroma of roasted chicken, peaches, and butter. He grinned. Robert elbowed him and the two men exchanged delighted smiles. Delilah exclaimed over how beautiful it all was and clapped her hands. Sadie found the seat with an upside-down crate on it and tried to climb up. Struggling, she turned to Casewell and raised her arms to him. He lifted her, and as her feet left the ground, he found himself tossing her into the air and catching her before setting her as gently as the finest china onto her seat. Sadie's laughter seemed to fill them all with a joy beyond understanding. They sat and joined hands to give thanks for this food.

❧

The next morning Casewell went to his workshop to hammer together a couple of extra crates for food deliveries. He was almost surprised to see the finished bed and tea table sitting exactly where he had left them two days earlier. He needed to let Frank know his commission was complete. He doubted Frank had a phone, so he wrapped the table in an old blanket and carefully wedged it into the front seat of his truck. He drove out to the Rexroad place, whistling absently through his teeth and thinking about nothing in particular.

Frank sat out front in an old kitchen chair with a frayed bottom. He wore threadbare dungarees and a thin undershirt. His feet were bare and his white hair gleamed in the morning sun. Casewell stopped well back of the house to keep the dust down. He'd driven over with the windows up to protect the table, and he could feel sweat gathering where his back pressed against the cracked seat.

Climbing out of the truck, Casewell raised a hand and called out. "Brought your table."

Frank nodded and waved him on. Casewell unwrapped the table and carried it over to set in front of the old man. He thought it made an interesting picture—the barefoot man in his broken-down chair and a handcrafted tea table, all sitting in a dusty, shadeless yard.

"Hope you like it," Casewell said, taking a step back and giving Frank room to make up his mind.

Frank lifted the tray out and clicked it back into place. He ran a hand over the inlay and stroked the scalloped edge. He nodded one time, emphatically.

"Son, you have earned your pay and then some," he said at last. He fished in his front pocket and pulled out a roll of bills. He peeled off what he owed and handed it over. Casewell took the cash, wondering that a man with no shoes would have a bankroll handy.

"I hope the lady you plan to give it to likes it," Casewell said.

Frank's head jerked up. "I didn't say I planned to give it away," he said sharply.

Casewell reddened. "I guess you didn't. I made an assumption there. My apologies." He began backing toward his truck. "Guess I'd better be getting on. Thanks for the work."

Frank laid a hand on the table again. "It is a gift," he said softly. Casewell stopped. "But I don't suppose it will make a bit of difference. There are some things you can never apologize for."

Casewell cleared his throat. He had the feeling Frank wasn't talking to him. "It's never too late to ask for forgiveness," Casewell said. "Even if you don't get it, I think it's worth asking."

"I don't know. It's been a lot of years since I tampered with not one heart but two." He pulled his hand back from the table. "Three, if you count mine. At first I was too mad to come home, so I traveled the world, nursing what I told myself was a broken heart. Then when I came home . . . well, what I found gave me the ammunition I needed for some good ol' righteous indignation. Crawling into a jug of moonshine seemed the answer back then. Now I tend to think the answer might be owning up to my part in the whole thing. Can't hardly change anyone but me, so thought I'd start there."

Frank nodded his head and patted the table. He looked up and seemed to shed his pensive mood like brushing away cobwebs. "You bring me some of that good food Perla's cooking down at the store." Casewell thought he saw a twinkle in the old man's eye. "I reckon I'm going to need my strength."

Perla needed to get away. She'd been cooking all week and she was exhausted. By Friday, a few folks were coming to the store to pick up their daily meal, but Casewell and Robert were still delivering most of the food. Perla wasn't complaining—she loved every minute, from the time she stepped into the kitchen area each morning until she sat down at the end of the day to consider the inevitable leftovers. Delilah kept Sadie occupied and the time flew like startled doves. But even so, Perla was tired.

Delilah stopped Perla as she started out of the house on Saturday morning.

"No, ma'am," she said, barring the younger woman's path. "Today is your day off. From what I hear, the food that's been delivered this week has supplied enough leftovers that folks can just reheat whatever they feel like today. You've been spoiling this town." Delilah looked thoughtful. "And they're mostly ungrateful, anyway. You go put your feet up somewhere. Sadie and I are going down to the store to see if anyone wants to buy a spool of thread or a cup of sugar."

Perla felt intense relief, although she tried not to show it. "That sounds nice, Delilah. I think maybe I will go for a walk."

Perla watched Delilah and Sadie as they headed out, and then she walked out the back door and began wandering aimlessly. Maybe she would find a nice spot down by the creek—or what used to be the creek—and just sit.

Even though the water had dried up, the trees near the creek banks had roots that ran deep enough to still be mostly green. Perla thought she was close to where the swimming hole behind the Talbots' used to be. The dark rocks still held some coolness, even in the absence of water. Perla picked her way among the stones and was startled when she heard the rattle of pebbles. Whirling toward the bank, she saw Liza Talbot seated on a stone.

"Did I startle you?" Liza asked.

"A little. I didn't expect to see anyone down here."

"I like to come here to think. I liked it better when there was water." Liza scanned the rocky bed and sighed.

"It seems like a good place."

"Oh, it is." Liza patted a rock next to her. "You're most welcome to join me."

Perla wasn't sure she wanted company, but she sat, anyway. Silence reigned for a time.

Eventually Liza looked over at Perla, almost as though she were surprised to see the other woman sitting there. "Have you ever been wrong about someone you thought loved you?" she asked.

Perla jerked as though Liza had slapped her. Liza didn't seem to notice. "I've been so very blind," she said. "Do you mind if I tell you about it? Somehow I feel safe talking to you."

Perla nodded jerkily and made a small sound of agreement. She had the feeling she didn't want to hear what Liza had to say, but she also felt deeply curious. She knew very well how it felt to mistake someone's love.

"When Frank began courting me, Angie didn't approve," Liza said. "She thought he would never amount to anything. Oh, he was such a fun-loving young man. And he could dance, which was generally frowned upon by almost everyone we knew. But Mama let us go to a country dance once, and Frank stood up with me. Well, I guess I fell in love with the pure joy in that man. He danced once with Angie, too, but Angie said he was too free with himself, and it would only lead to a broken heart." She darted a look at Perla. "I guess she was right.

"Frank came around all the time. Mama and Papa encouraged him. I guess they hoped to marry off one of us. I'd always been too shy to do much courting, and maybe Angie was too particular. At first I wasn't entirely certain which one of us he was courting. He flirted with me and teased Angie something awful. I never did know what to say to him, but Angie always had something smart to come back at him with. Eventually he started asking me to sit on the porch swing with him or to walk out through the pasture and along the creek. Angie came along sometimes, as chaperone, but she always kind of lagged behind.

"I pinched myself. I felt so lucky. Frank was handsome and fun and made me feel beautiful. I had never dared to imagine myself married or a mother, and the more Frank came around, the more I thought it was possible. It was almost Christmas in 1901 that Frank asked me to marry him." Liza got a faraway look and fell silent. Perla thought maybe the story was over. Then Liza resumed the telling.

"Angie and I were out cutting pine and holly to decorate the house. Frank planned to meet us and help. Angie was on the creek side of the house, where the big hollies grow, and I had gone up the hill out front to cut some cedar. I was coming back to the house when Angie came tearing around the side, looking mad as a wet hen. Frank trailed along after a few minutes later, looking kind of sheepish."

Liza paused and picked up a small round stone, which she rolled between her fingers. Perla was interested in spite of herself, but she didn't feel it was appropriate to speak.

"I guessed Frank went too far in his teasing. Now I wonder. Angie refused to speak to either of us the rest of the afternoon, and Frank didn't stay much longer. I heard him in the kitchen telling Angie he was sorry, but she didn't answer him. I heard her crying later that night, but I didn't ask her about it. I think I didn't really want to know what had her so upset.

"The next day was Christmas Eve, and Frank came to dinner. After we ate, he asked to speak to Papa privately. They talked and he came into the family room, knelt down beside me where I sat near the fire, and asked me to be his wife. I was never so happy before or since, even though Papa said we had to wait until I was eighteen. The next year he went off to roam the world with Buffalo Bill—said he was going to make our fortune. After a few letters I never heard from him again." Liza tucked the stone she had picked up into a pocket. Perla suspected she didn't even realize she'd done it.

"I was so sad, but since we didn't hear anything to the contrary, I hoped maybe he just wasn't able to get back to me some way. I guess I really thought he'd been killed. But I used to daydream about how he'd lost his memory and then one day it would all come back to him and he'd rush home to me and we'd get married and live happily ever after." Liza picked up another pebble.

"And then Angie told me she'd heard Frank married a girl in France. She said a friend of Frank's sent her a letter and that she was so mad she'd thrown it into the fire." Liza looked sad. "I've never in my life had reason to doubt Angie, but I wonder . . ."

Liza seemed to have run out of words. Perla laid a hand on her arm and squeezed gently. "What's got you questioning Angie?" she asked softly.

"I came home from my walk this morning, and Frank was in the living room with Angie. There was a fancy tea table sitting there, and Angie was crying. Frank was holding one of her hands and looking so very sad. As soon as I came in, Angie jumped up and jerked her hand away. She started talking about the table and how Frank had brought it as a gift for the two of us. She said over and over that it was for both of us, that it was Frank's way of saying how sorry he was for all the years we didn't know what happened to him." Liza stopped and closed her eyes. "And maybe for the years we knew but didn't understand.

"It just seemed odd somehow. I can't make sense of it all. He never was married, and why in the world did he think I would start courting someone else just like that? There's so much I don't understand." Tears streaked Liza's wrinkled cheeks. "I hate to feel suspicious of Angie, but I think there's something more to the story. I tried to talk to Frank once after he came back, but he was drunk and acted the fool."

Perla patted Liza's hand. "There's usually more to every story. And Liza"—Perla made sure the older woman was looking at her—"it's often not what we imagine."

Liza smiled. "Oh, Perla, you're right. My imagination is getting carried away with me. Thank you."

They chatted a little longer, and Liza insisted Perla come to see the tea table. Angie was sitting in the living room near the little table and rose to greet them as though she'd been waiting for them to arrive. Perla admired the craftsmanship of the piece.

"Frank told us Casewell made it," Angie said.

"He made our kitchen dresser, too," chimed in Liza.

"He's a gifted craftsman," Angie said.

"A shame he's still single," Liza added.

"Some of us are destined to be single," Angie said. "And that's just the way of it."

13

LATER, WHEN REMEMBERING WHAT HAPPENED at church that Sunday, folks talked about the day Pastor Longbourne tried to pry open the gates of hell and see who he could kick through the door. From the moment the first person stepped into the church, it was clear that this day would be different. Longbourne stood in front of the pulpit in his shirtsleeves, black suspenders taut against his bony shoulders. He didn't speak until the last parishioner slid into his seat. An uncomfortable silence reigned.

Casewell noticed that his parents had not come. He didn't know if his father was too ill or too ornery. Perla was conspicuously absent as well. Robert and Delilah sat a little ways back with Sadie between them.

Casewell realized that the pastor seemed to be breathing heavily, as though he'd been running. He took in a deep raspy breath and then exhaled with a great gust of air. "Pontius Pilate washed his hands of the Jews when they insisted on slaughtering the Son of God. And so I wash my hands of you."

He strode over to the small baptistery, sent the cover crashing to the floor, and sloshed his hands vigorously. He turned and slung water out over the first few pews. Casewell felt cool drops spray across his cheek.

"I have warned you. I have spoken truth from this pulpit. I have all but named the sinner in our midst." Longbourne seemed not able to take in enough air for a moment. "And you have turned from the light and into darkness. I gave you the Lord's manna, and you cried out for meat. I gave you the rules of righteous living, and you made yourselves an idol. You are foolish, wayward children, and I will have nothing more to do with you."

The congregation sat dumbstruck. Even the children were quiet. Longbourne stared unseeingly over their heads to the back of the building.

"Go," he said, pointing a long finger to the door. "Be gone from this place, and do not darken the door again." He took another shuddering breath. "Or get on your knees and crawl forward toward the light. Prostrate yourselves here at my feet and beg for forgiveness. I can't promise you'll receive it, but if you value your very soul, you will press your face into the dust and plead for mercy."

For several long moments, no one moved. Then Robert and Delilah stood and took Sadie out. A few others rose to follow. Casewell wanted to leave, too, but he felt frozen in place. He watched as the first few lowered themselves to the dusty floor and began moving forward, crouching or on their knees. Longbourne made a sharp, slashing gesture with his hand. "Down. Get yourselves down like the dogs you are." Congregants dropped to their hands and knees, trying not to make eye contact with one another.

Casewell could stand it no longer. He stood to walk out.

Liza and Angie sat in the back pew. He stopped and offered them each a hand. "I'll escort you out, if you like, ladies." Angie rose with dignity, hooking her arm through Casewell's. Liza seemed to flutter against his other side. They exited the church together.

⁂

The following week they abandoned the plan for feeding the masses. Perla was willing, but Robert and Casewell talked in private and decided that it might not be safe. Casewell tried to tamp down the anger he felt rising in him. People could be so foolish, and for someone who claimed to be a man of God, Pastor Longbourne seemed determined to sow hate and dissension. Casewell hoped to have a chance to speak to the pastor, to try to understand why he was trying to turn the people against Perla, and in doing so, turning them against one another. It just didn't make sense.

With time on his hands, Casewell tried to pick up his mandolin and occupy himself, but his fingers felt stiff and unwilling. He finally gave up and wandered out to his workshop. The bed still stood there, and as Casewell admired his own work, he realized that he didn't want to wait until Christmas. His father was likely dying. His mother suffered more each day. He would give them the bed now.

Casewell carefully loaded the pieces of the bed into his truck and covered them with several layers of tarps and blankets to keep the dust out. He drove slowly to his parents' house and backed the truck right up to the porch. Emily came out and raised her hand to shade her eyes from the glare. Casewell got out and walked over to meet her.

"I've brought you a present, Ma," he said.

"Why, Casewell, what in the world for?"

"I meant it to be a Christmas present, but with things the way they have been lately"—Casewell braced a foot on the bottom step and slapped at some dust on his pant leg—"well, I thought I'd bring it on over now. Where's Dad? I'd like to show it to both of you."

Emily bowed her head and knotted her hands in her apron. "He took to his bed the middle of last week," she said softly. "He says he don't reckon he'll get back up."

Casewell stepped back as though she'd pushed him. "Why didn't you call?"

"He insisted I leave you alone. He said you didn't need the distraction." She turned wide, sad eyes on her son. "He said you were doing God's work, and we should leave you to it. When he said that"—Emily choked a little—"it scared me worse than all the cussing and meanness."

Casewell moved up the steps to pull his mother into his arms. "It's a good sign, Ma," he whispered. "I don't know what it means, but I feel like it's a good sign."

They stood, holding each other for a few moments, but neither of them cried. Finally Casewell pulled away. "Now, let me show you what I've brought," he said.

Carefully pulling away the dusty coverings, Casewell exposed the headboard with its elaborate flower carvings. He heard his mother gasp.

"Is it a bed?" she asked.

"It is. I've always wanted to try my hand at something like this, and with so little work coming in, the time seemed right. Do you like it?" Casewell felt like a little boy bringing home a clay ashtray from summer Bible school. He suddenly wanted to make his mother happy more than anything.

"Oh, Casewell, it's the most beautiful thing I've ever seen. I knew you were gifted, but I had no idea . . ." The tears that hadn't fallen earlier now flowed freely. "And with your father staying in bed . . . if it weren't for him, I'd think it was too grand for us. But now, somehow all this beauty will be a comfort." She turned soft eyes on Casewell. "Thank you, son. Thank you so much."

Casewell went in and explained to his father that he was bringing in a new bed. He expected to meet with resistance, but Dad was surprisingly docile and agreeable. He let Casewell help him into an armchair, where Emily tucked blankets around him in spite of the heat. Casewell was shocked at how much weight his father had lost. Just a week ago he'd seemed a little thin, but now he was almost emaciated. Guilt swept over Casewell. Had he been so preoccupied with Perla and their plans to feed the community that he'd forgotten his own family? He feared so. He would not let it happen again.

In short order, the old bedstead was removed and the new brought in. Casewell topped it with the mattress and helped Mom remake it with fresh sheets and her wedding quilt. The quilt had a double wedding-ring pattern in soft pastels, which seemed to lend color to the flowers in the headboard.

When they finished, they stood back and admired the beauty of the bed in the sunlit room. Sheer curtains at the window billowed on a gentle breeze, and Casewell had to admit he'd done a fine job. He was glad he'd decided to give his parents the bed early. He turned to check his father's reaction and was shocked to see tears streaking the older man's face. Dad made no move to wipe his face or to speak. Mom sat down on the arm of his chair and wrapped an arm around his shoulders as she dabbed at his face with the hem of her apron.

"Isn't our son amazing?" she asked softly.

When his father nodded, Casewell thought his heart might burst. How could the barest movement of his father's head feel like the greatest compliment of his life? He just stood there, trying to take it in.

⁂

The next morning, Casewell received an unexpected call. When he answered the phone, he recognized the voice of Angie Talbot.

"Casewell, I was hoping you might be able to come call on me this morning," she said without preamble.

"I could do that," he said.

"If it's convenient, I'd like to see you promptly at nine fifteen."

Casewell agreed and opted not to ask any questions. Angie rarely sounded warm, but this morning she sounded particularly stiff and formal. Casewell marveled that he always felt like a schoolboy around Angie, while Liza tended to make him feel like a favorite nephew. He assumed the sisters needed something done around the house. Well, he had nothing else to occupy his time.

Casewell walked into the bathroom to tidy his beard before driving over and was surprised when brown water sputtered out of the faucet. He shut it off and walked out to the wellhead with a flashlight. He lifted the cover and shone the light down the stone-lined well. The rocks were shockingly dry, and his light glinted on what looked like little more than a mud puddle in the bottom. Casewell knew the well might go dry, and he'd been conserving water as best he could, but he hadn't expected it to happen so soon. There was an old well out back of the house that had been shut up because the water had a sulfur taint. Casewell needed to get on to the Talbots', so he'd try the old well when he got back. Poor water would be better than none.

Still scruffy, Casewell drove to the Talbots' and arrived promptly at nine fifteen. Angie stood inside the kitchen door. She pushed the screen open and waited for Casewell to pass through, then ushered him into the sitting room. He was surprised to see that Liza wasn't there.

"Liza is taking her morning constitutional," Angie said. "She always returns after about an hour and a half. Normally, I wouldn't invite a man to visit while I am alone, but you're an elder in the church, and I have a private matter I need to discuss."

Casewell realized his eyebrows had been climbing steadily higher. He made an effort to lower them a notch. "I'll be pleased to help in any way I can," he said.

"The Bible tells us to confess our sins, and although I have confessed over and over to God Almighty, I feel Him directing me to confess to someone who can help me discern His leading. I am not comfortable telling my tale to anyone but you." Angie swallowed hard. "You have been kind to my sister and me, and I have seen how forgiving you have been of Perla Long. I hope that I can trust you."

Casewell looked at his shoes and leaned forward, bracing his elbows on his knees. "Miss Angie, I'm honored that you have chosen to confide in me. I hope that I'm worthy of your trust."

"Of course, what I plan to tell you is in the strictest confidence," she said.

"Yes, ma'am. I will keep it entirely to myself." Casewell couldn't imagine what a seventy-year-old spinster would have to confess, and with the way folks had been acting lately, he was almost afraid to hear it.

Angie sat on the sofa opposite Casewell, who sat in an overstuffed armchair. She planted both feet firmly on the floor and placed a hand on each knee. When she was composed, she began to speak.

"The first time I saw Frank Post, I was little more than a child and smitten. I always assumed I would never marry. Papa was a fine man and I couldn't imagine anyone ever comparing to him. Frank was nothing like Papa, who was serious and worked hard. Papa's whole life was centered around God, his family, and his farm. Frank was fun-loving and full of himself. I thought he was frivolous. I thought he was often ridiculous. I doubted his faith and I doubted his intentions. But oh, how he made me laugh. No one made me laugh. I always thought hilarity was for the weak and foolish. And Frank Post made me feel very weak and not a little foolish. I'm afraid I enjoyed it, but I refused to let anyone—especially Frank—see how he delighted me.

"I think when he first began coming around, he intended to court me. In retrospect I think he found me to be a challenge. But I refused to be charmed, and he had his work cut out for him. Liza, on the other hand, was only too glad to laugh and cut up. The more I resisted, the easier it was for Frank to spend time with Liza. I think I was in love with him from the moment I saw him, but my stubborn pride drove him into my sister's arms."

Angie paused and hung her head, although she didn't move otherwise. Casewell eased back in his chair. This was beginning to sound like it might take a while.

"Liza was utterly innocent. She enjoyed Frank and her heart was always so open. It was inevitable that she would fall in love and that Frank would love her in turn. As I saw it happening, I told myself it was for the best. They would marry and be happy, and I would stay at home to take care of Mama and Papa. But my heart betrayed me. I began to resent Liza and was unkind to Frank as his affections were transferred to my twin.

"Just before Christmas that year, Frank came to help us gather greens to decorate the house. I was cutting holly." Angie nodded out the rear window, where Casewell could see the old trees still standing, though parched and dusty now. "There was snow on the ground, and it was so beautiful, and I was full of the spirit of Christmas. When Frank came around the corner of the house, I called out to him. I suppose I smiled and maybe was more welcoming than I should have been. His eyes lit up and he walked over, swept me into his arms, and kissed me on the mouth. When he stopped, he said that he'd always loved me and hoped my heart was softening toward him."

Angie kept her head down, but Casewell could see the furious blush rising in her cheeks. She clasped her hands together, twisting her fingers.

"I slapped him," she said finally. "I slapped him and told him he could not woo both of us. I said some hateful things to him—told him that he was a sinner and a vain rooster. Then I ran away. Liza saw me come around the corner of the house, and I can only imagine what she must have thought. The next day Frank proposed to Liza, and Liza was overjoyed. Papa said they would have to wait two years until Liza was old enough, but she still talked and talked about what their life would be like together, and I let her. She thanked me later for letting her go on and on. I suppose I would have normally cut her off at some point. I wasn't a very good sister before Frank, and I got worse after him.

"I did my best to seem happy about the engagement. I avoided Frank as much as possible. I tried to hate him for transferring his affection so easily. Then he ran off with that fool show. Liza wrote him letters almost daily, and he wrote back a time or two. She continued dreaming about the wedding—it wouldn't be anything fancy—but she was so excited. I came to dread the mention of his name. I thought my feelings would subside with him gone, but they grew stronger.

"I imagined what it would be like watching my sister and the man I loved making a life together. I simply could not bear it. I wrote a letter to Frank." Angie stopped and gripped her knees so hard her knuckles turned white. "I'm so ashamed of what I did, Casewell. I dread telling it, but it hangs so heavy. So very, very heavy."

Casewell tried to think of something to say. He could see where the story was headed, and it broke his heart, too. He remained silent. There wasn't anything to say.

Angie took a deep breath and began speaking again. "In my letter, I told him that I would never forgive him and Liza was courting a wonderful man I was sure would make her an excellent husband. I told him that I was sorry, but life goes on, and Liza suspected his affections were weak. I said that she probably sounded just the same in her letters, but it was because she found it too hard to tell him that she loved someone else. I told him he should make a life for himself somewhere else. Oh, I said so much. I think I could quote that letter to this day. I hoped that Frank would be angry enough to never come home. I hoped that by banishing him, I could find some peace."

She looked directly at Casewell with eyes that seemed dark and almost hollow. "He didn't come home—not for a long time. And instead of peace, I found my sins weighing heavier and my love festering inside. The day he came home and learned about my lies"—Angie looked out the window as if it were a door to the past—"I felt like the angel of the Lord had appeared with a fiery sword to cleave me in two. I was almost grateful when he took to drinking. I figured even if he told the truth, no one would believe him."

Casewell was riveted. "But didn't Liza keep writing to Frank?"

"She did for a while. I thought she'd give up if he didn't write back, but I began to worry that she wouldn't give up and Frank would become suspicious. So I wrote another letter and mailed it to myself. I made sure Liza knew I'd gotten mail, but I didn't let her see it. I told her it was from a friend of Frank's who thought someone should let us know that he had taken up with a woman over there in Europe and that he might have to marry her because she was with child. I said the letter made me so angry I burned it. Liza always trusted me . . ." Angie trailed off. She looked exhausted.

Clearing his throat, Casewell said, "Angie, I'm not sure what you want from me."

"Forgiveness," she said. "Punishment."

"I don't think it's mine to give," Casewell answered. "Have you told Liza this story?"

Angie crumbled then. "I can't. She would likely forgive me. She's such a good, loving woman, and I . . . I'm coldhearted and mean. I don't know if I could stand her forgiveness. I deserve to be punished, and loving-kindness from my sister would be a kind of torture."

"Angie." Casewell leaned forward. He felt the urge to reach out and touch the older woman's hand, but he wasn't sure she would allow it. "Maybe you've been punished enough these last fifty years. Maybe the person you need forgiveness from is yourself."

Angie cried silently. Her shoulders quivered and tears dripped from her chin, but she did not make a sound, and her only movement was a spasmodic clutching of her skirt. Casewell had no idea what to do, and then it came to him.

"Would you like me to pray?" he asked.

Angie nodded without looking up. Casewell bowed his head.

"Father, your daughter Angie is aching right now. She has carried the weight of her sin for longer than you or anyone would have asked her. Give her the strength to seek forgiveness from those she has hurt. Give her the strength to grant forgiveness to herself. You are the God of second chances, Father. Remind Angie that it's never too late. In the name of Jesus Christ, your Son, amen."

Casewell wished he'd been more eloquent. He wished he'd thought to pray for the right words to pray. He wished he could somehow open a window and let the sorrow and guilt that had built up in the room dissipate. He opened his eyes and saw Liza standing in the doorway.

Angie was looking, too. "Sister, when did you get back?" she asked.

"I've been here a little while," Liza said. "And if you want me to, I forgive you." She began to cry, as well. "Even if you don't want me to, I forgive you. I just can't think of anything else to do."

Angie held her arms out to her sister, and then they sat side by side on the sofa, clasping each other tightly. Casewell rose, making as little noise as possible as he left the house.

14

When Casewell got home and scratched his grubby scalp, he remembered the well was dry. The Talbots had driven all thoughts of water from his head. He walked out back and found the cover to the old well that hadn't been used in years. It would have been grown over with vines if the drought hadn't withered everything. He brushed dead stems aside with his foot and pried up the lid. He couldn't see much, so he found a rock and dropped it in, hoping to hear it hit bottom with a splash. He heard a dry thud instead. He felt like cursing.

Casewell stood and considered what in the world was left for him to do. Then a memory of the cold spring came to him. His father had taken him there when he was a boy. The spring was out back in the woods a ways and down a steep hillside. It had never been convenient to the house, but Casewell used to drink there when he spent long days hunting or just exploring the woods. Surely he could find it again.

Casewell went back to the house for a bucket and a shovel and then headed in the general direction he remembered. He was soon glad for the shovel, which he could use as a sort of walking stick on the steeper parts of the hill. After he thought he'd found the right place twice, he finally saw a tree with a branch that grew nearly parallel to the ground, making a sort of high bench. *Aha*. He remembered sitting there more than once after getting a cool drink from the spring.

And there it was, water bubbling out of the ground in a clear, cold stream. As soon as he got close, he knew it was the right place. A narrowing streak of green fell away from the source where the dry land sponged up the water as quickly as it burbled out. Casewell bent and scooped up a handful of water. He lifted it to his lips, smelling it first and then taking a tentative sip. It was just as cold and pure as he remembered. It had no flavor but somehow reminded him of moss and dark rich soil. He scooped again and drank more deeply. He felt so good that he thought for a moment he might have discovered the fountain of youth.

Grinning, Casewell set his bucket aside and began carefully digging out a basin where the spring emerged. There had been a small declivity before, but it had filled in over the years. Soon he had a small pool, about two feet by one. He carefully deepened it a little and then found stones to fortify the edges. He whistled under his breath, enjoying the work and wishing someone were with him to share his delight in the water. Perla would laugh to see this gift from the side of the mountain. And little Sadie would dip her fingers in it and squeal at how cold the water was.

Nonsense. Casewell stopped whistling. What in the world had come over him, imagining those two out here in the woods with him? He stood back to survey his work and felt pleased. The pool was just deep enough to fill his bucket almost to the rim. Of course, getting the water back up the hill was going to be a chore, but it was worth it for the water.

As he lifted the shoshing bucket, he saw something golden out of the corner of his eye and realized there was a stubby peach tree growing just above the spring. A break in the woods sent sunlight skimming over its surprisingly green leaves. And there, amongst the green, were a half dozen or so ripe peaches. He laughed aloud. Not only did he have fresh water, but he also had just about the best gift he could offer Perla. He remembered her cobbler and thought how glad she'd be to get fresh fruit. Stripping off his shirt, he fashioned a sort of sling and loaded it with warm peaches. He slipped the makeshift sack over his shoulder and picked up the bucket, brimming with cold water.

Life-giving water, Casewell thought. Then another idea struck him. He carried everything back to the house and set a pan of water to warming on the back of the stove. He stepped into the bathroom and found the shears his mother used to trim his hair. He grabbed his beard and began snipping.

Casewell felt a little self-conscious when he stopped by Robert and Delilah's to give Perla the peaches. She came outside to greet him and stared at his clean-shaven face for a moment but didn't comment. He showed her the fruit, still wrapped in his shirt, and she gathered them one by one into her apron. They somehow seemed more bountiful there—bigger and brighter, more perfect.

"I can make cobbler enough for everyone now," she said with a shy smile.

Casewell felt like he'd done something brave and wonderful, but he reminded himself it was just peaches.

❧

The drought had gotten so bad that cattle were dying and some families were talking about moving. They'd heard there had been some rain down in North and South Carolina, thanks to storms coming in from the Gulf of Mexico. No one really wanted to go, but it was looking desperate. Clouds rolled in a time or two with a breeze that might have been a little bit cooler, but it never amounted to anything.

Casewell caused a bit of a stir with his face clean shaven. But Delilah proclaimed him more handsome than ever, and some of the fellows guessed he must be thinking of doing some courting. Casewell ran a finger along the scar that was somehow less pronounced than he remembered and kept his thoughts to himself.

The gift of peaches seemed to reignite Perla's desire to feed the community, and once she resumed cooking, it was the only thing that kept many families going. But her abilities stretched only so far. The store of food at the Thorntons' slowly but clearly diminished. Tensions ran high. Although Pastor Longbourne didn't attempt a repeat of the previous Sunday's performance, his sermons took on a theme—Bathsheba brought down King David, Delilah ruined Samson, and, of course, Eve took much of the brunt of his rage against sinful and lascivious women.

Casewell continued to help Perla with cooking and distributing food. After a couple of weeks, most folks got used to the idea that she had a strange knack and were grateful for the help. And then someone—no one was sure who first said it—suggested the food was a miracle. In a community where everyone was worried and where the news had all been bad for so long, the idea of a miracle was more than welcome.

People soaked up the idea that Perla was a miracle worker like the dry ground would soak up water. Before the rumor, only a few folks came to the store for food, while Casewell and Robert delivered the rest. Now people were willing to come and wait for hours to get a bowl of stew or a biscuit, and it seemed the more that came, the more food there was. Surely it was a miracle, Casewell decided.

The crowd that just a few weeks before had wanted to run Perla out of town, except for the fact that they would starve without her, were now treating her with a strange kind of reverence. And then Cathy Stott brought her toddler to the store. The child had been plagued with ear infections since birth, and Cathy couldn't afford surgery. Little Travis always seemed to be miserable and crying. He was sobbing the day Cathy pushed her way through the crowd, waiting for their share of barley soup.

Cathy fell to her knees in front of Perla and held the child up. "Bless him for me, miss. I'm begging you," she said.

Perla just stood there, soup ladle in one hand and eyes wide.

"I've seen the miracle you've worked with the food," Cathy said. "Won't you work a miracle for my baby?"

"I don't know a thing about miracles," Perla said, stumbling over the words. "I'm just cooking."

Delilah stepped over from her place in the serving line and took little Travis in her arms. He wailed all the louder. "Let's you and me say a prayer over this little one," she said, moving in close to Perla. "Father, you know little Travis here has had sore ears pretty much from the day he was born. We know you're the miracle worker in this room, and we ask that you heal Travis and give both him and his mother some peace. Amen."

While Delilah prayed, Perla reached out and laid a soothing hand on Travis's head. She smoothed his hair back from his hot face and, in the way a mother will, leaned over and kissed his forehead. He stopped crying and looked at her with wide eyes.

Cathy climbed to her feet. "I think that done it," she said. "That there was a holy kiss. Thank you. Thank you, miss." She sort of curtsied, scooped Travis back into her arms, and left.

"But I didn't . . ." Perla trailed off.

"I'm sorry." Delilah grimaced. "I was trying to diffuse the situation, but I think we may have just made it worse."

Perla shoved the ladle she was still holding into Casewell's hand and fled the building. The crowd watched her go in undisguised wonder.

Perla ran straight to John and Emily's house. Emily often watched Sadie while Perla and Casewell worked at the store. She claimed the child cheered John, although Perla had never noticed that John seemed any less closed in and quiet no matter who was around.

Her thought was to take Sadie and run away, but as soon as she came in the door and saw her child helping Emily polish the furniture, going over the legs of the table with a soft cloth, she knew her thought was foolish. Perla burst into tears and fell into one of the kitchen chairs. She buried her head in her arms on the table and sobbed.

She heard Emily take Sadie into John's room, where she spoke in a low voice. Then Perla felt Emily's hand on her shoulder.

"Let it out, dear. Have yourself a good, long cry. Goodness knows those tears are the closest thing to rain we've had in a long time."

When the sobbing began to subside, Perla looked up at Emily, sitting patiently, hands folded in her lap, as if she had nothing to do but wait to hear whatever Perla might say. Perla suddenly knew how Liza felt when she poured her heart out sitting on a creek rock that day. A listening ear was all it took.

"They think I can do miracles," Perla blurted. "Some woman brought her child so I could cure him. Delilah stepped in, but when that little boy stopped crying, they acted like I somehow did it."

"Oh, child," Emily said, taking one of Perla's hands. "People are so hungry for something good right now. They'll come to their senses once we get some rain. A year from now, folks will hardly remember what it was they were so riled up about."

"What if others come?" Perla asked. "What if other people come to me thinking I can heal their bunions and make their headaches go away? When people talked about me being a witch . . ." Emily tried to protest, but Perla didn't let her. "No, I know what they were saying. And when they said it, I thought my heart would break, but I determined to love them, anyway. I told myself that so long as the people who mattered most loved me, I could stand the talk. I told myself that as long as Sadie was happy and thriving, I wouldn't leave. But now, once all those people realize I can't do miracles, they'll turn against me worse than before. I'll have no choice but to leave."

"But you can work miracles, Perla." Emily squeezed the younger woman's hand. "I've seen them with my own eyes. Oh, maybe it's not the miracles people are asking for, but I've seen how Casewell has stepped up to help you help the very people who have held your shortcomings against you. Once upon a time he would have refused to do something like that." Emily looked down at the table, brushing away imaginary crumbs.

"His father taught him to be rule bound, and I let that happen. John believed in an Old Testament God who was unforgiving and a terrible taskmaster. I'm afraid he was that kind of father to his own son all too often. But in the past weeks I've seen Casewell change. I've seen his heart softening, not only toward God, but toward being accepting of you and your . . . situation."

Perla was crying again. She protested softly, "But the people—"

"People are a stubborn lot. And I know stubborn." Emily shot a glance at John's room. "I also know God can use anything for His purpose, and I trust that He has a plan." Emily stood and put an arm around Perla's shoulders. "I'm not saying you've made the right choices in life, but I am saying that you have to keep going in spite of the past."

Perla sniffled and wiped her tears before going to collect Sadie. Emily's words had been comforting, but at the same time she had the feeling that the older woman didn't quite approve of her. And why should she? At least Emily loved and care for Sadie. And being held accountable for her past mistakes by someone who cared about her had to be a good thing.

Walking through the doorway into John's room, Perla saw that Sadie had climbed onto the bed with her doll. The child chattered away.

"Sadie, it's time to go," Perla said.

"But I want to stay and play with Mr. John," she said. "He feels better when I'm here."

John reached out and cupped the little girl's cheek. "She's right. I do. But Sadie, girl, you need to do what your mama says. You go on now, and we'll play another time."

Sadie smiled, and Perla marveled at the softness she saw in John's eyes. She knew John's reputation for being a hard man, but Sadie seemed to bring out the best in him.

"Okay," Sadie agreed. "But first we should pray."

"Pray?" Perla seemed surprised. "You want to pray?"

"Yes, Mama, Mr. John is sick, and you said that when someone is sick or hurt, we should pray for them. Now pray."

Sadie slid off the bed and pulled her mother closer to John. She took her mother's hand, then John's. "Pray," she repeated.

Perla shuffled her feet uncomfortably. She wasn't very good

at praying. She took Sadie to church and told her Bible stories. She taught her daughter to pray and to be kind to others, but she generally felt like a fraud as she instructed her child in religious things. She often felt her own faith was fragile and too easily broken. Deep down, Perla suspected that God wasn't really all that interested in her. He had remained silent on so many counts in recent years.

Perla looked at Emily, who had come to the doorway and then to John, who nodded once and bowed his head. The expectancy was like something tangible in the room. Perla cleared her throat and squeezed her eyes shut.

"God." Her voice sounded too loud in her own ears. She took a breath and started again. "God, we know you're looking out for us even when things don't seem to be going right. John is sick, we're having a terrible drought, and times are hard. We ask that you heal John and send some rain. We thank you for your blessings, even when they seem few. We have enough to eat for now, and we have roofs over our heads. Thank you for that, Father." Perla cracked an eye open and peeked at John, who was propped up with pillows. He sat unmoving, head bowed. Emily nodded. Perla didn't know what to say next.

She was surprised when John began speaking. "And, Father, we thank you in particular for this child you've sent to us. She has brought the spirit of love among us, and it has been better than a quenching rain. Thank you."

"Amen," Emily said, and Perla quickly echoed her.

"Amen," said Sadie. "Are you better now, Mr. John?"

John smiled and patted her on the head. "I am, Sadie. Thank you."

Soon after that, Casewell heard a rumor that Perla healed John's cancer. Sadie told Delilah that her mama prayed, and Mr. John felt better. Delilah knew better but couldn't help mentioning it to some of the ladies who had begun to come by the store to help with the cooking and dishwashing. Casewell knew she only meant to tell it as a sweet story, but a few of the ladies grabbed hold of the tale and began to elaborate. By the time the story reached Pastor Longbourne's ears, a miraculous expulsion of demons had taken place. Serena Ward carried the exaggerated tale to him in the churchyard.

"And when she finished praying, he begun floppin' around in that bed like a fish outta water. He choked and gasped and coughed, and afore they knew it, he hocked up a big ol' ball of something black. Spit it out right there on the coverlet. Way I heard it, that black stuff oozed out and started burning a hole through the bedding when Emily grabbed it up and run out in the yard with it. I reckon they burned that cancer up, bedding and all.

"Now John is spry as a grasshopper—hale and hearty and a changed man. Reckon you oughta get on over there, pastor, and make sure whatever they done to him was done right. I'd hate to think it was devil work disguised as something holy." Serena said this last with a glint in her eye, like devil work would be about the most exciting thing that had happened in Wise in a long time. Casewell bit his tongue and clenched his fists.

Casewell knew the best thing he could do was ignore the stories. But the look on Pastor Longbourne's face somehow chilled him. He had a terrible feeling the pastor might take things to an extreme.

15

AT CHURCH THE NEXT SUNDAY, Longbourne pulled Casewell aside as he shook the pastor's hand on the way out of the sanctuary.

"I'd like to speak with you. Privately," he added.

Casewell waited until the congregants all made their way home. They tended not to linger long in the dry, dusty churchyard in these dog days of August. Pastor Longbourne waved Casewell back into the sanctuary. Casewell wasn't at all certain that he wanted to hear anything the preacher had to say but walked in and sat in a rear pew.

Longbourne paced up and down the center aisle. "I hear your father has been healed," he said. Casewell didn't respond right away. "And I see that he did not bother to come to church today. I fear that Perla Long has been working her witchcraft on your family, and I feel it is past time I intervened. Healing is not always of the Lord. A devil's healing can trick good people into acts of foolishness."

Casewell finally found his tongue. "My father has not been healed," he said.

"And so you confess the truth," Longbourne said. "I am grateful for that at least. When can I visit the poor man and help you convince him, as well."

"Pastor, no one thinks my father has been healed. He's dying. And Perla Long is a good woman."

"Blasphemy," Longbourne cried. "She has worked her witchery on you, as well. I wonder, Casewell, can you be trusted?"

Casewell felt bewildered. "Pastor, I have no idea what you're talking about. Perla has become a friend to our family. She's a friend to this whole community. If it weren't for her, some families would have starved by now."

"The sins of this community have been visited upon the people." Longbourne spoke as though reading from the book of Revelation. "If they had turned back to God rather than to the devil's minion, we would have had rain by now. False prophets," he said, shaking his head. "I feel that all is not lost with your family, Casewell. Will you take me to your father?"

"Pastor, I'm not sure my father would welcome you."

"That's why I ask you to take me to him. I need your help." Longbourne stopped his pacing at the end of the pew where Casewell sat. He braced himself in the opening, and somehow Casewell felt penned in, trapped. "I insist that you take me to him."

Something clicked in Casewell's brain. Why was he fighting this? Why not take the pastor to his father's house? It would be interesting to watch Dad tear into Longbourne. It might even give the dying man some spunk.

"Fine. Let's go."

Longbourne looked as close to happy as Casewell had ever seen him. He rubbed his hands together as though the idea of tussling with the devil was the best thing he'd had to look forward to in a long time. "The Lord is softening your heart, son. Thank you."

Casewell snorted softly. He was pretty sure it was the devil telling him to take this crazy preacher to see his father.

Casewell had never knocked on the door at his parents' house in his life, but he did on the day he brought the preacher to witness his father's imaginary healing. His mother came to the door just as Casewell eased it open.

"Why, son, you don't need to knock," she said, peering over his shoulder at Longbourne. "And neither do you, Pastor. You're both as welcome as the sunshine on a rainy day."

Casewell smiled as best he could and eased into the kitchen. Longbourne slithered in behind him.

"Would you'uns like a glass of tea?" Mom asked. "It's hot enough, although I think I feel a touch of cool in the air today. Maybe fall isn't so far off, after all."

"Mrs. Phillips," Pastor Longbourne intoned. "Thank you, but this is not a social call."

"No?" she said.

"No, ma'am. I'm here to witness your husband's alleged healing," he said.

"Healing." The one word, uttered without inflection, was somehow a complete statement that summed up all of Mom's suffering in recent months. "Are you suggesting he's been healed?"

"No, ma'am, but folks in the community have said so, and I feel that I had best witness this so-called miracle and determine if it's God's will or the devil's work."

Mom looked as though she simply couldn't take this in. "Pastor, I'm not sure what you're talking about, but you're welcome to go in and talk to John. He's had a bad morning, but maybe visitors will perk him up."

Casewell led the pastor into his father's room. The bed he had crafted with his own hands looked magnificent. Sun shone in through the window and caught the petals of a flower on the headboard. For just a moment, the flower looked real, as though the petals were soft with morning dew. Casewell breathed in and then out before he let his focus move down to where his father lay against the crisp sheets. Each time Casewell visited, he could see the ravages of the disease in his father's face. The shadows grew deeper and darker, skin grew more taut, and his eyes were somehow brighter with each visit. How anyone could think there had been a healing was beyond Casewell.

"Brother John." Longbourne pushed past Casewell to take the sick man's hand. "I have come to witness your healing."

Casewell thought Longbourne's eyes were too bright, his handshake too eager.

"I ain't been healed that I know about," Dad rasped. "I reckon somebody's been pulling your leg."

"You'll forgive me, brother, if I have to determine what has happened to you on my own. If you have been touched by evil, what you say can't be trusted."

Dad did seem to perk up at that. "Evil?" he cried out. "I reckon so. Evil has took up residence in my body, and it will be the death of me. Why you've come to see it now, I don't know."

"Did the witch Perla Long lay hands on you?" Longbourne asked.

"I don't know no witch." Dad hitched himself up a little higher on his pillow.

"I have heard that Perla came here and laid hands on you, prayed over you, and claimed a healing."

"You're a fool, man, and forever more full of crap." Dad

wasn't quite yelling, but he spoke louder than Casewell thought he could. "Perla Long is a good woman and a good mother."

Longbourne shot a dark look at Casewell. "I see that she has infiltrated the whole family. Evil is an insidious thing."

Dad reached out and clamped a hand down on Longbourne's arm. The preacher winced. "Speak plain, man. Tell me what you've come here for, so I can send you packing."

"I have come to ferret out the devil," Longbourne said. "I have come to undo the spell that witch has cast on you and your family. Do not forfeit your soul just for the comforts of this world. She is a harlot, a blasphemer, and a sinner. Beg my forgiveness, and perhaps you can yet be saved."

Casewell could see the skin of Longbourne's arm twisting under his father's hand. Longbourne seemed determined to stand it but grimaced and tried to shift his arm away. John only gripped tighter.

"Your forgiveness is little more than the dust kicked up by a dog," he said. "I have asked the Lord's forgiveness for a lifetime of sin, and He has granted it to me. He has spoken to me—not through the likes of you—but through the child of that woman you call 'harlot.' The good Lord has seen fit to show me His ways through the simple love of a child who does not have a man to call father. She has accomplished what you never could."

Beads of sweat stood out on Longbourne's upper lip. He licked at them and tried to shift his arm. He finally could stand it no longer. "You are hurting me, Brother John," he said. "Release my arm."

Dad flung Longbourne's arm from his grasp. "You're not worth hurting," he spat out. "You're not worth the air you breathe." He fell back against his pillows, clearly exhausted.

He looked toward Casewell standing at the foot of the bed, his face a mass of confusion. "Son?"

Casewell felt tears spring to his eyes. "Yes?" he whispered.

"I need to tell you something. There's something I need you to know." John's eyes tracked back and forth, as though he was looking for something moving through the air that he couldn't pin down.

Casewell realized he was holding his breath. He sensed that whatever his father wanted to say was important. But then Dad grimaced and closed his eyes.

Neither of the men noticed Pastor Longbourne easing toward the door. He was poised for flight before he spoke. "I have seen enough to know that evil has gained a strong foothold in this place," he said. "I will root it out." And with that, the preacher fled.

Casewell felt a momentary chill, wondering what Longbourne would do.

On Monday Frank came by the store as folks were lining up for the day's meal. Casewell saw him and stepped over to greet the older man. He could almost forget that Frank used to be the town drunk. Especially now that he knew he traveled with Buffalo Bill.

"I've come with good news." Frank grinned broadly. "I went to see Angie and Liza the other day, and they told me what happened all those years ago to drive us apart." The smile faded but didn't disappear completely. "I had to own my part in all that mess. My playing one sister against the other was where things started to go wrong. I reckon I didn't deserve either one of those fine ladies. I played with fire in them days, and I sure enough got burnt. I didn't mean for them to get burnt, too." He sighed and looked wistful. Then the smile broke out full force once again.

"We talked and maybe fussed a little until Liza got to giggling about three old folks wrangling over a love triangle—that's what she called it, love triangle—and then I reckon we all began to see the humor in the thing. Before you knew it, we were laughing fit to bust. Can you imagine? Three wrinkled, white-headed old folks tangled up over who loved whom and which one lied first and who was more wrong all those years ago.

"Well, we decided we might as well be friends. We shook on it and then had us a fine dinner of green beans and peas out of the cellar. There's nothing like being forgiven to add a tang to your dinner."

Casewell clapped Frank on the shoulder. "I'm glad to hear you worked it out," he said. "All three of you are mighty fine folks. I'm glad you can be friends."

"That's not all my news. I went ahead and bought the Rexroad place. Old man Rexroad's daughter has no interest in coming back to Wise, and with the drought and all, she didn't figure on ever getting the place sold. I made her a fair offer, and she snapped it up."

Robert joined them in time to hear this last piece of news. "Well, that calls for a celebration. Soon as I run across a fatted calf, we'll have us a feast."

"Robert, I have a proposal for you," Frank said. "I've got quite a collection of books I've gathered over the years. Seems a shame to leave them in boxes out there at the house. I was thinking, since you have some empty shelves around here"—he waved a hand at the sparse store shelves—"we could start us up a lending library."

"Why, that's a fine idea," Robert said. "And I 'spect Delilah would enjoy being the head librarian. She always has had a love for the printed word."

"Excellent." Frank rubbed his hands together. "Casewell, what say you and Robert come on out to the house after you finish up here, and we'll start loading up books."

The three men continued to talk about plans for the library, clearing shelves and rearranging things as the hungry crowd swelled and then thinned out to nothing. Delilah was thrilled when they shared their plan and immediately began wiping down shelves and planning how she would keep a record of who checked out which books.

Emily came by to pick up dinner just as Perla finished serving the last guest. Emily and Perla cleaned up the kitchen area together, and when they finished, they offered to help with the lending library.

"Oh, but I suppose I can't," Emily said. "I need to take John and Sadie their dinner. He probably won't feel like eating, but that child will be hungry."

Perla jumped in. "Emily, you stay. I'll take dinner and then Sadie and I can walk home. You don't really need my help here, and I'm guessing it'll be nice for you to get out of the house for a little while."

Emily smiled, allowing some of the fear and worry she now lived with each day to show in her eyes. "It would be a nice distraction. If you'll just stay until John falls asleep, he should be fine."

"I'd be glad to. I'm beginning to feel a real kinship for John. Maybe it's the way he's gotten so attached to Sadie. You have a good time setting up the library here."

When Perla got to the Phillipses' house, she found John already sleeping. Sadie sat at the foot of his fancy new bed, playing quietly with her dolls. It occurred to Perla that leaving a child alone with a dying man might not be the wisest plan, but then Sadie put her mind at ease. The child crept out of the bedroom and led her mother into the sitting room.

"Mr. John fell asleep and Ms. Emily went for supper," Sadie whispered. "Mr. John needs his rest. He said to wake him up if there's an emergency, but there wasn't one." She nodded her head for emphasis and went to climb onto one of the kitchen chairs. "I'm glad you're here. I'm hungry."

Perla smiled and sat down to eat with her daughter. It was nice enjoying the quiet of the kitchen in someone else's house. There were no dishes to wash, no meals to plan, nothing to do but listen to her child's prattling and John's light snoring from the other room. It was the picture of peace.

As they ate, Perla noticed Sadie's eyes getting heavy. She still took an afternoon nap most days, and Perla suspected there hadn't been one that day. Finally Sadie's spoon clattered to the table, and her head nearly fell into her bowl. Perla scooped her up and carried her to Casewell's old room, where she placed the child on a narrow twin bed with a quilt folded at the foot. Perla supposed she ought to go to the house, but she was too tired to carry Sadie and hated to wake her sufficiently to walk. Casewell would eventually bring Emily home, and then she was sure he would take them to the Thorntons'.

Perla went into the kitchen and rinsed the two bowls she and Sadie had used. John's dinner had gone into the Frigidaire. She would warm it up when he woke. Walking into the sitting room, Perla eased herself onto the sofa and folded her hands in her lap. She tried to remember the last time she just sat down and did nothing. She leaned her head against the curved back of the sofa and examined the light fixture in the ceiling. There was a cobweb there that Perla suspected wouldn't have lasted long before John's illness. Now she was amazed that Emily got anything done beyond caring for her husband. She closed her eyes for just a moment and was startled awake by the door opening and footsteps coming though the kitchen.

"Emily?" she called out. "Sadie and I are still here. Can . . ." she trailed off as she realized it wasn't Emily or Casewell standing in the kitchen doorway.

Pastor Longbourne let his eyes run up and down the length of Perla. There was something in his look that made her feel she'd been caught doing something unseemly in public.

"Why, Pastor," she said, "you must be here to see John. I'll wake him for you."

Perla began to rise but Longbourne stepped forward with his hand out to still her. "No need," he said. "I am here to speak to you."

"How did you know . . .?" Perla felt weak.

"Your movements are no secret to me, witch." Longbourne curled his lip. "You think you have won the people of Wise over with your sorcery, but I am not so easily swayed."

"I'm not a witch," Perla whispered.

Longbourne moved to stand over her on the low sofa. She tried to stand but he leaned forward to push her back down. "Stay where you are," he said. "You need not rise on my account." His smile was grotesque, and Perla realized she could hear her heart pounding in her ears. She tried to tell herself she had nothing to be afraid of, but deep inside something cried out, *"Run!"*

Before Perla could attempt to move again, Longbourne stepped forward and pushed one leg between her knees. She was so astonished, she barely resisted. There was no question of standing now.

"You need to be broken, witch," he said. "You need to be cleansed from all unrighteousness."

Perla didn't know what to do. She felt certain that this was not a man who could be reasoned with. Words hardly seemed appropriate at this point, but what else could she do?

"We are all sinners," she said, wishing her voice wasn't quivering.

"Yes," roared Longbourne, "and you are the worst among us. Repent. Repent or die."

Perla felt a shiver make its way up her spine. Almost involuntarily she tried to shift sideways, away from the man. He jammed his leg further between her knees and clamped a hand down on her thigh. Perla began to shake in earnest.

Longbourne's eyes were like hot coals burning into her. He reached down with his free hand and began to push the hem of her skirt up her leg. "You must repent, harlot," he grated out. "And I will help drive the demons from your body."

Tears began to run down Perla's face. She struggled, but Longbourne's grip was like a vise, and she was afraid to cry out. She was afraid to wake her daughter and expose her to this horrible scene. She closed her eyes and tried to pray.

And then, as though God had heard her prayer, Longbourne staggered sideways and went down on the floor at Perla's feet. As he fell he tore the hem of her skirt, exposing her left leg. Perla clutched the torn fabric and looked wildly around the room. John stood nearby, holding a stick of firewood and panting as though he'd been running.

"You all right?" he asked.

Perla nodded and looked down at the fallen pastor. There

was a skinned place on his head that oozed blood. He wadded the piece of skirt that had come away in his hand and pressed it to his skull. His eyes were full of hate.

"Preacher, I reckon you'd best go," John said.

Longbourne crawled a little ways and used an armchair to pull himself up. "I don't know what you think you saw, John Phillips, but you had no call to hit me." He spoke slowly, as though the blow to his head had made it hard to formulate the right words.

"I saw someone who claims to be a man of God trying to take advantage of a young woman who has committed no worse sin than caring for the people around her."

"That's a lie," spat Longbourne. "I'd like to see you convince my flock that I would do such a thing." He flung the blood-soaked rag to the floor and pressed his own handkerchief to his head. "And I imagine this wound will show them how I was attacked by a madman who probably was out of his mind with illness." Longbourne smirked.

John bent down, grimacing with pain, and retrieved the discarded bit of cloth. "I'm thinking this bit of the lady's frock soaked in your blood will be a little harder to explain," he said.

Longbourne paled and took a step forward as though he would snatch the bit of evidence from John's hand. But he froze when he heard Casewell and Emily coming in through the kitchen door.

"Perla, are you still here?" Emily called. She appeared in the doorway and stopped so suddenly that Casewell bumped into her. "Why, John, what in the world are you doing out of bed? And Pastor—are you injured?"

Casewell quickly took stock of the situation. "Mother, Perla is crying and I think Dad needs to sit. Let's ease on in here and get everyone situated so we can hear what's happening." Casewell guided his mother to a seat beside Perla. He snatched up a dish towel and folded it to make a compress for Pastor Longbourne, who took it and began edging toward the front door.

"I'll be on my way," he said. "Probably need to get this little cut on my head looked at. I'll be praying for—"

Casewell planted himself between Longbourne and the door. "I think you should stay," he said. "Never know when someone's going to need some pastoral counseling."

Dad collapsed into an armchair. Soaked in sweat, he panted like a man who'd just run a race. "Son, that man is evil. I say we let him go." Longbourne looked hopeful. "I say we let him go a long, long way from here with the promise that he will never attempt to lead a church again."

"Hold on, now," protested Longbourne. "All you got against me is the word of a harlot and a dying man. John Phillips, you ain't never been one to make friends around here, and I ain't the first to call that woman there 'witch.' You're acting awful high and mighty, considering what little you got to go on."

Casewell thought the preacher sounded a lot less educated all of a sudden. "Longbourne, it's pretty clear to me what happened here, and I'll be speaking to the elders about it before the sun sets."

"*You!*" Longbourne said the word like he was expelling something disgusting from his mouth. "You've been stepping out with that slut. You, I can do battle with."

Casewell doubted Longbourne would survive the battle, but he did not relish the idea of dragging what he feared had happened out into the public eye. He looked from Perla clutching her torn dress to Longbourne and considered what to do next. And then his mother took care of everything.

"Pastor Longbourne," she said, standing, "I knew your wife well before she passed. She confided in me and told me things she felt she couldn't share with another soul. I swore to her that I would never break her confidence. But I see that the evil you forced her to live with is still in you, and I believe she would forgive me for sharing her secrets now. I see what you tried to do here today, and while the good Lord can forgive and forget, I doubt the people of Wise will be quite so willing. I beg you, Pastor, leave this place and try to find your way back to our Savior. He is the only hope for your soul."

"Lies," Longbourne whispered, backing into the corner of the room. "How can I stand against all of these lies?"

Mom moved toward him and held out her hand. "There is no standing," she said. "You have already fallen. Now, please go."

Longbourne circled her as though coming into contact with that outstretched hand was more than he could bear. He darted through the kitchen and banged out the back door.

"He could still try to turn the people against us," Casewell said.

"I don't think so." Mom's voice was laced with sorrow. "I don't think we'll ever see him again."

16

THE NEXT DAY CASEWELL GOT WORD that there would be an impromptu meeting of the elders at the church that afternoon. He walked in just behind Steve Cutright, who grabbed Casewell's arm as he passed through the door.

"I hear the preacher done run off with that Perla Long," he said. Casewell stiffened and freed his arm.

"I think you'll find you heard wrong," he said, moving forward to join the other men gathered in the front pews.

Casewell and Steve were the last to arrive. Robert called the meeting to order by clapping his hands and offering a prayer.

"Now, there are rumors aplenty about why we've come together this afternoon. Let me clear it all up for you. Pastor Longbourne has left town. Alone," he added, shooting a look at Steve. "He spoke nary a word to anyone, just left a note, which I will now read to you. It's short if not sweet.

"I am no longer able to serve a pastorate where my parishioners are intent on defying the wisdom of God. I have done my best by you all, and now I wash my hands of you. If lies

are spread about me after I am gone, I trust God will punish the offenders.

Longbourne

“That’s it. He packed up what little he had in the parsonage and left. Last night, as best we can tell.”

“Maybe we oughta fetch him back,” Steve said. “Don’t seem likely we’ll find a new preacher, things like they are around here.”

“No one knows where he went,” Robert said. “He’s got no family since his wife passed, and I couldn’t even make a guess at where he might be headed.”

Casewell shifted his feet and spoke. “It just might be we’re better off with him gone.”

“Ah, you just don’t like him ’cause he was so rough on that woman you’re sweet on,” Steve said.” I thought he was on to something, what with the drought and all. The Lord works in mysterious ways.” He nodded his head and looked pensive. Casewell thought the look didn’t suit the fiddle player.

“Regardless,” Robert said, “what we need to do is figure out how to fill that pulpit”—he pointed to the front of the church—“until we can hire a new pastor.”

The men looked at one another and then at their hands and finally at their shoes.

Robert cleared his throat. “Seems to me we’re in line to preach for the time being,” he said. “We’re all ordained as elders, and that means we’re qualified to give the message.”

Steve laughed. “There’s qualified and there’s able. If it’s a fiddle concert you’re after, I’m the man. For preaching, you’d best look elsewhere.”

The other men nodded their heads. They were farmers, carpenters, and store owners, unaccustomed to the spotlight.

Robert nodded his head. "I thought you'd feel that way. I guess I can take a stab at it, but I'll admit I was hoping Casewell here might be willing to step up."

Casewell jerked his head up. "Me? You want me to preach?"

"Well, of all of us, I'd guess you know the Bible best, and I'd be surprised to hear you were nervous about talking in front of a crowd. So yes, I think you should preach."

Casewell shifted, as though the hard pew had just gotten harder. He was surprised but also flattered. More than once he'd thought of good topics for a sermon and even imagined how he would go about delivering his message. Of course, at the moment he couldn't think what any of those topics were.

"Well, I'll confess that I might even enjoy delivering a talk or two from up front," he said at last. "Of course, I'll expect you all to stay awake."

Steve slapped Casewell on the back. "Now you're talking. Can't wait to hear your first sermon."

Although Casewell had initially felt a rush of excitement at the prospect of filling the pulpit, by Tuesday evening he was having second thoughts. He wasn't qualified to teach, preach, or anything else. Sure, he'd read the Bible—several times. He'd listened to countless sermons and had some interesting discussions with friends about interpretation and meaning. But he had no training—no formal education—no authority. What was he thinking?

Casewell had hardly spoken to Perla since her run-in with Longbourne. She was still cooking at the Thorntons' store, and Casewell continued to help, but he was trying to keep a little distance between them. He hadn't realized that so many folks in the community were beginning to pair them up. He admired Perla and he enjoyed her company. He even accepted her fatherless child, but he didn't want to give her the wrong idea about his intentions. He only meant to be friendly.

As Casewell cleaned up the kitchen area after the communal meal Thursday evening, he was oblivious to the people around him. He was too busy tormenting himself over a sermon topic and his unworthiness to deliver anything he could think of to realize that Perla had slipped in and worked by his side.

"Penny for your thoughts," she said.

Casewell jumped and looked at her like he'd just woken up. "Oh, I guess I was pondering what I could talk about from the pulpit come Sunday."

"Seems like there'd be no shortage. The Bible's a long book." Perla smiled. "Too long, some have said when they got to the begats."

"Well, it's not that I can't come up with something. It's more like I can't come up with the right something. This is the first time I've had the chance to speak from the pulpit. I want to do it right."

"Have you asked God for guidance? "she asked. "Seems to me He could put something on your heart, and if you speak from the heart . . ." She paused and her eyes softened. "You can't go wrong."

Casewell looked at Perla as though for the first time. "That's wise counsel. I think I'll take it. Suppose you can get along without me tomorrow?"

"I think we'll be fine," she said. "You go write that sermon."

Friday morning Casewell got up early, made a pot of coffee, and got down on his knees to discuss his sermon with God. He prayed pretty steadily for fifteen minutes or so and then sat, Bible in hand, waiting for inspiration. He flipped through the Old Testament, read snatches of the Gospels, and dipped into Revelation. Nothing seemed right. He got out a pad of paper and started writing about the Sermon on the Mount. That was chock-full of food for thought. But after several paragraphs, Casewell realized there was too much. He was going to have to narrow his topic down.

Around noon, Casewell slung his notebook into the corner of the room and strode outside. Though September, it was still hot, without a hint of a breeze. He gazed across the barren landscape. The drought had taken such a toll. He thought of pictures he'd seen in *National Geographic* of the Midwest Dust Bowl during the Great Depression. *Not so long ago,* he thought. Looked like they were headed for another one.

If it weren't for Perla feeding people, they would be in an even harder place. Casewell knew the crops were lost, and by the end of the month he feared most of the livestock would be beyond saving, too. Some folks had gone ahead and butchered what they could spare. It was the wrong time of year for it, but Perla had used the meat as it was killed.

Killed. Casewell felt the weight of death hanging over the landscape. In a way, he had avoided thinking about how desperate their situation was. He'd kept busy with the unfolding tale of the Talbot sisters and their lost love, with his father's illness, and with Perla. Casewell realized that the more he tried to put distance and space between himself and Perla, the more he seemed to think about her.

Even now, he thought about how she was daily giving all she could to a suspicious group of people who scorned her. He thought about how she seemed to have no animosity for the father of her child. He remembered how she had boldly shared her story with him and how he had turned away, only to be drawn back to her again. He thought about how she loved her child. The same child who many would say was a source of pain and disgrace. Words began to form in Casewell's mind, then sentences, then paragraphs.

He ran inside and snatched up his pad and pencil and made notes for a full hour, flipping back and forth through the pages of the Bible, talking to himself and smiling. Sweat bloomed on Casewell's shirt and streaked his forehead. When he stopped writing, he fell to his knees again, and this time offered up a prayer of thanksgiving. So much had become clear to him. His path was suddenly straight and true.

The lending library at the Thorntons' store turned out to be a hit with the local community. Delilah was only too delighted to take over as librarian and even created her own little catalog and offered recommendations to nearly everyone who came into the store, whether they wanted them or not.

On Saturday she cornered Casewell as he was heading home and insisted that he take a book for himself and several for his father.

"He'll welcome a good book to keep his mind occupied while he's laid up in bed," she said.

"Dad never was much of a reader." Casewell tried to get

away without having to pick out any books. "I wouldn't know what to take him."

"I imagine he didn't read much simply because he didn't have time for it," Delilah said. "And don't worry about what to take him—I have some books right here." She picked up three volumes lying on the counter and handed them over. Two were Westerns by someone named Louis L'Amour, and the third was a book of poems by Robert Frost.

"I don't know that poetry is quite right for Dad these days," Casewell said.

Delilah harrumphed. "There's a poem in there about mending fences. I put in a marker." She pointed at a slip of paper sticking out. "I think he'll like that one in particular."

Casewell smiled his thanks and stowed the books, along with a pot containing beefsteaks stewed in tomato sauce, on the floorboard of his truck. He'd been planning on going by his parents' house all along.

He mulled over his sermon as he drove the short distance. He very much wanted his parents to be in attendance on Sunday, if his father was well enough, but he also felt a little nervous. His father may have finally begun to soften, but Casewell still feared his judgment. What if his father didn't like what he had to say? What if no one did? What if Casewell made a fool of himself in front of the whole town? It was enough to wear a man out.

Casewell carried the food and books from his truck, and as he walked up the dusty path to the door, he felt a coolness caress the back of his neck. If he didn't know better, he would have said it was the kind of breeze that brings rain. Scanning the sky he noted that it was that cloudless, blue-white of a late-summer day. It looked as if it had been bleached by the unrelenting sun, and he turned his eyes to the house, somehow wishing he hadn't taken notice of the desolate sky.

"Ma, I've got dinner," he called, pushing into the kitchen. He heard laughter in the bedroom, so he put the pot down on the table and carried the books back to his father's room. He stood in the doorway for a moment, watching his mother where she sat on the edge of the bed, leaning toward his father. She spoke in a low voice and smiled. She kissed his father, and he reached an arm up to pull her closer. Casewell felt a lump form in his throat and wished he could live in that moment forever. He would never preach, his mother would always smile, it would never rain, and his father would live forever. Yes, he could accept that.

"Come on in, son." His father's voice sounded weaker than Casewell remembered. "I was just telling your mother that I'd go ahead and die if it didn't mean leaving her."

Casewell was almost shocked by the love he could hear in his father's voice. It was palpable. "And you, too, son. It'll mean leaving you, and I swear I thought I'd get more time to . . ." He seemed unable to catch his next breath, as if something stopped up his throat. "To love you."

Casewell stumbled on the doorsill and dropped the books he was holding. Emily smiled and leaned down to scoop them up. "I know," she said and patted Casewell's arm. "I've always known who your father really is. I'm just glad you get to meet him this side of heaven."

"Heaven," Dad laughed. "I will say I'm mighty relieved to know we'll get back together there before we know it. I can't say I was so sure of it a month ago. Can't wait to thank the Lord in person for sending that little'un to show me the way." Dad coughed with a violence that made the roses carved on the headboard look like they were swaying in a spring breeze.

The fit passed and Casewell glanced at the carving again—he could have sworn that the flowers continued to flutter for a moment. He rubbed his eyes and moved toward his father.

"Dad, I don't know what to say . . ."

"I reckon not, son. I've been an ornery, ill tempered fool most of your life. And for a while there after that dang doctor told me I was dying, I determined to prove I could be even meaner than anyone thought. And I reckon I did prove it. But that little tyke of Perla's has found the soft center of me. I meant to hate her, too, being that she's a woods colt. But I somehow couldn't do it. I began to see something in that child that reminded me . . . well, of the good I've seen in this life. Innocence, purity, wonder. She's as fresh as a January snowfall, and some way or another, just being around her made me feel clean, light, maybe even hopeful. Though it took me a while to figure out what it was I was hoping for."

Mom sat on the far side of the bed and laced her fingers through Dad's. "Don't wear yourself out talking," she said. "We can talk later if you need to."

Dad glanced at his wife and squeezed her hand. "Thank you, but I reckon I'd best go ahead and get this out. I want Casewell to know before he preaches on Sunday." He turned to look at his only child, a grown man, standing beside his bed.

"Son, I thought I was a Christian most of my life, though I didn't see as that guaranteed me a spot in heaven. I figured that dunking I got when I was a boy made me good enough for church, but maybe not good enough for God himself. Well, I ain't good enough. Never have been, never will be. But God's been talking at me through that child, and I finally paid Him heed. I still ain't good enough, but I reckon so long as I walk through the pearly gates on Jesus' coattails, I don't hafta be.

That's what I'm trying to tell you, son. I'm sure of heaven for the first time in my life. And if you're as sure as I think you are, then we'll be getting together again real soon."

Casewell was crying now. He hadn't cried in front of his father since he was a boy and had been whipped for lying. Even then he'd struggled not to let his father see how weak he was. But now weakness washed over him and made him strong enough to cry for the years of wishing and for the joy of knowing his father was saved. And loved his only son.

"I'm going to go dish up that supper while you two have a minute alone." Mom stood and shook out her apron.

As she started out of the room, Dad called to her. "Emily," he said, stretching out his hand. She stepped back, gave his fingers a squeeze, and turned to go, but Dad held on and pulled her toward him. "Emily, listen to me. Everything is all right." Casewell thought he saw a tear in his father's eye. "It always has been," he said. "But now I know it."

"As do I." Emily squeezed her husband's hand in her own one more time before going into the kitchen.

Sunday morning Casewell woke refreshed and eager to get to church. He hummed as he dressed and polished his boots. He didn't know why he bothered—they would get dusty again as soon as he set foot outside. He thought back to that Sunday morning when he first laid eyes on Perla Long. He'd been hungry that morning, embarrassed by his stomach's growl. Now he knew a man could be hungry for a great deal more than food. He could be hungry for God, hungry for love, and hungry for forgiveness. Yes, thought Casewell, there were worse things than an empty belly.

The lightness Casewell woke with left him as soon as he set foot inside the church. The crowd seemed larger than usual. Of course, people would come just to hear him. Some curious, some wishing him well, and some hoping to see him make a fool of himself. Casewell set his jaw. They just might get that satisfaction, the way he felt right then.

Robert served as liturgist, calling out the hymns, praying, and asking for the collection to be taken up. Not that anyone had much to drop into the plate, but it went round just the same. Finally it came time to read the Scriptures.

"Matthew, chapter six, verses fourteen and fifteen. 'For if ye forgive men their trespasses, your heavenly Father will also forgive you: But if ye forgive not men their trespasses, neither will your father forgive your trespasses.'" Casewell only stumbled a little as he read. "Let us pray," he said and bowed his head.

Casewell had never been entirely comfortable praying aloud, and now he felt a moment of panic as a bead of sweat rolled down and dripped off his nose. The words would not come.

And then he felt a gust of wind from an open window curl around the back of his neck. It gave him the same feeling as the breeze the day before—that rain was in the offing. Casewell knew it was wishful thinking, but the distraction unstuck his brain.

"Father, thank you for the opportunity to gather in your house to hear your Word. We thank you for the blessings of fellowship, especially in difficult times. Open your Word to us this morning, Father, and speak to our hearts and minds through your Spirit. In the name of Jesus Christ we pray, amen."

The breeze cooled Casewell's sweaty neck and brought a

sense of calm. As he raised his head his eyes found his father's in the front pew. *What a blessing,* he thought. And he began to speak.

"A little further on in Matthew, Jesus told the story of the unmerciful servant after Peter came and asked Him how many times he should forgive his brother. Peter seemed to think seven times ought to be plenty, but Jesus said to forgive a man seventy-seven times. By that I guess He meant to just keep on forgiving as long as it's needed.

"Well, the unmerciful servant owed his king ten thousand bags of gold, and he didn't have it. So the king planned to sell the servant and his whole family to make up the debt. But the servant begged the king not to do it and said he'd pay him back soon enough. The king felt sorry for the servant and canceled the debt." Casewell felt like he was moving along nicely now.

"Later on, that same servant ran into another servant who owed him a hundred silver coins. Well, the servant whose debt had been forgiven grabbed hold of the second servant and started to choke him, demanding he pay up." Casewell made a strangling motion in the air and then dropped his hands down to brace against the pulpit.

"That second servant went down on his knees and begged for more time to pay. And what did the forgiven servant do? Why, he had that other fellow thrown into prison. Some of that second servant's friends went to the king and told him what had happened. The king was so mad that the servant whose huge debt had been forgiven wouldn't forgive a little debt that he threw him in jail to be tortured until he paid every penny back." Casewell paused and looked out over the congregation.

"That's how God does us. He'll forgive us anything—all we have to do is ask Him. I know I've had to ask Him for plenty of forgiveness here lately. He doesn't hold it over me, He doesn't carry a grudge, and I don't think He even remembers what I needed forgiveness for. All He asks is that I forgive other people the same way He's forgiven me."

Casewell smiled and leaned into the pulpit. "I know. Easier said than done. Somehow other people's sins seem to look worse than mine." His eyes flicked past Perla. He was trying hard not to look at her. He didn't want her to know that he'd ever judged her so harshly. "But in God's eyes, sin is sin, whether it's murder or telling a little white lie. We all need forgiveness just the same.

"And we all need to dish out forgiveness just as quick as we dish out judgment and condemnation. Jesus made it pretty clear that God's forgiveness depends on our forgiving one another. In Luke, chapter six, He said, 'Judge not, and ye shall not be judged: condemn not, and ye shall not be condemned: forgive, and ye shall be forgiven.' I've seen people forgive things that I would want to hold on to. Cruelty, spite, mean-spiritedness. It takes a gentle spirit to turn loose of all that, but it's no less than what God calls us to do.

"I don't know about all of you." Casewell really looked at the congregation for the first time. Did some people look uncomfortable? Maybe. Maybe they needed to. "But I don't want to be judged or condemned by God. I know I'll come up short. So I plan to try real hard to forgive when I need to. And I'm going to start by forgiving Pastor Longbourne for the trouble he stirred up. I reckon he's got enough pain bottled up inside him that there's no need for me to hold anything against him. And if there's anyone else out there who wants my forgiveness, though I don't think I have anything against even one of you, consider it given."

Casewell moved out from behind the pulpit and stepped off the dais. He raised his hands into the air. "Go forth this morning and search your hearts to know if there's anyone you need to forgive. Find them and give them the same gift God is so glad to give to you. Peace be with you." He dropped his arms and walked toward the back door so he could shake hands. He hoped no one would notice his sweaty palms.

But before Casewell had taken more than two steps, he heard a rustling and then a voice—his father's voice.

"Son, forgive me."

Casewell stopped and turned as though afraid of what he might see. His father stood, hunched over and leaning against the pew in front of him. "I have not been the father"—he looked at Emily—"or husband I should have been. Forgive me."

Mom leaned forward and pressed her cheek against his father's hand where it gripped the pew. Tears washed over the worn knuckles. Casewell didn't know what to do. Should he speak? Should he go to his father? And then it was as though he lost the ability to decide for himself, and he rushed to wrap his arms around his father's frail shoulders. He thought he might hurt the sick man, he was squeezing so hard, but his father wrapped an arm around Casewell and squeezed back just as hard. Casewell could feel every bone beneath Dad's taut skin. His father had the feel of a man who might break. Then again, maybe he was finally broken.

That afternoon Perla left Sadie playing quietly at Delilah's feet so she could close herself alone in the room she shared with her daughter. Casewell's sermon had touched her in ways she did not expect. "I must forgive him," she whispered. "I must forgive them both."

She fell to her knees on the braided rug and clasped her hands at her breast. She closed her eyes and began to pray aloud.

"Father, I came here to escape the censure of men, but that is not what I most wanted to escape. People will judge me, and it is, perhaps, no less than I deserve. I was trying to outrun your judgment, Father. I blamed . . . him . . . for loving me when he was not free to do so. But I loved him back, even when I knew it was wrong. And I turned my back on you as though that would prevent your seeing. You have forgiven me, Father, but I have not forgiven him. I have heaped blame on his shoulders, attempting to lessen my own load. I forgive him now. Please bless him." Perla squeezed her eyes more tightly shut. "And bless his family." She gave one tearless sob, then composed herself again.

"And, Father, I forgive Casewell, too. It wasn't until this morning that I knew there was anything to forgive. I've carried anger toward him for judging me. He is a good man. I had hoped . . . well, you know my hopes and dreams, impossible, as I know they are. Amen."

Perla remained kneeling, hands now limp. She felt lighter, easier. A breeze slipped in the window and caressed her face. She felt beloved by God, if by no one else.

17

CASEWELL ENJOYED SUNDAY DINNER with his parents. They ate leftovers from Perla's last round of cooking.

"I'm proud of you, son," Dad said.

Casewell felt a surge of joy that made the top of his head tingle. He grinned, something he doubted he'd done at the dinner table since he was in a high chair.

"It was the best sermon I ever heard," his mother said.

"Ma, you'd say that no matter what."

"Of course I would, and I'm allowed. The other mothers wish their sons could do half so well."

"Don't go and indulge in pride now," Casewell teased. "If I'm going to be the preacher, I'll have to hold you accountable."

The three laughed together and finished off the meal with the most lively conversation Casewell ever remembered them having.

After dinner Mom helped Dad back to bed. Casewell realized that his father seemed to have trouble lifting his feet. He dragged into the bedroom, and Casewell helped his mother get him into a nightshirt. Then Mom excused herself to tidy up the kitchen.

In the quiet left behind, Casewell could hear his father's breathing. It was raspy and seemed slow. He really looked at his father for the first time in a long while. The older man's white hair had long been striking against his sun- and wind-darkened skin. But now his face was almost as pale as his hair, the ruddy flush of sun and hard work long gone. The lined skin seemed to have pulled tight against Dad's skull, giving his flesh an almost translucent quality. Casewell noticed the throbbing of his father's heartbeat in the fragile skin of his neck. He wished the beat were faster.

"Do you hear that, son?" Dad turned his head toward the window, which was closed in a futile effort to keep out the dust.

"Hear what?" Casewell moved to look outside.

"Open the window," he commanded.

Casewell moved to obey the order even as he argued against it. "It'll just let in more dust, Dad. There's hardly a breeze to make it worthwhile."

But as the window cleared the sash, a gust of cool air surged into the room, sending the lacy curtains billowing out over the bed. Casewell looked out the window and saw that the formerly barren sky was now scudding with great cottony clouds. It wasn't just a breeze that had kicked up. It was wind.

"The rain sounds so good after all this time," Dad sighed. "Thank God for the rain."

"It's not raining, Dad." Casewell glanced at the window. "And even though there are clouds, I don't hold out much hope. We've seen clouds before that didn't amount to anything."

"Oh, the sweet sound of rain on a tin roof." He smiled. "Your mother and I hid out in a barn in a storm like this once. That's when I kissed her the first time. Can't help but think that sound is the purtiest I ever heard."

Casewell glanced out the window again and looked back at his father. Going to church and having dinner must have been too much for him. He was hallucinating. Casewell wondered how to snap him out of it, but the more he thought about it, the more he felt it would be cruel to interrupt such a pleasant notion.

"It does sound good," he said at last. "Been too long since we heard rain like that."

"Ain't it the truth," Dad said, closing his eyes.

Casewell noted the rise and fall of his father's chest. It was slow, but it was there. And then, as he watched his father breathe, he did hear something. It sounded like thunder, distant thunder. Probably just heat lightning way off on the horizon. It happened like that in the evenings sometimes. And then he heard the unmistakable splat of water on a pane of glass.

Casewell whirled toward the open window and saw it was true. One fat drop after another splatted against the upper panes. Drops came through the open window and made a pattern in the dust on the sill. Casewell reached out a shaking hand and felt the cool water bless his skin. He turned to show his father, but the rise and fall of Dad's chest had ceased. His father lay still, smiling, as Casewell stretched out wet fingers to anoint his brow.

The rain came like a petulant child given permission to play. It came in sheets with crashes of thunder and lightning, then eased down to a sprinkle—teasing—before revving up again for an hour of slow, steady blessing.

Casewell opened all the windows and doors in his parents' house while his mother lay down next to his father and whispered he knew not what. After opening the house, Casewell slipped back into the bedroom and placed a hand on his mother's shoulder.

"I called the funeral home. They'll come for him after the rain eases up. The roads are rivers with all the water trying to soak into the parched ground. Marvin said he'd just about need a boat to come right now."

"I'm in no hurry." She had cried but only a little. Now she lay curled on her side, stroking her husband's hair. "I know he's not in there," she said. "But I'm going to miss touching him so very much. I always loved to feel his hair, though he didn't like me to do it unless we were alone. I guess this is the first time I've run my fingers through his hair while someone else was in the room." She gazed past her husband into nothingness. "I don't suppose he minds."

Casewell sat on the foot of the bed. He would have expected being in the bedroom with his dead father and living mother to be strange, but somehow it was friendly. His mother began humming "I'll Fly Away," and he wished he had his mandolin to play along. The patter of the rain, the warmth of the room, and the song conspired to make Casewell drowsy. He thought it was probably awful of him to think of sleep at a time like this.

Jerking upright, Casewell realized he'd dozed off. He felt disoriented and out of sorts. He sat up and realized his father still lay in the bed. His mother had straightened Dad's shirt and arranged the covers so that they turned down under his arms. His hands were crossed on his chest. Casewell's gaze traveled to his father's face and he startled, not recognizing him for a moment. He knew his father was gone, but now that he studied his face, he realized just how long gone. Although the shape of the nose, the thick eyebrows, and the lips—surprisingly full for a man—were all the same, he no longer looked like John Phillips. That man had surely departed.

His mother bustled into the room. "Marvin called to say he's on his way. I'm betting that's what woke you. I was going to let you nap a little longer."

"It's just as well. The stories people would tell if Marvin caught me sleeping at my dead father's feet."

She kissed him on the forehead. "People will talk no matter what you do." Turning to the window, she said, "The rain's stopped. It surely is fresh outside. Come and see."

Casewell walked out onto the front porch with his mother and inhaled deeply. The sky was the brilliant shade of blue that often came in October, and the air smelled like clean laundry. The yard, with its brittle, brown grass, was a maze of puddles that had yet to find a way into the hard-baked soil. The trees were still leafless, the earth was still brown, the garden was still a wasteland, but somehow the world looked brighter. It was certainly cleaner with the rime of dust rinsed off everything, including Casewell's truck parked in the yard. The windows were down, but he couldn't bring himself to care. At this point water, anywhere, was welcome.

"It's a miracle," Mom said. "How many times has rain spoiled some plan of mine, and now I see that it's a miracle. Not just after a drought, but every time it rains." Emily linked her arm through Casewell's. "Your father knew the rain was coming. I think he knew because he was standing next to Jesus, and you can see everything from there."

Marvin Tomlyn pulled his makeshift hearse into the yard and backed up to the porch. Casewell opened the rear door and tried not to think too much about what would happen to his father's body after this. Marvin hopped out and strode around the vehicle to shake Casewell's hand. The undertaker stood maybe five feet four and was built like a bull, with a broad chest and bandy legs. He looked tough as a mule, but everyone who knew him had experienced his softhearted kindness.

"How you holding up, son?" he asked.

"I'm doing all right. Ma's taking it pretty well, too. He'd been sick for so long . . ."

"I understand. Just let me tell you one thing. Right now you can't quite take all of this in, and thinking things like 'he's in a better place,' and 'he's not suffering anymore' might seem like a comfort. But trust me when I tell you that two days from now some well-meaning folks will say those exact same words to you, and you'll want to shove their teeth down their necks. The best advice I can give you or anyone else who's just seen someone they love die is to take it one day at a time. Don't go beating yourself up for all the different ways you'll feel between now and next week. It's all normal, son."

Casewell felt like he couldn't get a breath. Then his lungs filled all at once, and he smiled. "I guess I've been feeling six or seven of 'em just today," he said.

Marvin slapped him on the back. "There you go. You'll be all right. Now let's get this business taken care of. We'll go just as fast or slow as you and your mama want."

As it turned out, Mom had finished saying her good-byes, and Casewell felt oddly detached from the body that was once his father. It was easier than he expected to help Marvin load the body into the hearse and slam the door. Marvin sat with mother and son as they sorted out the arrangements. There would be a viewing Thursday afternoon with the service at five o'clock. In the absence of a preacher to do the burying, Casewell would speak, along with one or two of the other elders. Dad had never been one to build close friendships with other men, but he'd won the respect of most everyone. Casewell didn't think it would be hard to get some folks to read Scripture or to say a few words. Mom suggested Casewell play his mandolin at the service, which surprised him.

"I don't know if Dad would think that was appropriate," he said. "Even if I play a hymn, it's a little jaunty for a funeral."

"Oh, Casewell, I don't suppose he ever told you, but he was so proud of your playing. He told me more than once that you'd been blessed with a gift, and he was so proud of how you used it to bring joy to people. He would want you to play."

Casewell blushed at the unexpected praise and agreed. He felt inordinately pleased, as if his father himself had asked for the music.

Finally, with everything sorted out, Marvin headed for the car, hoping aloud that he wouldn't get bogged down in the rain-wet yard. Then he turned, as if just remembering something. "You'uns probably don't feel much like getting out, but word is going 'round that folks are gathering at the church this evening to give thanks for the rain. I can pass on word about John, if you'd rather."

Casewell thought about it for only a moment. Something prodded him to go to the church and share this news himself. "No, that's all right," he said. "We'll tell the news."

Marvin raised one meaty hand and dropped it to his side. Then he climbed into the car and eased out of the yard, spinning his tires only a little. Casewell thought about how his father would not have liked the ruts left behind. He smiled to himself. He'd fix them tomorrow.

Casewell called Robert and Delilah to let them know about his father's passing and asked Delilah to come sit with Emily. She preferred to stay home from the church celebration, and though she said she'd be fine by herself, Casewell hated the idea of her sitting in the lonely house. Delilah said of course she would come, and Robert offered to read from the Psalms at the service on Thursday.

As Casewell hung up the phone and washed his hands and face before driving over to the church, he felt a weight lift. Someone else knew his father was gone. Somehow it seemed it would be easier to tell the next person and then the next. By the end of the week he thought he might have gotten used to the news himself.

Casewell heard Robert and Delilah come in and speak to his mother. Their tones were low and soothing. He heard his mother laugh softly and marveled that she could do that with her husband so recently gone. He was grateful she could.

"Casewell, come on," Robert called.

"I'm right behind you." Casewell stepped out of the bathroom, running his fingers through damp hair.

"Why don't you ride with me? I'll have to come back here and get Delilah after we finish whooping it up over the rain."

"Well, my windows were down when the rain started, so I guess I'd appreciate a ride." Casewell walked over and put a hand on his mother's shoulder. "I'll see you shortly," he said. "Thought I'd spend the night."

"You don't need to do that, son," she protested. Then she put her own hand over Casewell's where it gripped her shoulder. "But I guess I'd be more than glad to have you."

Casewell gave her a final squeeze and trailed out after Robert.

⁂

After dark now, light poured from the windows of the church. Drops of water suspended from leafless trees sparkled. Casewell felt a lump rise in his throat. He supposed it was the loss of his father combined with the blessing of the rain. As Robert parked, Casewell felt a shyness wash over him. He didn't know how to tell these people about his father's passing in the midst of their celebration. He wished he could find Perla and tell her first.

As though in answer to his wish, Perla appeared outside the car window. She was holding tight to Sadie's hand, and the light from the church caught in her blond hair, seeming to form a halo around her face. Casewell felt enchanted for a moment, as though he had the power to make his own dreams come true. Perla smiled when Casewell stepped out of Robert's car, and Sadie threw her arms around his right knee.

"Dad died today," Casewell blurted. "Delilah's with Mom."

"Oh, Casewell, I'm so sorry," Perla's face softened and her eyes seemed to plumb the depths of his. He felt she understood the mixture of sadness and joy he was experiencing, that she knew what it was to be glad a thing had happened and sorry at the same time. The urge to take her in his arms and cry with her almost overwhelmed him, but some other folks came by, and the spell was broken. She squeezed his arm and smiled through tears.

"And on the day the rain finally came," she said. "All too often sorrow and joy come skipping into your life holding hands."

Casewell nodded mutely. Robert beckoned them on to the church, and they walked into the spill of light coming through the open door.

George and Steve were at the front with their instruments, and Casewell felt somehow naked without his mandolin. Robert made his way to the front of the jam-packed church and waved his arms for quiet. Casewell and Perla slipped into the outside of a middle pew.

"Before we begin offering praise tonight, I have some important news to share," Robert said. "Casewell Phillips has joined us this evening, even though his father, John, passed earlier today."

Casewell felt grateful to Robert for solving his dilemma about how to tell folks, although he was also embarrassed to have attention drawn his way. Perla placed slender fingers on his arm and squeezed gently before folding her hands in her lap once more. He felt her warmth linger on his skin as someone in the pew behind patted him on the shoulder and those in front turned to nod or offer up sad smiles.

"We'll gather back here tomorrow for the viewing and the burial. But like it says in Ecclesiastes, there is a time for everything. 'A time to weep, and a time to laugh; a time to mourn, and a time to dance.' This whole summer has felt like a mourning time, with the world withering and dying all around us. Now it's time to rejoice in God's grace in sending the rain."

As Robert finished speaking George and Steve began playing "Shall We Gather at the River?" The congregation rose to their feet and sang as though they wanted heaven to hear.

> "Yes, we'll gather at the river,
> The beautiful, the beautiful river;
> Gather with the saints at the river
> That flows by the throne of God."

As he sang, Casewell glanced down at the top of Perla's golden head. He could see that she was smiling and tapping her foot in rhythm to the music. Little Sadie had taken her mother's hand and was swinging it to the beat. They both looked happy and peaceful. Casewell marveled, thinking of all Perla had gone through to keep this child with her. He had judged her sinful at one time, now he judged her brave and bold . . . and beautiful. Casewell felt joy and sorrow twine together in his heart and form something he had never experienced before. He thought it might be love. He thought it might be the feeling a man had when he looked at his beloved family. All he knew was that he wanted to go on feeling it.

> "Soon we'll reach the silver river,
> Soon our pilgrimage will cease;
> Soon our happy hearts will quiver
> With the melody of peace."

That night Casewell enjoyed a deeper and more peaceful sleep than he had in months. Maybe ever.

But when he woke in his parents' house the next morning, he realized he still needed to think of what to say at his father's funeral.

❧

As Perla washed the dishes that evening, she remembered how good it felt to imagine, if only for a moment, that she offered comfort to Casewell. When she squeezed his arm, it felt like her fingers belonged there, touching his skin. Like she had a right to touch him, which, of course, she didn't. But for those few moments when circumstance placed them side by side in the pew while they celebrated the rain and Casewell mourned his father, Perla had felt a kinship, a closeness that she allowed to linger, even though she knew it was just her imagination.

As they walked out into the rain-fresh evening, she'd seen Melody Simmons laughing with some other young women. Casewell had glanced at her, and Perla thought it had been an admiring look. Why wouldn't it be? Melody was lovely, though she'd never impressed Perla as being especially quick-witted. But maybe that would suit Casewell—a simple wife who didn't fill his life with complications. She sighed and walked to the back door to throw out the dirty dishwater. Sadie and Delilah were there, examining a praying mantis.

"Don't touch it," Delilah admonished. "Just look."

"Mommy, it's a praying bug." Sadie ran to pull Perla closer to see. "What is he praying for?"

"He's probably giving thanks for the rain." Perla caught Delilah's eye over Sadie's bent head. "Maybe he's giving thanks for such a nice place to live."

And maybe she should say her thanks—at least to the people who had been kind—and then move on. The people of Wise probably wouldn't need her anymore now that the rain had come. Maybe it was time to go home. She missed her mother, and she hoped her father would be ready to forgive her by now. She'd seen the miracle of forgiveness between Casewell and John, so she knew it was possible. She kissed the top of Sadie's head. Yes, going home was a good idea. It would save her having to see Casewell make a match. Closing her eyes, Perla tried to ignore the stone that was her heart.

18

CASEWELL FACED THE DAY with a mixture of dread, sorrow, and inexplicable joy. He wanted to honor his father with just the right words, but he didn't know what they were. Casewell took a deep breath, like a man surfacing after being underwater. He could taste the air. It seemed cleaner, richer somehow. He supposed it was from the rain. Casewell headed for the kitchen where he smelled coffee. He trusted he would think better after a stout cup.

As he passed through the front room with its windows thrown open to the rain-freshened air, Casewell tried to put his finger on what was different about the morning. It was more than just rain and his father's passing. A wren landed on the windowsill and sang with all her might.

Birdsong. The morning rang with birdsong. The drought had driven the birds away, hopefully to someplace greener, but overnight they had returned and seemed determined to celebrate. Casewell smiled and stopped to admire the wren's soft brown feathers and watch her tilt her head back to warble. He thought the birds might be rushing things a bit—it would take a while for the landscape to green back up, but he was glad just the same.

He stepped out onto the porch. The landscape was still desolate, but it looked somehow hopeful this morning. He looked more closely at a sugar maple growing off the corner of the porch and saw leaf buds swelling along the branches. Even as he watched it seemed like a burgeoning bud pushed a dead, shriveled leaf off the tip of a branch. It fluttered to the ground like a sigh at the end of a long, hard day. Casewell looked around the corner of the house at his parents' garden patch—he didn't much enjoy gardening—but the once parched rows called to him now. He had that spring feeling that it was time to get seed in the ground, time for a new season to unfold.

Casewell headed inside for a cup of coffee with his mother. He thought he might have an idea of what he wanted to say at the funeral.

That afternoon they held the viewing for John Phillips. Of course, the primary topic of discussion was the recent rain. Casewell had never seen a happier group gather for a funeral. Even his mother smiled as she placed a handkerchief embroidered with her initials in the casket beside his father. She leaned in and whispered something, then smoothed the hair back from his forehead. She turned and came to stand next to Casewell so the long line of mourners could clasp their hands and say well-meaning things.

The typical exchange ran along the lines of "I'm so sorry about John, but he'd been sick for a long time. What d'you reckon he'd make of this weather? He'd surely have something to say about it."

Casewell and his mother nodded and agreed and marveled over the miracle that had watered the land. They were grateful when well-wishers moved along quickly and tried to be patient when they wanted to linger and talk. Time for the service grew near, and the line dwindled. Casewell took the opportunity to step outside for a breath of air. Perla appeared with Sadie just as he was about to go back in.

"We're late." Perla wrinkled her brow.

"No. I suppose you're right on time." Casewell was rewarded with a smile.

"We've been picking violets along the creek—I guess they never quite died back all the way, and with the rain . . . Well, I've never seen so many, and Sadie was having such a nice time."

Casewell looked down at the child and noticed she was wearing a wreath of the flowers in her hair. He'd never noticed that violets had much smell to them, but there was the loveliest aroma in the air. He knelt down and admired Sadie's halo.

"Aren't they nice?" The child tilted her head this way and that to give Casewell a better look. "Can I give them to Mr. John to say good-bye?"

Casewell raised his eyebrows and cocked his head. "I don't see why not. Let's take them in."

Sadie wrapped her tiny hand around Casewell's third and fourth fingers, which was all she could manage. They approached the casket, and Casewell worried that seeing a dead man might disturb the child.

"Do you want me to put them in for you?" he asked.

"No. I can do it."

Casewell saw that she couldn't, so he lifted Sadie as she removed the wreath from her hair. She laid it on his father's chest and gave it a little pat. "Good-bye, Mr. John," she said. "I love you."

Casewell knew it was only his imagination, but he heard his father's voice whisper, *"I love you, too."* Casewell knew who his father was talking to.

Setting Sadie back on the ground, Casewell turned to Perla and took her hand. He kneaded her fingers between his own. "I," he began. But Marvin walked in and said they'd better get on in there and start the service.

"We'll talk later," Casewell said to Perla and followed Marvin into the chapel.

⁂

Robert opened the service with "Sweet By and By." Casewell listened to the words, confident that God was even now holding his father's hand.

> "There's a land that is fairer than day,
> And by faith we can see it afar;
> For the Father waits over the way
> To prepare us a dwelling place there.
>
> "In the sweet by an by,
> We shall meet on that beautiful shore;
> In the sweet by and by,
> We shall meet on that beautiful shore."

Casewell watched his mother cry as she sang, but in spite of the tears she somehow looked happy. She smiled and seemed to be looking up at something that pleased her. Seeing her like that made Casewell glad.

Steve came up and read the Twenty-third Psalm. Then Robert called Casewell to the front. He stood and felt unsteady for a moment. He had been so sure of what he wanted to say that he hadn't felt the need for notes. Now his mind was a blank. Then the image of his father asking for Casewell's forgiveness just the previous Sunday came to mind. That was it. Casewell stepped up to the pulpit, pausing to lay a hand on his father's now-closed casket.

Casewell gazed across the crowd. Everyone was there. Frank sat between Liza and Angie, the trio looking pleased just to be in one another's company. Delilah sat with Perla and Sadie. Casewell thought he'd never seen three prettier girls lined up in a row. His mother sat on the other side of Delilah, and in spite of the sorrow she carried, there was a softness to her face that had been missing for a long time. Casewell supposed it was the absence of worry.

The rest of the crowd looked more like they had gathered for a tent meeting than for a funeral. Casewell credited it to the drought ending and the land beginning to heal. The rain had eased fears people didn't even know they carried. Casewell became aware of the wind rustling the branches of a dogwood outside the open window to his left. It was a relaxing sound, and he closed his eyes for a moment to enjoy it better. Then he opened his eyes and began speaking.

"I reckon most of you were as glad as me when that rain came. Seemed like Dad could hear it coming before anybody. Maybe that's because he was on his way home." People shifted and a few sat up a bit straighter.

"Last Sunday those of you who were here saw my father stand up in that pew right there." Casewell pointed to where a family of four now sat. They looked a little uncomfortable, as though they shouldn't have taken the dead man's seat. "He stood up and asked me to forgive him for being less of a father than he thought I deserved." Casewell bowed his head and gripped the sides of the pulpit. "He was wrong. He was more of a father than I deserved. Who among us"—Casewell's head swung up and his eyes shone—"really and truly deserves a father who would . . ." He paused, feeling the tears rise in his throat, and he cleared it before trying again. "My father was not one to show much emotion. I don't think he told me he loved me until just a few days ago. But I knew he did." Casewell looked at the congregation and let the silence stretch a moment. "He showed me every day of his life. He showed me in the hard work he did, the sacrifices he made, the way he treasured my mother." She beamed through her tears. "He showed me in a thousand ways, and while I will always be glad he *told* me he loved me, I did not doubt it."

"Look out there." Casewell gestured to the windows. "A week ago it seemed like the end of the world. If it hadn't been for the food dished out at the store, some of us might have starved. We likely would have been forced to leave this place just to find enough to eat and water to drink. A week ago, it looked like God hated us. It looked like He was finally giving us what we most likely deserve—the hard back side of His hand.

"My own father gave me that a time or two over the years. I don't blame him a bit." Casewell smiled at his mother. "I reckon I was a handful coming up." She smiled back and gave her head a little shake.

"I guess I needed to be kept in check by a firm hand. A hand like John Phillips's. I deserved to be taken down a notch when I was a boy full of mischief. Just like maybe we all deserved a season of drought. But my father showed us what God requires when he stood up here last week. We have to ask for forgiveness, and what's more, we have to give it." Casewell hesitated, then looked out and met Perla's gaze. She smiled and he felt a surge of energy enter the general area of his heart. He smiled back.

"A few days ago, my father asked for my forgiveness, and then he died. I don't know that I said the words out loud, but I want you all to hear it. I forgive my father. The rain ushered him into heaven. And now it's like spring out there—trees budding, grass coming up, birds singing—God's gift to all of us." Casewell kneaded his hands. "John Phillips was not perfect. He was a father and a husband, and I loved him. John Phillips is sitting at the feet of God, forgiven. Hallelujah." The last word came out a hoarse whisper. Casewell bowed his head and dropped his shaking hands to the pulpit. Silence reigned.

THE CONGREGATION SAT as though holding its collective breath. And then Robert leapt to his feet and clapped Casewell on the back.

"George, Steve, get on up here and let's have a song. What'll it be, Casewell?" He turned to his friend.

"Are You Washed in the Blood," Casewell said without having to think. Someone handed him his mandolin, and George started them off.

> "Have you been to Jesus for the cleansing power?
> Are you washed in the blood of the Lamb?
> Are you fully trusting in His grace this hour?
> Are you washed in the blood of the Lamb?"

The song swirled around Casewell. He played it with scarcely a thought for the tune. The congregation began clapping their hands in time to the lively music. Casewell felt washed cleaner than he had ever been in his life. Guilt, shame, anger—all sluiced out through his fingertips as he plucked the strings.

When the song ended, George whispered, "Trust and Obey." And Casewell knew that this song was also the right one.

By the time they finished the second song, most of the congregants had risen to their feet and were singing with arms raised and throats tilted heavenward. The last note died away along with the upraised voices, and the congregation sat without being asked. Robert stepped back up to the pulpit.

"Friends, we came today to bury a man many of us have known for a long time. But I think what we've done is resurrect our own spirits in the assurance of a forgiveness that brings life everlasting. John Phillips may have left this world, but we'll be seeing him again. 'Weeping may endure for a night, but joy cometh in the morning.'

"I don't think I've ever been to a more joyful funeral. I thank you all for coming to honor a good man's life. Now please join us in the cemetery for the burial."

Casewell, Robert, George, Steve, Frank, and Marvin stepped forward to carry the casket out to the cemetery. They moved slowly over the uneven ground until they reached the gaping hole that Casewell and other men had dug the day before. The job would have been nearly impossible in the midst of the drought with the sunbaked dirt. But thanks to the rain, their shovels slid through the dirt and clay like a child digging in sand. Even now, there was a little water puddled in the bottom of the grave, and Casewell imagined it would be like a baptism, dropping the casket into that water.

Everyone gathered around the grave site. It was customary to say a few words, but Casewell felt his had run out. The men placed the casket over ropes arranged on the ground. He looked at the other pallbearers and nodded. They seemed to understand that he wanted them to go ahead and lower the casket.

Casewell watched the box containing what was left of his father descend into the cool brown earth. He had no sense that his father was actually in there. It seemed only that he was honoring the temple that had housed the man he loved most in this world, tucking it away now that his father was done with it.

Once the casket was situated, Casewell drew his mother forward, and each of them took up a handful of dirt to rain down on the closed lid. The clods of dirt hit with hollow thuds. Traditionally, the family would leave before the grave was filled in, but Casewell took up a shovel, handed it to Robert, took another for himself, and began filling in the grave. Other men stepped forward to help. George began singing.

> "Some glad morning when this life is o'er,
> I'll fly away. . . ."

His sweet tenor was punctuated by the sound of dirt hitting the casket and then, dirt hitting dirt lending a rhythmic sort of beat to the song. The rest of the group joined in until the whole crowd was singing verse after verse of "I'll Fly Away."

Casewell could hear Perla's sweet soprano and his mother's alto mingling. He imagined his father was flying about now. And it was good.

After the funeral, people went back to the Phillipses' farm, bringing what food they had. Although the land was beginning to heal, they still didn't have gardens or much left in their cellars. But Perla took over the kitchen, and Casewell knew there would be more than enough.

Neighbors and friends stayed all evening—eating, talking, laughing, even singing. The funeral had been better than any revival. Eventually Casewell eased away and closed himself in his parents' bedroom for a moment of solitude.

He ran a hand over the woodwork on the headboard he'd made for them. Joy swelled his heart at the thought that his father had enjoyed his craftsmanship right up until the last moments of his life. He noticed that the window he opened at his father's request just a few days earlier had not been adjusted since. The night air held an unexpected coolness. Autumn would come soon.

Casewell heard the door ease open and turned to see his mother slipping through. She gave him a tired smile and sat down in a rocking chair near the window.

"Some of those folks may stay the night," she said. "I've never seen people linger over a funeral so long."

"A lot has happened this week." Casewell scrubbed a hand through his hair. "Probably they just want to be together right now."

"Can't say as I'm looking forward to being alone myself. It's well and truly alone I'll be now."

"I've been thinking, Ma. What if you came to stay with me?" Casewell wasn't entirely sure he wanted his mother to move in with him, but he'd been thinking it would be the right thing to do.

His mother reached out to take his hand where he stood looking out the window. "No, thank you, son. I'll confess it's tempting, but this is my home. This is where my memories are stacked up like kindling for the winter." Her eyes twinkled, surprising Casewell. "And anyway, I've never cottoned to living in a house with another woman."

"What are you talking about? It's just me."

"Today maybe, but I have high hopes for the future. You

need a good woman who will fill your house to overflowing with love. Seems to me there's more than one young lady in these parts who would be glad for a man like you."

Casewell took a breath to speak, but Mom squeezed his hand and gave it a little tug. "No, hush now. This isn't the time to discuss it one way or the other. It's time you settled down. I think I've maybe held you a little too close, discouraged your marrying. Just know it won't hurt my feelings if you find someone." She released his hand. "Now go on out there and see if you can't get at least half that crowd to go on home. I'm going to rest my eyes for a spell." She inhaled deeply and closed her eyes, letting her breath out slowly, as though reluctant to release it. She smiled and Casewell thought she might be asleep already.

He eased the door open and then shut it with a soft click. He wondered if his mother's tune would change if she knew who haunted his dreams.

The living room had already thinned out a good bit without his having to ask anyone to leave. If the exodus had begun, surely the momentum would continue, and they would have the house to themselves again soon.

Casewell shook a few hands, suffered shoulder pats and squeezes, and finally saw the last guest off the front porch. Just Robert, Delilah, and Perla remained in the kitchen. Sadie lay curled on the sofa, sound asleep with her doll strangled in the crook of her arm. Casewell tugged the afghan his mother had crocheted off the back of the sofa and draped it over the child. The tenderness he had experienced in church on Sunday rose in him to a degree that he could hardly absorb. He confessed to himself that he wanted this child for his own, and he wanted her mother with her. The need for these two females to belong to him was almost overwhelming. Casewell dropped to his knees next to the sofa and began a whispered prayer.

"Lord, you know the depths of my heart. You know the desires of my soul. You know what is good and right and proper. Father, I beg you to grant me this. And if you choose not to, please take this longing from me. I can't bear it much longer. Amen."

When he raised his head, Sadie blinked at him sleepily. "Are you talking to God?" she asked.

"I am."

"Tell Him 'hey' for me," she said and closed her eyes again.

Casewell squeezed his eyes shut. "Your daughter says 'hello,'" he whispered. "Please make her my daughter, too."

Casewell stood and moved into the kitchen where Robert slouched in a chair at the table while Perla and Delilah finished drying and putting away the dishes. Perla slid a cake of gingerbread out of the oven.

"We pooled ingredients to make cakes," she explained. "This is the last one. Would you like a piece?"

Casewell realized he was ravenous. He thought back to the day he met Perla, when his stomach growled in church. She'd been feeding him ever since. She'd been feeding them all.

"I'd be pleased if you'd help me some," he said. Robert shot him a look, and he thought he saw Delilah smirk.

"Robert, I think it's time you and I went and sat on the porch a spell," she said to her husband.

"But I was going to have some of that cake," Robert protested.

"You've had plenty. Get on out there and enjoy the cool of the evening with me."

Robert grumbled but pulled himself to his feet and ambled out onto the porch. As he passed Casewell, he slapped him on the shoulder and said, "Reckon she wants me to romance her a little. Women." He winked at his friend and grinned.

Perla cut out a hunk of the warm gingerbread and put it on a plate for Casewell. "Wish I had some lemon sauce to go with this, but lemons are scarce these days." She set the plate in front of Casewell, and before she could bring him a fork, he picked up the cake and sank his teeth into its warm spiciness. He sighed and smiled.

"You are the finest cook I've ever met."

Perla blushed and sat opposite him at the little kitchen table. Casewell realized that he was sitting in his father's chair and Perla was in his mother's.

"Seems like I've always been able to cook. I just wish my food didn't . . . didn't go on like it does. I don't understand it and some people . . ." Perla trailed off.

"I know. But a lot of folks would have gone hungry this summer if not for you." Casewell finished his cake in two huge bites. He swallowed and wiped his mouth with the back of his hand. "Seems to me you have a talent just like anybody else. I have a knack for making things out of wood. George can play the banjo like a miracle. Marvin somehow makes folks feel all right when somebody they love dies. Your knack is just a little less . . . common than most."

Perla smiled. "Thank you for that. Once upon a time I wouldn't have expected anything quite so philosophical from you."

"Guess I've had a lot to make me thoughtful this year. And that's not all I've been thinking about." The words popped out before Casewell could catch them. He felt cold sweat bead on his brow. Was he going to declare himself to Perla? Right here and now on the day they'd buried his father?

"Oh? What else have you been thinking about?"

Casewell's mouth was suddenly drier than the creek had been a week ago. He coughed and Perla fetched him a glass of water. She handed it to him, worry in her eyes. Casewell realized her eyes were the color of the tiny blue dayflowers that bloomed in the yard every summer. He wanted to gaze into them all day, but he gave himself a shake. This wasn't the time. He might admit to himself that he loved Perla Long, but he needed to do more than just tell her so. He needed to court her properly.

"I've been thinking it's time we took Sadie on a picnic," he said at last. We'll get Delilah and Robert and take Ma along. It'll cheer her up."

"That sounds lovely. Just let me know when you'd like to go."

That night Perla tucked Sadie into the bed they shared. As soon as she heard the child's steady breathing, she slipped from under the coverlet and padded out onto the porch. She could have sworn Casewell meant to say something important to her that afternoon. Something far more important than a picnic.

Perla stared at the night sky. A shooting star streaked low on the horizon, and she gasped at how bright and distinct it was. But even so, it lasted only a moment. And that was how love seemed. Only God's love shone on and on like the sun. Perla loved Casewell and she had forgiven him for judging her. This feeling she had that he might have changed his mind about her was frightening in a way she hadn't expected. Especially now that she was determined to go home.

Perla sat on the porch steps and drew her knees up under her nightgown. She could see dew sparkling on the grass that was sprouting here and there. She was surrounded by miracles. Surely that was enough? She'd had the love of a man once, and it had been ephemeral. This time she would be risking not only her own heart, but Sadie's, as well. No, although Casewell was a good man, she suspected she would do well to keep her distance. Let him find a fresh woman who had lived less. A woman who didn't carry such burdens. A woman like Melody Simmons. Perla decided that the more she loved Casewell, the more she should be willing to let him find a wife worthy of him. Even to push him in that direction if necessary.

She gave a little nod, as though offering final approval of her plan. She stood, stretched, and went back in to sleep. For just a moment she hesitated and thought perhaps she should pray over this. But no, she knew without having to ask God that Casewell's finding someone better to love was just good sense.

20

CASEWELL MET FRANK at the Talbot sisters' house to help put in a late garden. Even though it was September, they hoped to get a few crops. He'd already plowed his mother's plot and planted collards, spinach, broccoli, turnips, beets, and carrots. Thankfully, his mother never threw out a seed and always kept more from year to year than she needed. Even now, he had a pocketful of her leftovers to share with Liza and Angie.

"Oh, two strapping men to work the garden," trilled Liza as they came up the front walk. "Angie, aren't we the luckiest girls in the county?"

"Luck, I'll grant you," Angie said, "girls, is a stretch. Come on, fellers, we've got work to do."

Casewell grinned. While Angie may have softened a bit once the sisters sorted out their romantic entanglement with Frank, she hadn't changed all that much.

"Here you go." Angie shoved a box of yellowed envelopes at Casewell. He lifted them out one by one and noted that the newest seeds looked to be several years old. "We planted all the new seed we had last spring, so this'll have to do." Angie looked like she was daring Casewell to criticize her supplies.

"This'll do just fine." Frank took the box from Casewell, winked, and headed out to the garden. In short order they had plowed under what was left of the old garden and were putting out Emily's seeds along with Casewell's and some Frank had scrounged up. The men tipped the good seed into the envelopes in Angie's box so the sisters wouldn't know.

"I don't even half know what's in there." Liza squinted at the envelope in Casewell's hand.

"Turnips. And this one here is radish," Frank said.

"My, you are smart to know what a seed is by looking at it."

Casewell grinned at the flirtatious tone Liza used. Angie harrumphed and said they ought to get busy filling buckets from the well. "Now that the well has something to offer other than dry leaves and worm carcasses."

Once the women were busy cranking buckets of water up out of the well, Casewell turned to speak to Frank. The older man seemed to be having some sort of spasm. Casewell rushed to his side and took his arm. Frank slung him off and wrapped his arms around his belly.

"Are you ill? What can I do?"

Frank gasped and sputtered and then guffawed. "Lordy, those two women will be the death of me yet. I don't think they even know they do it. Liza flirts and Angie disapproves. I suspect they wouldn't know how to live otherwise." He wiped a tear from the corner of his eye. "Keeps me young." He laughed a little more, then slapped his knees and stood upright. "Come on, boy, let's tote water."

Once the garden was planted and watered, Casewell sat under an oak tree with Frank. For a long time they sat in silence, taking in the green valley and the old farmhouse, where the voices of the two women carried across the yard on the occasional breeze.

"It's a good life," Frank said.

"What is?"

"This." Frank waved an arm to include all they could see. "Good land, good people, running water. I've traveled the world over, and I'd trade most everything I've seen for this right here. 'Course, I had to get sober to appreciate it."

"You'd trade everything?"

"Well, there was that China girl . . ." Frank laughed. "Yes, son, everything. I suppose what I'm really talking about is the peace that comes when you've spent the day in good company doing good work. Satisfaction—real satisfaction—is hard to come by."

"But what about marriage, children, a family?"

"Looks like I missed out on all that." Frank ran a hand through his hair, making it stand on end. "Oh, looking back on it from this height, I can see that I would have done well to marry one of those gals in there. Probably would have had a mess of children to take care of me in my old age. But might-have-beens never appealed to me much. Sometimes I feel like there's nothing but this moment right here we're living in. No past, no future, just right now. And this right now suits me like lemonade on a hot day."

Casewell felt somehow dissatisfied with Frank's philosophy. "Even so . . ."

Frank turned to face Casewell head-on. There was a strange light to his eyes, and his wild hair reminded Casewell of how he used to look when he was drinking. It flashed through Casewell's mind that angels weren't lovely gossamer creatures, but fearsome messengers of God. He leaned back a little.

"Son, I think you have something—or maybe someone—specific on your mind. I've made it a habit to never regret anything. With the life I've lived, I won't live long enough to get over my mistakes. I can't change things now, and it surely doesn't make me feel any better to moon over what might have been. But I will tell you this." He took a deep breath, and fire lit the depths of his eyes. "If you find a woman you can love, a woman you can marry and rear children with and live out your days in abiding peace with, then for the love of God, do it."

The old man seemed to subside against the trunk of the tree. He smoothed his hair and brushed some dirt off the left knee of his dungarees. "'Course, that's just my opinion," he said with one of his winks.

As Wise settled into a normal autumn cycle of rain and sun, gardens slowly began to offer a late October harvest. Cattle fattened and began giving milk again. Hens laid eggs, and while the people weren't exactly feasting, the sense of impending doom began to fade.

In the absence of a preacher, church became a weekly sing, with Bible readings and prayer. Occasionally, either Casewell or Robert gave a short homily. No one seemed to be in any hurry to find a new preacher. And although there was more to eat now, people still came to the store for Perla's cooking a couple of times a week. But now folks rarely came empty-handed. They would bring a handful of turnip greens or some spinach. There were even a few root vegetables—small yet, but all the sweeter for it.

Perla welcomed the variety in her cooking. Robert promised a hog-killing after the first cold spell in November, and she caught herself planning ahead to make cracklings and roast pork and sausage, even though she assumed there wouldn't be a need for her cooking anymore by then. Although she still felt a long way from welcome, the community seemed to have decided to take her ability in stride. No one marveled over it or commented on it, and no one asked Perla for miracles or accused her of witchcraft. Casewell took it as proof that people will get used to anything.

And then, one day no one came for food. Casewell was helping, as he often did. He noticed that there seemed to be less food than usual.

"Perla, why are you cooking less today?"

"Am I? I thought I was doing everything just the same."

"Seems like a lot less to me." Casewell looked over the bowls of cabbage sautéed with onions, spinach salad with hard-boiled eggs, and buttered carrots with honey. "It looks good. There just seems to be less of it."

Perla came to stand beside Casewell and surveyed the food. "I think you're right. But it's always been enough, so I guess we should trust it still is."

They waited for someone to come and eat, but no one did. Finally, they got Casewell's mother and took all the food to the Thorntons' house, where they ate their fill. Perla laughed as she cleared the table.

"What did I tell you?" she said, tipping a bowl toward Casewell to show him the little bit left in the bottom. "Enough and then some."

Casewell smiled at the woman he loved and watched her put away the little bit. He spent time with Perla as he could, but he wanted to court her, and he wasn't sure how to go about it. Every time he tried to get close, he felt her shy away. It was as though she had decided against him but didn't have the heart to say so. As if she were being polite by having him around.

Well, he wasn't going to give up without a clearer sign than he'd gotten so far.

Perla put away the last dish and turned to walk out onto the porch.

"Perla." Casewell said her name, surprised by how tender it sounded in his mouth. "Would you walk out with me?"

"Oh, well, I'm pretty tired."

"Too tired to walk out in the cool of the evening and watch the stars come out one by one?" Again Casewell surprised himself. Where did that come from?

Perla grinned. "When you put it that way . . ."

Casewell hopped up from the table and moved to hold the screen door open for her. He wasn't going to give her a chance to change her mind. She plucked a sweater from a coat-tree near the door and draped it around her shoulders.

They set off down the lane, strolling along in no particular hurry. Casewell stuffed his hands into his pockets, and Perla clasped hers behind. Silence reigned. Casewell finally decided it was probably his job to say something.

"I can't get over how lush the fields have gotten," he said at last. "George is cutting hay over on his place, and he'll cut for Ma as soon as he's done. It'll still get lean this winter, but it's surely more than we had."

"Will your mother keep farming?" There was a note of surprise in Perla's voice.

"No. We'll sell off the cattle. Probably in the spring. Dad wanted to sell them last spring, but I dragged my feet, and it never got done. They're still too puny to sell right now. We'll see if we can get 'em through the winter and then go to market."

"So you don't want to take over the farm, then."

Casewell scratched his chin. He heard the scrape of whiskers and stopped. "I thought about it. But what I love is making things with my hands—furniture, music. Farming is good work, but I don't think it's for me. Dad and I talked about selling the cattle off once he was gone. He just wanted Ma to be taken care of. I don't think the herd meant much to him."

"And the land?" Perla seemed determined to follow this line of conversation.

"Oh, well, the land. That's our heritage, I guess. Been passed down through Phillips men for five generations. We'll keep the land. Who knows," Casewell grinned, "I might have a son who wants to farm it one of these days."

Perla had nothing to say to that.

This time Casewell had to think harder to break the silence. "What about you? Now that your stint as town cook seems to be winding down, what will you do with yourself?"

Perla looked up at a swallow flying home late. They could hear a whippoorwill call and another answer it somewhere beyond the tree line. "I'm going home," she said.

Casewell stumbled over nothing in particular and tried to recover without looking awkward. "Home?" he echoed.

"Yes." Perla slanted a look at Casewell and then turned her eyes back toward the dirt road they walked along. "I think it's time. I came to Wise because I wanted to get away from all the talk. Seems like the talk here has been a thousand times worse, and I've survived. Running away didn't do me any good. And it might even have done me harm. It's time I took Sadie back to her grandmother."

Casewell found himself speechless. She couldn't go now. Not when he was ready to win her. He swallowed hard and tried to think what to say. "Folks will miss you."

"Folks? Oh, I suppose Delilah and Robert have gotten used

to having us around. Still, they must be ready to have their home their own again."

"Not just them." The words burst from Casewell.

Perla laughed. "Who else? I haven't exactly been given a warm welcome around here. People ate my food, sure enough, and I suppose they've accepted me, but I'm not leaving any close friendships behind."

Casewell wanted to ask, *What about me?* more than anything, but he couldn't do it. He ran the words around in his head until they sounded so awkward and strange that he wasn't even sure they made sense anymore.

Perla stopped and watched the moon where it seemed to tangle in the branches of a locust tree. "I am tired, Casewell," she said. "Let's head back."

Casewell nodded and pushed his hands deep into his pockets again. He was a fool, and he didn't know what to do about it.

21

I hear Perla's going home." Casewell's mother pulled a pan of biscuits out of the oven and placed them on a trivet on the kitchen table. Casewell planned to spend the day checking over his parents' cattle. Normally, he and his father would be administering a dewormer around this time of year, but with the drought, any parasites should be long dead by now. While Casewell was glad he wouldn't have to round up helpers to administer medicine to uncooperative cattle, he found himself wishing his father were there to be glad with him.

"That's what she says." Casewell split a hot biscuit, slid a generous pat of butter inside, and put it on his plate next to several fried eggs.

"Seems a shame, though it might be for the best. She's been so important to us, what with feeding the whole community and all. Even so, it seems right for that child to be with family, especially since—well, it just seems right." Mom settled into a chair and spread her biscuit with last year's grape jelly.

"I'm not sure she feels she's been important." Casewell searched for the right words. "I think folks made her feel like an outcast when she got here, and once they found out about her cooking, no one knew how to talk to her."

"I should have done better by her, but with John . . ." Emily set her half-eaten biscuit down. "I'm going to call Delilah right this minute and invite her and Perla over for cake and coffee." She made her way to the phone mounted on the wall in the hallway. Casewell heard his mother's side of the conversation. The invitation seemed to be met with enthusiasm. Emily returned to the kitchen.

"There. It's probably too little too late, but at the very least, Perla will know she's meant something to this family." Tears welled in her eyes. "Not to mention Sadie. I never knew your father to be sentimental, but that child meant the world to him. I'm so glad they got to know each other."

She gave herself a shake and dabbed at her eyes with her napkin. "Enough of that. I'd better get to making a cake. No, I think I'll make tea cakes."

Casewell watched his mother as she began to gather ingredients and set the oven to heat. She had her moments of melancholy, but she also seemed to be getting on with life.

"Ma," Casewell spoke spontaneously, "do you mind living here with Dad gone?"

His mother stopped with eggs in her hands and turned to look at Casewell. "You know, I thought I would, but somehow I can't imagine living anywhere else. He's here." She waved the eggs around. "In the chair he always sat in, in the hint of cigarette smoke when I walk out on the porch, in his tools out in the building. I guess it's what I have left of him."

She put the eggs down and dusted her hands before setting them on her hips. "Now," she said with a smile, "get on out there and check on those cows while I get ready for my hen party."

Casewell spent a couple of hours counting the cattle and checking each one for any problems. He cleaned out the water trough and replaced the salt block. The herd seemed generally healthy, though still on the thin side from lack of good feed over the summer. The survival of the herd, small as it was, made for another miracle. Though they'd survived the drought, Casewell expected to lose a few after the rains started. Cattle were prone to fog fever when going from poor forage to rich pasturage. As quickly as the fields recovered, Casewell had felt certain some of the cattle would get sick, but not a single one had.

Because of the drought, his father had decided to put off breeding the cows over the summer. He liked to breed in late June or July for spring calves. But a cow stressed by drought was likely to abort or fail to conceive altogether. Casewell wondered if he should bring a bull in now. He decided against it. The cows still might not take, and he'd be selling them before they calved anyway. He slapped a particularly docile heifer on the rump. She rolled an eye at him and went back to cropping the new grass. Casewell realized he would miss having cattle. Maybe he'd get a Guernsey milk cow and keep it at the house. If he ever did marry and have children, it would be good to have fresh milk.

Still pondering the ins and outs of animal husbandry, Casewell headed back to the house, forgetting his mother would likely have company by now.

As he stepped into the side yard, Sadie called out to him from the back porch. "Mr. Casewell, we're having tea and cookies. *Real* tea and cookies." Her eyes shone and he felt a stab of joy to see her.

"I heard. Is your mama inside?" Casewell felt oddly shy and wasn't sure he should go in with the ladies.

"Yup. She cries at night. She tries to be very, very quiet, but I hear her. I think it's because we have to go home now. I don't want to go, but Mama says we have to." Sadie heaved an overly dramatic sigh and hugged her doll tighter in the crook of her arm. "She says God will take care of us wherever we go. I don't see why He can't take care of us here."

Casewell felt something like anger roll over in his belly. Why did Perla insist on being obstinate? There was no reason for her to leave, and here she was dragging this poor child off. He had an urge to go inside and give that woman a talking to. Casewell felt the anger drain away as quickly as it had come. What would he say? That he loved her and wanted to marry her? Would that be a good enough reason for her to stay? It would if she loved him in return. But he had no reason to think she did.

His mother's voice floated out through the screen door. "Casewell? Is that you? Bring Sadie in here for some cookies."

Casewell summoned a smile and took Sadie's hand. Her fingers were so tiny. She gripped Casewell's ring and middle fingers, which fit her palm like they'd been shaped for just such a reason. He remembered she'd done the same thing at his father's funeral. Tears pricked the backs of his eyes and he blinked rapidly. He didn't know which female had him more tied up in knots—the mother or the child.

Inside, his mother sat at the kitchen table with Perla and Delilah. The table was covered by a linen cloth with scalloped edges. Casewell knew his grandmother had made it, and his mother saved it for only the most special occasions. She was also using his grandmother's china—some fussy pattern with pink and blue flowers. He guessed it was pretty, but he'd rather drink coffee from a stout mug any day.

"Won't you join us?" Delilah asked. "I expect we can talk cattle almost as well as any man."

Casewell grinned and sat in the empty chair that had always

been his father's. Sadie climbed on his knee and reached for a teacup.

"No, that's easy to break." Casewell reached out a hand to stop the child. Her lower lip protruded.

Emily intervened. "Of course she can have her own cup. Sadie is a careful child, and even if she breaks every single cup and plate, she's worth more than any set of china."

Casewell studied his mother. She never would have allowed him to handle her china when he was small. He hardly dared attempt it now. This woman at the table, pressing a fragile cup into a chubby little hand, seemed different.

And witnessing that one small act, Casewell felt the magnetic north of his whole life shift. What, after all, was important? Being a fine musician? A skilled carpenter? A good son? Casewell turned his head and saw that Perla was watching him. He met her eyes and smiled from the bottom of his soul. He felt an almost overwhelming urge to clasp Sadie to his chest, to hold her tight and refuse to let her go. And he saw that Perla understood. He saw that Perla had been holding this precious child close since the day she first knew she would be a mother. Perla knew what mattered, and Casewell hoped she could see in his eyes that he did, too.

"Tea cake?" His mother's voice broke over Casewell like cool water after a hot day working in the hayfields.

"Yes," he said, taking one for himself and putting a second in front of Sadie. "I'd enjoy a tea cake."

Perla tucked Sadie in that night, then slipped outside to enjoy the October bite in the air. What had she seen in Casewell's eyes? It had been . . . breathtaking. She thought she might have gasped when he looked at her and smiled. The light, the depth. It had been like looking into a murky pool of water that suddenly cleared so that she could see the shape and size of every stone on the bottom. She'd noticed his honey eyes the first time she saw him, but this time the color was, well, liquid and sweet. She wanted to gather more of that honey.

Perla squeezed her arms harder. What was happening to her? She felt . . . beloved. But how could that be? She had been beloved only once before, and it had been a mistake. A sweet, tender mistake that had brought her the greatest sorrow and the greatest joy of her life. She shivered.

She could not hope. She dared not hope. Her plans to return home were final. Her mother was expecting her, though she hadn't sounded happy about it. Perla supposed she would need to find another place to disappear. This time she'd look for somewhere no one knew her. Maybe this time she could escape the gossip. *And live a lie.*

Why would it be so hard to lie? Why did that thought make her feel shriveled and small inside? Surely it would be a relief to live in a place where people respected her, maybe even pitied her a little, if they believed she was a young widow trying to get by. And she would cook only for Sadie and herself. No one ever again need know what she could do with a handful of beans.

Perla realized that tears coursed down her cheeks. She tasted the salt and wondered that she could have so thoroughly wet her cheeks without realizing it. She inhaled deeply, letting the air out quietly so as not to disturb the night. She loved Casewell Phillips with all her heart. For just a moment, she allowed herself the luxury of believing that he loved her and somehow it would all work out. Then she went inside to lie down beside her slumbering child and cried herself to sleep.

22

CASEWELL KNEW WHAT TO DO. It was up to him to court and win Perla Long. He had been tentative to this point, waiting for a sign that she would welcome his advances. No longer. God had filled his heart with love for a woman with a child, and he would move forward in the knowledge that God had already blessed them.

He walked into the living room and picked up his Bible from the coffee table. He flipped to the first chapter of Matthew and read the account of the angel visiting Joseph. Casewell felt for the first time that he could begin to understand how Joseph felt. The woman he loved was pregnant and would give birth to a child not his own. Casewell smiled. Perla was no Mary, but he supposed that she, like everyone else, was ultimately from God. And whether God had blessed Perla with a child or simply took her sin and used it for good, Sadie was clearly a gift. A gift he would be only too glad to claim as his own, just as Joseph had claimed Jesus. The only question now was how to go about it.

Casewell drove down to the Thorntons' store. He knew Perla

had been spending less time there now that her cooking was no longer in demand, and he hoped to find Delilah alone. Robert was behind the counter, and Delilah was reading at the end of the row that now served as a lending library. Casewell nodded to Robert and began thumbing through the books as though looking for something of interest.

"Can I help you, Casewell?" Delilah asked.

"Oh, just browsing. Though if you had a book about how to court a woman, I guess I'd take it." He snuck a look at Delilah out of the corner of his eye. She closed her book and moved toward him.

"Really? Well, I'm pretty sure Frank never did collect anything like that, but there's better ways to find out than books."

Casewell turned toward her with raised eyebrows, hoping he wouldn't need to say anything else.

"As a matter of fact, depending on the woman, I might be able to help."

"Now, that would be fine. Books probably wouldn't apply to our country ways, anyhow. What would you suggest for courting a woman who is, well, reluctant to be courted?"

"Do you know why she's reluctant?" Delilah stuck the book in her hand onto the shelf at random and turned her full attention on Casewell.

"I think it might have to do with the fact that she's . . ." Casewell looked up and scratched his chin. "Well, this might not be her first go-round."

"A widow?"

Casewell suspected Delilah was playing with him, but he could play, too. "Not exactly, but let's make that assumption for the sake of discussion."

Delilah beamed and then recovered herself and looked serious again. "Well, then, she's no blushing maiden to be tiptoed around. I reckon you can go straight to the heart of the matter." Delilah held up a finger. "Though every woman, no matter how experienced, likes a little romance. I'd venture you could tell her straight out how you're feeling, but just the same she might appreciate some flowers or candy along with sweet words. Even us old married ladies like sweet talk." Delilah showed dimples that Casewell had never seen before. "And if, say, there were a child in the mix, a gift for the little one would go a long way toward winning the mama, I suspect."

"So bring her some flowers and candy, a gift for her child—if she has one—and just tell her straight out?"

"I think that will get you pretty far along, Casewell. Women are less complicated than you think." Delilah dimpled at him again and pulled a book off the shelf—not the one she'd been reading before—and headed back to her chair, where she buried her nose between the pages.

Casewell strongly suspected that Delilah wasn't very interested in *South Sea Tales* by Jack London, but he'd been wrong before. He laughed. He'd been very wrong before. But Delilah had given him an idea, and he was looking forward to carrying it out.

❧

His next stop was the Talbot sisters'. Angie was famous for her divinity. Around the holidays the crunchy, meringue-like candies were a staple in the community. Maybe he could sweet-talk her into making him a batch.

When he pulled his old truck into their yard, Liza was sitting in a swing hanging from the huge old oak tree in the side yard. Frank was leaning against the trunk. He waved at Casewell.

"I've been trying to get Liza here to let me give her a push, but she seems to think I might get carried away."

Liza laughed. "Isn't it marvelous? We haven't had a swing in this tree since I was a girl. It was Frank's idea to hang one. I don't think Angie likes it too much, but she didn't put up a fuss. I swan, I feel like I'm twelve years old." She pushed herself back and kicked her heels up into the air. Her skirts fluttered, and she squealed as the swing began its gentle back and forth arc. Frank grinned, as did Casewell. They could see the child Liza had been and, somewhere deep down, still was.

"I bet if we could get Angie in this swing, she'd let me push," Frank said.

"*Pshaw.* You won't get her in the swing. She's too proper a lady," Liza scoffed.

"Who says?" Angie stood, arms akimbo, on the edge of the porch. "Just because I don't have a penchant for foolishness doesn't mean I'm not willing to kick my heels up now and again."

"Come on, then." Liza stood and made a sweeping gesture toward the empty swing. "Show us."

Casewell realized he was not only seeing the fun-loving child Liza had once been, but he was also seeing the way the sisters had likely baited each other as children. He wished his mother could be here for this.

Liza marched over and gingerly settled herself in the swing, grasping the ropes firmly and pushing off with one foot. She swung like the pendulum on a grandfather clock, slow and steady. Chin high, she shot a defiant look at her sister.

"But will you let Frank push you?" There was a teasing note in Liza's voice.

"Certainly." Angie bit the word off and raised her chin a notch higher. "Frank, if you would be so kind."

Frank grinned and waggled his eyebrows at Casewell. He stepped behind Angie and held his hands near her bottom. Then he hesitated and moved them up a bit. Grasping her waist like he might handle a newborn pup, he eased her forward. Once she was moving a bit, he gave her several gentle pushes.

"Oh, for heaven's sake, I won't break." Angie began pumping her legs back and forth. She was surprisingly limber for a woman her age. Soon she had the swing going, if not high, then higher than Casewell would have expected. She closed her eyes as her hair worked its way loose from its bun and fluttered over her cheeks. Then Casewell saw her smile. Not a half smile or a pleased look, but an expression that curled her lips, plumped her cheeks, and crinkled her eyes. It was a look of utter delight, and Casewell felt oddly humbled seeing it. Angie laughed long and loud, then let the swing coast to a stop.

"Oh my. That was wonderful. Frank, you are an old fool, but even old fools have good ideas now and again. Thank you for our swing." She stood and brushed her hands against her skirt, then smoothed wisps of gray hair back into place. "Well, now, Casewell. You will have something to talk about come Sunday."

But Casewell didn't think he would talk about it. Seeing the twins here in the yard with the man they both had loved, getting on with life and enjoying it—well, it was too tender a thing to share. He might tell Perla one day. She would see the beauty. She wouldn't think it was a great joke, two old women finding joy in being childish. He reckoned they all could do with being a little more childlike.

Angie started toward the porch, but turned back. "Casewell, I'm thinking you didn't come here to watch us act the fool. Did you need something?"

"Yes, ma'am. I need a batch of divinity."

"Oh, well, I've got everything but the pecans. Problem is, divinity never does right when it's humid, and with all the rain lately I doubt I can get it to turn out. Now, if you'd come to me during the drought, I could have made the perfect batch."

Casewell must have looked crestfallen. "But if you can get me enough cream and butter, we can make caramels—they're supposed to be a mite sticky."

"Ma makes those sometimes." He perked up. "As a matter of fact, if you're willing to part with your recipe, I can probably get Ma to help me out."

"Come on in and I'll write it out for you." Angie beckoned him inside. "We'll leave the young'uns to their play."

Liza giggled from where she had resumed her seat on the swing. "Push me, Frank," she said.

Recipe in hand, Casewell headed back to the Thorntons' store. The ingredient list and directions were less complicated than anticipated. He could do this by himself. He had cream, butter, and sugar already, so all he needed was some corn syrup and vanilla.

Robert raised an eyebrow when Casewell told him what he needed.

"Shopping for your ma?"

"Oh, just stocking up now that your shelves are full again." Casewell didn't want to lie, but he also didn't want to explain.

Delilah swooped in with a small bottle of vanilla in hand. "Leave him alone. If all the men around here would get a little more familiar with supplies beyond coffee and cornmeal, the world would be a better place." She plunked the bottle down next to the corn syrup Casewell had found on his own.

"Whatever you say." Robert looked confused, but he rang up the items and Casewell headed home, whistling. Step one was accomplished—well, nearly.

The next morning, Casewell walked out to the pasture while the dew was still on. He carried a pocketknife and a Mason jar with some water in it. He began cutting the flowers that had sprung up as fast as the grass. There were daisies and black-eyed Susans, Queen Anne's lace, and butterfly weed. He debated cutting some Joe-Pye weed, but decided it was too big a flower. He settled on some little blue asters and decided it was aplenty. The Mason jar was stuffed with flowers, and he wondered how he might go about arranging them better. He decided to look for something prettier than an old jar to put them in when he got back to the house.

Plopping the flowers on the drain board, Casewell set out his ingredients for caramels. He dumped everything but the vanilla into an extra large saucepan and lit the gas flame under it. This was going to be easier than he thought.

Fifteen minutes later, Casewell knew he was in trouble. The mixture in the pan seemed to be taking forever to come to a rolling boil—whatever that was—so he jacked the heat up. He'd just turned away from the stove for a minute to look for a better container for the flowers when the caramel boiled over, spattering the stove with a residue that seemed to turn to stone. He'd gotten the flame under control and saved most of the contents of the pan, but a great deal of what was in there seemed to be adhering to the sides. Angie had explained that he could test to see if the candy had reached the hard ball-stage by dropping a little bit of it into a glass of cold water.

He'd done that, but all he got was a gummy wad of gunk that wasn't a hard ball of anything. He decided enough was enough and dumped what he could into a buttered pan.

Then he nearly cursed. He'd forgotten to add the vanilla. Grabbing the little bottle, he sloshed some into the pan of candy. The liquid pooled across the top and then seemed to mostly evaporate. Maybe that's how it worked. Casewell jammed the hot, sticky saucepan under the faucet and filled it with cool water. He reached in to loosen the residue with his fingers and found that it had hardened to a satiny sheen. He considered whether he really cared about keeping that pan. Probably he could get by without it.

Caramels finished, Casewell turned his attention to the flowers. He found an old blue-speckled coffeepot that he thought would look better than the Mason jar. He filled it with water and began trying to arrange the flowers. Somehow it didn't look quite like he'd pictured, but he guessed it would do.

He poked a finger at the candy and found it to be the consistency of soft taffy. Maybe Angie had been right about making candy when it was humid. He stuck the pan in the Frigidaire and hoped for the best. After cleaning up the kitchen and throwing out the saucepan, Casewell considered the third element he needed to win Perla. Words.

He began to suspect the candy and flowers had been the easy part. Surely if he could preach a sermon, he could tell a woman how he felt. Thinking about his sermon gave him an idea. Maybe the Bible would have some words he could use. He flipped to the Song of Solomon. He'd never found cause to spend much time in this particular book, but it was the love story of King Solomon and his bride, so surely there was something good in here. He browsed until he came to the seventh chapter. And there he read King Solomon's description of his beloved and, blushing, decided that this was no help at all.

He scrounged up a piece of paper and a pencil, which needed sharpening. He pulled out his pocketknife and gave the lead a good point. Then he sat at the kitchen table, flowers at his elbow, and gave his full attention to writing down what he should say.

Maybe if he started it like a letter. *Dear Perla*. There, a beginning. *I wanted to tell you that I* . . . That he what? Loved her? That seemed kind of blunt. Wasn't he supposed to warm up to something like that? Aha . . . *admire and respect you*. Good. But that was all he could come up with. He could tell her he liked her cooking, but he liked his mother's cooking. He could say she was a good mother, but that seemed too far afield from what he really wanted to say. And what was that? Casewell flung the pencil down and cradled his head in his hands. He just wanted her to know that he didn't want to live another day without her.

He heard a sound and jerked his head up.

"Casewell?" A woman's voice wafted through the screen door.

"Come on in." He folded the paper and crammed it into his breast pocket.

Perla stepped into the kitchen, wearing a soft-yellow dress that made her hair look as golden as a late autumn field. But her blue eyes seemed almost gray today, like creek water reflecting storm clouds overhead. Casewell marveled that he could think thoughts like that but couldn't write a simple love letter.

"I found this pan outside." Perla held the ruined saucepan. "Shall I clean it for you?"

Casewell jumped to his feet and reached for the pan. "No, no. I was, uh, putting it out for the critters to eat."

Perla looked skeptical but relinquished her hold. "Oh, how lovely." She spied the flowers on the table, and her eyes brightened just a bit.

Casewell felt off balance. This wasn't how it was supposed to go. He threw up a quick prayer to heaven, something he should have done before he embarked on all this nonsense, and turned to pull the bouquet closer.

"They're for you," he blurted.

Perla seemed to lose what little color there was in her cheeks, and then they flushed pink. "Why, thank you," she said, reaching out to cup a blossom. "I have to say I'm surprised, but it's very thoughtful of you."

"You should have flowers every day of your life." Now Casewell flushed. Where had that come from?

Perla seemed to be amused. She gave a little smile and raised one eyebrow. Were her eyes getting bluer? "Really. Every single day? Even in winter?"

Casewell grinned. He liked her spunk. "In winter you should have a different snowflake for every hour of the day."

A soft smile spread across Perla's face. "Why, Casewell, that's practically poetry."

He decided there was no time like the present. He opened the refrigerator door and pulled out the pan of caramels. "I made you candy, too." He plunked the pan down on the table and rifled through a drawer for a butter knife. "Here, I'll cut you a piece."

"Caramels? I love caramels."

Casewell thought Perla looked younger and prettier by the minute. He thrust the knife into the candy and found it to be the consistency of cold molasses. He must have looked like he needed rescuing, because Perla took the knife from his hand, scooped up a bit of candy on the tip, and popped it into her mouth.

"Delicious," she said. "Try some."

She handed him the knife, and in that small act of sharing, Casewell realized that he couldn't keep from speaking his heart another moment.

"Perla, I don't want you to leave."

"I'm not exactly anxious to go, but I really do think it's for the best. Actually, that's why I'm here. I came to tell you good-bye. I've been putting off going long enough, and I just wanted to . . . to thank you, I suppose."

"What in the world for?"

"For being such a help serving food. For being my . . ." She hesitated. "My friend when so many people treated me like I was some kind of bad luck. And for being so good to Sadie. I know she needs a father, and you and John and Robert have been such wonderful examples of godly men for her. I appreciate that."

She looked Casewell fully in the eye for the first time since she came in the door. He thought he saw something there—a question?

"I want to go on being an example." He spoke in a hurry, as though the words he'd been searching for had arrived all at once. "I want to be more than an example for that child. I want to protect her and love her and be there for her when she falls out of trees. I want to hear her laugh and hold her when she cries. I want to be a father to her."

Perla's eyes were decidedly blue now—like icicles against a winter sky. Casewell began to wonder if he'd said something wrong after all.

"Well, you can't just decide to be her father." Perla's voice was clipped. "There's more to it than that."

"I know." Casewell reached for Perla's hand, which she let him take, although she didn't soften her posture. "I think I started in the wrong place. There's so much I want to say to you. I'm not good at knowing where to begin." He tugged her to a chair at the table and scooted a second chair around so it faced her. He sat and took both of her stiff, cold hands in his own. They were small and soft, though not without calluses. He noticed a burned spot on her right wrist—probably from reaching into a hot oven.

"Perla. I love Sadie, but more importantly, I love you." He had to stop a moment and catch his breath. There, he'd said it. Perla relaxed the tiniest bit, her back curving a little into the kitchen chair. "I thought about loving you the first time I saw you, and then I found out you had a child, and no . . . well, you know what I found out. I judged you and before I do anything else, I need to ask you to forgive me for that. I was wrong about so many things." He waited and looked into her eyes.

"I forgive you," she whispered.

"Thank you. Now, once I decided you weren't . . . appropriate for me, I chose not to love you. But God has been working on my hard heart and so have you. Watching you feed all those people. Watching you love people who scorned you. Watching you love a child that some women might have wanted to abandon. I can't help loving you."

"No." The word came out of Perla sounding harsh. "No," she said again more softly. "I'm not worth loving. I think God's cursed me with the ability to feed people as a way of doing penance for my sin. And I will do that penance. Loving you would be more good than I deserve." She turned her head away.

Casewell wanted to pull her into his arms, but he just got a firmer grip on the fingers she was trying to slip out of his hands.

"If we only got what we deserved, this world would be a sorry place. I used to think I was a good man. I thought my father was a good man. But we sinned against each other by withholding our love and our forgiveness. It took his dying for me to understand that God loves us so much He'll give us eternity with Him, even though we fail Him every day. Dad and I figured it out just in time. Please don't spend the rest of your life waiting to find out that you're loved whether you deserve it or not."

Tears streamed down Perla's cheeks. "I'm afraid," she sobbed.

"Of what?"

"Of losing you. Of giving myself to you and then losing you."

Casewell stood and drew her to his breast. "I vow that I will love you as long as I live and that we will spend eternity together in heaven. I know it's not perfect, but it's the best I can do."

Perla cried harder. Casewell could feel her tears soaking through his shirt and wetting his skin. He relished the intimacy of that.

Perla hiccupped and tried to take a few deep breaths. "Casewell Phillips?" she said at last.

"Yes, ma'am?"

"Are you asking me to marry you?"

Casewell laughed. "Leave it to me to forget the most important part. Yes. Perla Long, will you be my wife and bless me with your daughter and your cooking for as long as we both shall live?"

"I will." Perla sighed, leaning her cheek against the dry side of Casewell's shirt.

23

CASEWELL WOKE THE NEXT MORNING, his heart full of praise. It was raining again and the soft patter of drops on the roof made him want to tarry in bed. He had a brief thought of how he would be sharing his bed soon and found himself very much awake. It was just as well. He had work to do.

While his plan to court Perla hadn't gone exactly as planned, he did still think Delilah had given him good advice. And there was one element of the plan he had neglected—a gift for Sadie. He brewed some coffee, ate a couple of slices of bread and butter, and dashed through the rain to his workshop. He would make the finest dollhouse any child had ever owned.

Casewell had been working several hours when he heard a knock on the open doorframe. He looked up, feeling a little dazed by the unexpected shift in focus.

"Well, howdy, Robert. I didn't hear you drive up."

"She's gone, Casewell." Robert looked grim.

"Who's gone?"

"Perla packed up and left early this morning. She made me promise I wouldn't tell you, but Delilah near about pulled a gun on me to make me come over here and let you know. She seems to think you'll mind."

"I don't understand." Casewell held a piece of wood unheeded in his right hand.

"What I'm saying is, Perla lit out of town with little Sadie in tow. I reckon she's gone home to her family, but she didn't say for sure. Lordy, but the place is quiet without them." Robert shook his head and kicked at the doorframe.

"But she's going to marry me."

Now it was Robert's turn to furrow his brow. "Marry you? Casewell, did you ask Perla to marry you?"

"I did, and she said yes. Just yesterday. She came to say good-bye, but I asked her to marry me, and she said yes. You must be wrong about her leaving. She's just gone for a walk or something."

"With her luggage in tow? I doubt it. Son, sounds to me like you scared her clean out of the county."

"I have to find her." Casewell dropped the wood he was holding and ran for the house, nearly knocking Robert over as he went. "When did she leave?" He hollered the question over his shoulder.

Robert jogged across the wet yard behind Casewell. "Round about eight this morning. Got an early start. Frank come by the house to give her a ride. Guess you could start by tracking him down."

Casewell stopped so suddenly Robert nearly crashed into him. "Frank? Why in the world would he drive her?"

"Guess she asked," Robert said with a shrug.

"You know if he's back?"

"Nope. But I ain't been looking for him."

Casewell grasped his friend by the shoulders and looked

him in the eye. "Thanks for coming out to tell me. Delilah was right to send you. I don't think I can live without that woman." Then he rushed into the house, grabbed his truck keys, and was spinning out of the yard before Robert could speak.

Casewell sped down dirt roads to Frank's house. He leapt from the truck and onto the front porch without losing much speed. He pounded on the door.

"Hang on, hang on. Whose barn is on fire?" Frank came to the door with a book in his hand. "Casewell. Come on in. I'm in the mood for some company."

But Casewell remained on the porch. "Where did you take her?"

"Take who?"

"Perla. How could you—" Casewell couldn't finish the sentence.

"I took her to the bus stop, son. I thought you might not be glad she was going, but I've learned that when a woman says she's going to do something, it's best to let her."

"But she said she'd marry me." Casewell knew he sounded like a tired child, but he couldn't seem to think through this situation.

"Well, then. No wonder she hightailed it out of the county on a Greyhound bus. Marriage."

"What do you mean?" Casewell was almost begging, but he didn't care.

"Casewell, that woman thinks she's ruined herself in the eyes of God and man. I expect the worst thing you could have done to her was propose. The surest sign of her love for you is this running-away business. If she didn't care about you, she'd marry you and give that child of hers a father. But I'm guessing she cares too much to saddle you with her fatherless child." Frank slapped Casewell on the back. "Son, I'd guess she loves you even more than you love her."

"I don't understand." Casewell sounded like a little boy who wasn't going to the circus after all.

"No, it'll take you more years than you've got to understand. Just go after her. She'll like that."

"Where?"

"I dropped her off at the station in Parson Springs. She didn't say where she was going, and I didn't ask, but you might could find out."

Frank was still speaking as Casewell slammed the door of his truck and spun out of the yard.

It took forty-five minutes to drive to Parson Springs. Casewell roared into the parking lot at the Greyhound bus station and strode toward the ticket office. A small man with a large mustache drowsed behind the counter. Casewell came to a stop in front of him and realized he wasn't entirely sure how to proceed.

"Can I help you?" The little man blinked at him. He spoke with a slight accent, and Casewell wondered for just a moment where he was from.

"I'm looking for someone."

"Ah-ha." Casewell thought the ticket man pulled back a notch. "I'm not sure I can help you."

"She's my fiancée." Casewell felt pride and desperation battle in his breast at the word. "I'm afraid she thinks I don't love her and she's running away." Was that a flicker of interest? "I do love her." Casewell leaned across the counter. "I need to find her and let her know how much."

"And what if she still wants to be away from you?" The man gave Casewell a sidelong look.

"Then I'd have to let her go. But I can't lose her to a misunderstanding."

The ticket man looked thoughtful. "Only one woman has come through here without a man this morning, but she had a child with her."

"That's her." Casewell felt excitement rise. "With her daughter—the most wonderful little girl. Please help me find them."

"*Humph.* Well, the miss bought a ticket for Ohio. Seemed very sad about it, too. And the child didn't act like she wanted to go—not that she was complaining. Maybe they need chasing down."

"Where in Ohio?"

"Pittsboro. Bus left here at ten this morning." He rifled through some papers. "Let's see. It is almost two now. She should be changing buses in Parkersburg. She'll be in Camden in another hour. There's quite a layover there—looks like three hours. You will perhaps catch her . . ."

Casewell had an ancient map of West Virginia in his glove box. He'd rarely traveled so far north in the state, and he couldn't risk getting lost. It looked like Camden was about sixty miles beyond the West Virginia state line—thankfully it was big enough and close enough to show up on a map of West Virginia. It would likely take him five hours to get there, and he reckoned he had four. He began pushing the old truck as hard as it would go.

Casewell was grateful for the new West Virginia Turnpike. Without it, his drive would take another two hours. Even so, the new highway only went so far, and he would eventually have to leave it and pursue winding mountain roads. He pressed down on the gas pedal.

After driving without stopping for nearly three hours, Casewell crossed into Ohio. He knew he could never cover the remaining sixty miles in the time he had left. He took off his watch and threw it on the floorboard. He prayed that he would somehow make it in time.

"Casewell."

Casewell's eyes widened and he looked around the cab of the truck. He was alone.

"She's the one, boy. Go get her."

Casewell swallowed hard. It was his father's smoke-roughened voice. He knew he was imagining it, but he could hear it plain as day.

"If you were ever going to do a thing right, now's the time. Drive faster."

Casewell laughed and pushed the truck a little harder. Leave it to his dad to talk tough from the grave. He imagined his father sitting in the truck beside him, enjoying this adventure. Casewell drove faster and began speaking aloud.

"She is the one, Dad. And she's afraid. I guess I'm a little scared, too, but I'm more scared of losing her than I am of what people will think about us getting married." He smiled. He never would have admitted to being afraid while his dad was alive. So Casewell kept talking to his father now. He talked about his dreams and how Perla and Sadie fit into them. He talked about his mother and how strong she was, even though she seemed meek and mild. He talked and he drove and by the time he saw the bus station, he was hoarse and desperate for a drink of water.

As Casewell pulled into the parking area, he saw a silver-and-blue bus with the iconic racing dog on the side pulling out of the station. It stopped to allow several cars to go by, and Casewell leapt from his truck, leaving it running, to hurry across the pavement and pound on the door. A surprised driver slid the door open.

"You about missed us," he said. Casewell jumped up the steps in one bound and scanned the seats.

"Take a seat. I'm already running late." The driver sounded a little testy.

"I'm looking for someone—"

"I don't have time for your looking. Sit down or get off."

Casewell didn't see Perla or Sadie. "Sorry," he said to the driver, backing down the steps, eyes roving among the seats. "Maybe I've got the wrong bus."

The driver grumbled something unintelligible and closed the doors in Casewell's face with a whoosh of air.

He told himself it was the wrong bus. He told himself Perla was almost certainly inside the station. He shut off his truck, then walked toward the front door, trying to move fast while still taking in every inch of his surroundings. Another bus sat off to the side, but it was clearly empty. He headed on into the station. If she was still here, he would not miss her.

The euphoria of Casewell's proposal had worn off all too soon. Who was she trying to fool? He was a good man and she didn't deserve him. He would marry her because he was the kind of man who would never go back on his word. But he would live to regret it. She wanted his love, craved it. But now that he had offered it to her, she realized how impossible it would be to accept it. She was a fool, but that was nothing new.

She closed her eyes and remembered how it had felt to cry in Casewell's arms. His hands were so strong against her back, and even as the tears flowed, she had felt a shiver of pleasure at his touch. Opening her eyes, Perla admonished herself. She had allowed her feelings to overcome her good sense before. She wasn't going to let that happen again.

After leaving Casewell, Perla went back to the house and for an hour or two floated on air. But then the reality of the situation gradually became clear. She couldn't marry Casewell. He was a pillar of the community, and she was a fallen woman. People who had been less than welcoming before would be downright angry if she married one of their own. She could hear their voices accusing her of using feminine wiles to trick Casewell into marrying her just to give her child a father.

She needed to make plans, but she couldn't discuss them with anyone. Delilah tried to draw her out, but Perla insisted she was fine, just thinking about the return trip to her family. Although she had originally planned to leave the following Monday, Perla realized she needed to go immediately. It would be too hard to see Casewell again, knowing that she could not marry him. Pretending with him would be harder than leaving him.

That night she waited for Sadie to fall asleep and then waited another hour for good measure. She eased out of bed and quietly packed their things. They didn't have much—clothes, her Bible and a devotional book, Sadie's few toys. When she reached for the doll furniture Casewell had made, tears burned the backs of Perla's eyes. She knelt on the floor and cradled the little chair in her lap. His hands had touched the wood, had shaped it and smoothed it and stained it. The time and love he had put into a simple toy gave Perla pause. Maybe . . . but no. She could not condemn him to life with an adulteress. She would leave him because she loved him too much to stay.

The next morning Perla got up early. She went to the store with Robert and waited, knowing Frank stopped in almost every morning to drink coffee and talk to anyone around. If no one was around he joked that he could always visit with his books. He came in five minutes after Robert unlocked the front door.

"Am I too early for coffee?" Frank asked. "Something made me want to get down here early this morning."

Perla tried to smile. Surely that was a sign she was doing the right thing.

"Let me get you a cup," she said. "Robert's in the storeroom, but he'll be along in a minute."

"Well, I'd rather have coffee from the hand of a pretty woman any day. Join me?"

"Sure." Perla's hand shook as she poured the coffee into two thick mugs. She usually added enough sugar to fight the bitter, but this morning she sipped her coffee black. Penance, maybe.

"Frank, I need a favor." She'd tried to think of a way to introduce the topic naturally but figured direct was best.

"I'll be glad to help any way I can."

"Will you drive Sadie and me to the bus station over in Parson Springs?"

"Surely. When are you needing to go?"

"As soon as possible. Now, if you're able."

"Now? I'd heard you were talking about going home, but I didn't realize you were in a hurry."

"Something's come up and I need to go. Dragging things out . . . well, it's not good for anyone."

"I hate to be the one to help you leave, but I've got no other plans." He thumped his nearly empty coffee mug down and slapped his knees. "I'm ready when you are."

"Thank you. I'll let Robert know we're leaving, and we can go pick up Sadie and our luggage."

Perla disappeared into the storeroom and came back out almost immediately. "All right, let's go."

Perla was pleased to find a bus leaving for Ohio that morning. Her family was in central West Virginia. She would not return to them. She would travel north until she found work. She could clean houses, keep children—she'd even cook if she had to. She had a little money that her parents had given her when she came to Wise. At the time, it had felt like hush money. While it wouldn't take her far, she hoped it would take her far enough.

Sadie was enthralled with the ticket man's mustache. He seemed equally taken with Sadie and gave her a peppermint drop.

"Where are you headed, missy?" the man asked.

Sadie piped up. "North, but we're not excited about it."

"Ah, well." The man seemed reluctant to pry, which made Perla grateful. "Not all travel can be for pleasure." He looked at Perla and nodded. "Hope everything turns out well for you, ma'am."

In that moment, Perla had the oddest feeling that everything would turn out well. But as the day progressed, her doubts mounted. Sadie, normally docile and easy to manage, wanted to run up and down the aisle of the bus. She whined when Perla made her sit and complained about being hungry, tired, and bored. Perla felt exasperated and done in by the trials of the day. When Sadie finally fell asleep with her head in Perla's lap inside the station during a short layover to change buses, Perla caught herself dozing a bit, as well. She jerked awake with a start and looked around as if she'd been caught stealing. Sleeping in public. How mortifying.

Glancing at the clock on the wall across the room, Perla panicked. It was after the time her bus was supposed to leave. Scooping up Sadie, she ran for the door. The bus was gone. A man behind the ticket counter called out to her.

"Was that your bus? I seen you get off earlier, but I thought you was back on there."

"My bag is on that bus. What do I do?" Perla almost wailed the question.

"Easy now. They's another bus headed the same way in fifteen minutes. Two lines come acrost of one another here and go the same road for a piece. I'll do you up a new ticket. Where was you headed?"

"Pittsboro."

"Oh, that'll be fine, then. Might get there later than you planned, but you'll get there all right. I'll call up to Camden, and they'll hold your luggage."

"Thank you." Perla fought tears.

"Now, none of that. I got a girl about the size of that 'un." He pointed at Sadie with his chin. "Only glad I can help."

The later bus meant she would arrive in Pittsboro after ten o'clock. The ticket man gave her the name of a boardinghouse that was likely to have a room. "Cheap but clean," he called it. Perla said a prayer and climbed aboard another bus.

Thankfully, Sadie slept all the way to Camden, where there would be a long wait. Perla decided she wouldn't even get off the bus this time. She wasn't taking any chances on missing a ride again. When the bus pulled into the station in Camden, Sadie stirred but didn't wake. Perla leaned back against the window and cradled her daughter in her arms. They were beginning a new life. She tried to see it as an opportunity.

Staring out the window, Perla saw a man who looked very much like Casewell stick his head out the front door of the bus station and look around. He ducked back inside before she got much more than a general impression of him. She turned firmly away from the window. She would not start imagining things. She had come too far to have second thoughts now.

24

Casewell didn't find Perla inside the station. He asked if anyone had seen a woman traveling with a child, but no one had. Could she have changed routes? Did she not get off the bus and just keep going? He learned that the bus she was on had left about ten minutes before he arrived, but the ticket agent was certain there hadn't been a woman and child traveling alone. Where could she be? Casewell sat. He paced. He went outside and looked around. He had a terrible feeling that Perla had somehow disappeared into thin air. But that was impossible.

He approached the ticket man with the slicked-back hair at the counter again. He thought the man looked a little annoyed, but he didn't care.

"Look here," the man said as Casewell stepped up to the counter. "I ain't seen 'em. Don't tell me some sob story about your woman running off, neither. Odds are if she run off she had a good reason."

Casewell felt like he'd been dashed with cold water. Did she have a good reason? And then an odd sort of assurance washed over him.

"That's not it," he said to the man. He read the nameplate on the counter. "Harold, it's like this. She had a child even though she didn't have a husband. I want to marry her, and she's running off because she thinks she'll bring shame on me. But I love her. And I intend to find her no matter how far she goes."

The man sniffed and lifted his nose slightly. "Huh. Guess it's up to you, but I wouldn't want no other man's leavings."

Casewell felt a surge of anger, followed closely by an unexpected peace. "I do," he said, looking the man in the eye. "She's a jewel beyond price."

Casewell heard a stifled gasp and turned. Perla stood behind him, holding a sleepy Sadie's hand. "What did you say?" she asked, her voice catching.

"You're priceless." Casewell swept her into his arms, tears gathering in his eyes. "I thought I'd lost you."

"You did," Perla said, collapsing into his arms. "But now I'm found."

Perla's luggage had been left at the Camden station for transfer to the second bus to Pittsboro. Perla saw a porter carrying her bag outside and intercepted him. It was soon stowed in the back of Casewell's truck. Perla took Sadie to the ladies' room—the whole reason she'd gotten off the bus in the first place—and then climbed into the truck with Casewell for the long ride back to Wise.

"It's going to be very late when we get home," Casewell said as he pulled out of the lot. "But I don't think it would be quite right for us to spend the night anywhere." He glanced at Perla and smiled. "Even if you are my fiancée."

Perla gave a wry laugh. "They could hardly talk about me

any more than they already do, but you're right. It's best we get back."

She settled Sadie, who sat between them, against her side. To keep the child comfortable, Perla turned in so that she was almost facing Casewell. She admired his profile and decided she was glad he'd shaved his beard. She wasn't sure about kissing a man with a full beard. Blushing, she decided she needed another line of thinking.

"Why did you come after me?"

Casewell looked at Perla and then turned his attention back to the road. "I love you."

"But marrying me . . . it may be complicated."

"No more complicated than any other two people putting their lives together. Seems to me everyone has something about them that could give a potential spouse pause. Ma says I snore something fierce."

Perla laughed. "But what will people think? What will they say?"

"Oh, some will say I could have done better," he looked at her again. "And some will say you could have. I don't really give a hoot one way or the other."

"I imagined what it would be like if you came after me." Perla ducked her head and smoothed hair back from Sadie's sleeping brow. "I determined that I wouldn't go back with you, no matter what."

"What changed your mind?"

"I heard what you said to the ticket man. I didn't think you'd admit to anyone what . . . what I am, much less stick up for me. You said I was a jewel beyond price."

"'Her price is far above rubies.' It's from the Bible."

"I know. It's from the thirty-first chapter of Proverbs. It's talking about a virtuous woman. You took me by surprise saying that."

"Why?" Casewell flashed her a puzzled look.

"I'm hardly virtuous."

"Virtuous—upstanding and moral. I'd say that describes you."

Perla swallowed hard and was silent a moment. Casewell began to wonder if the conversation was over. Maybe she was dozing. He looked at her again. Her left hand held Sadie in place while her right was over her face. He thought she looked to be crying, and his heart lurched. What had he said or done?

"Perla? What is it?"

"I'm soiled, Casewell. Unworthy, shameful. I don't deserve you or marriage or any kind of happiness. God has been generous in allowing me to love this child. I can't ask for any more than that." She struggled for composure and lowered her hand to her mouth. She whispered from behind her fingers. "How is it that you want me?"

"'As far as the east is from the west, so far hath he removed our transgressions from us.' That's from the Psalms. Before that it says, 'The Lord is merciful and gracious, slow to anger, and plenteous in mercy. He will not always chide: neither will he keep his anger forever. He hath not dealt with us after our sins; nor rewarded us according to our iniquities. For as the heaven is high above the earth, so great is his mercy toward them that fear him.'" Casewell took one hand off the wheel and laid it over Perla's where it cradled Sadie. "God's forgiven you. I have nothing to forgive. Seems to me the only one holding anything against you is you."

Perla felt tears stream down her face. She was acutely aware of Casewell's large calloused hand caressing her own.

She lifted his hand and pressed it to her lips. "Thank you," she whispered.

Perla must have fallen asleep. When she woke, she saw a gas pump with a small filling station beyond. Casewell and Sadie were gone, and for a moment Perla panicked. But then she saw the pair walking toward her across the pavement. Odds were, Sadie had to use the bathroom again. Casewell handed the child back up into the cab of the truck. She was holding a bottle of grape Nehi with a straw sticking out.

"Hope it's okay that I took her into the men's room." Casewell flushed a little. "I hated to wake you, and she seemed pretty anxious to go."

Perla smiled and shook her head. "And now you're giving her a refill." She looked down at her daughter's purple grin and found that she didn't mind a bit.

"Hope that's okay, too." Casewell hopped up into the truck and looked at Perla as though he couldn't get enough of looking at her. "You're real pretty when you sleep," he said.

It was Perla's turn to blush. "I doubt that. Probably had my mouth hanging open, and I wouldn't be surprised to hear I snore."

"You looked like an angel."

"Where are we?" Perla asked, if only to change the subject.

"About five miles outside of Wise. Lucky we found a filling station open this early in the morning. This old truck was running on fumes." He started the engine and eased out onto the two-lane road.

"People will be up," Perla said, the color draining from her cheeks.

"Yup. I suspect they will." Casewell had his eyes on the road.

"They'll think . . . what will they think?"

He darted a glance at her. "Can't say. People tend to think what they want to think."

"But to see us out together so early in the morning—as though we'd been together all night . . ."

"We were." Now Casewell had a boyish grin on his face. "Of course, we had a chaperone." He ruffled Sadie's hair.

"Oh, Casewell. My reputation was never worth saving, but I can't bring talk like this on you."

Casewell eased the truck off the side of the road where they could look out across a pasture and see the sun peeking through the trees. "You see that sun shining through over there? Makes me think of a piece of poetry." Casewell turned and took Perla's hand in his. "The thing that hath been, it is that which shall be; and that which is done is that which shall be done: and there is no new thing under the sun."

Tears welled in Perla's eyes. "That's beautiful, but what does it mean?"

"King Solomon wrote that about a thousand years before Christ was born. Even back then nothing was new. I doubt we're breaking new ground here. And I expect that no matter what people think, their thoughts won't be original. I, for one, don't plan to waste my time wondering about it. Promise me you'll do the same?"

Perla looked deep into his eyes and promised.

25

CASEWELL SOON LEARNED ALL TOO WELL that people's thoughts about his pending nuptials weren't the least bit original. Somehow, within hours of their arrival back in Wise, the entire community knew about the engagement and felt free to share their opinion of it. And true to his word, Casewell didn't care what anyone thought—until he told his mother.

Robert and Delilah learned that Perla would marry Casewell when he dropped her off with a drowsy Sadie cradled in his arms. Delilah opened the front door before any of them even stepped onto the porch.

"I've never been so worried in my life," she said without preamble. Then she flew down the steps and wrapped Perla in her arms. "I didn't know what to think when you were just gone like that. It was a terrible thing to do."

"I know," Perla said. "I planned to write, but I thought if I told you ahead of time, you'd talk me out of it."

"I would have, too." Delilah leaned back, hands still on Perla's shoulders. "Now what's this Robert says about an engagement?"

Delilah's mood went from anger to laughter so fast Casewell couldn't keep up.

Perla blushed and looked at Casewell. "I told Casewell I'd marry him, though I'm still not sure why he wants me."

"Stop fishing for compliments," Delilah chided. "Now get that baby on into the house, and we'll have some breakfast before we start planning the wedding."

Casewell moved toward the door and spoke over his shoulder. "I appreciate the offer, Delilah, but I'd best get on to the house and tell Mom before you let the rest of the world know about this."

Delilah laughed and let him go. Ten minutes later he stepped up to his mother's screen door. He could smell coffee and bacon, and for just a moment he expected to see his father sitting at the table, eating his breakfast. For the first time since he was a boy, Casewell wished he could share something with his father. He whispered a prayer and pushed open the door. He wasn't entirely sure how Emily Phillips would feel about gaining a daughter-in-law with Perla's reputation.

"Why, Casewell, you're out and about early. Come eat some breakfast with me." His mother added more bacon to the pan before Casewell even opened his mouth.

"Glad to," he said, pouring himself a cup of the strong, black coffee sitting on the back of the stove. He settled at the table and watched his mother, her robe wrapped around her trim waist. She was still a lovely woman, and it occurred to him for the first time that she might meet someone and remarry one day.

"Ma, I have some good news."

"It must be good for you to come over here this early. Either that or you were out of breakfast fixins'."

"I'm getting married."

Emily turned toward her son, spatula in her right hand. "What in the world?"

Casewell felt like a kid. "Perla said she'd marry me." He wanted to laugh, saying it aloud like that. He'd never been so happy in his life, but first he needed to see how his mother would take the news.

Emily leaned against the chair closest to her and then eased around and slid into the seat. Casewell began to feel some concern.

"Son, I don't know what to say."

"Well, congratulations would do." He tried to grin, but his mother's pale face worried him. "Are you okay?"

"Oh, well," she said as she waved the spatula in the air. "I'm not so sure this is the best idea."

Casewell leaned back in the chair as if he thought she might try to swat him with the spatula. "Not the best idea?"

"Perla is a lovely young woman, but she's . . . well, she has that child, and there's no father to speak of. Have you really considered this?"

Casewell felt disappointment rise in him. "Ma, are you saying I shouldn't marry her because she has another man's child?"

Emily's tone sharpened along with Casewell's. "I'm just saying that you should think long and hard before taking on a woman, who, well, who didn't see fit to save herself for marriage."

"Ma, you know Perla. I guessed you thought highly of her. You treat her well, and you dote on Sadie when she's around."

"Son, the Lord said to love sinners. He didn't say anything about marrying them."

Casewell sagged in his chair. He knew it might be like this, but he'd hoped . . .

Emily jumped to her feet to save the bacon from burning. She reached for eggs piled in a blue enamel bowl. "Over easy?"

"Ma."

She began cracking eggs into the hot grease.

"Ma, look at me."

His mother sighed and her shoulders slumped. She turned to Casewell with an empty eggshell in her hand.

"Ma, I'm going to marry Perla. And I think Dad would be proud of me for it."

A tear slipped from the corner of Emily's eye and caught in the wrinkles around her mouth. "You're probably right," she said. "I'll get used to the idea, too. She is a lovely woman. I just wish . . ."

"I know." Casewell stood and wrapped an arm around his mother's shoulders. "Jesus died for her sins just the same as for mine." Mom took a breath as though to speak, but Casewell continued before she could. "There's no hierarchy of sin, Ma. The Bible doesn't say one sin is worse than another. 'The wages of sin is death.' That's any sin—from little white lies all the way to murder. And Jesus wiped them all away on the cross. It's like starting over fresh." He smiled. "Perla and I will start over fresh. Only"—his smile broadened—"only we get Sadie out of the deal."

Casewell knew when he proposed to Perla and when he drove through the night to fetch her home that people in the community of Wise would likely frown on their union. He knew marrying a woman with a child who wasn't a widow was bold. But he also knew that Perla was the woman for him. Even so, he was surprised by the vehemence some of his neighbors expressed when the news got around. Hardly anyone was critical to Casewell's face, but he got cold shoulders, curt conversations, and an absolute halt to any woodworking business he might have done.

"Wish I needed you to build me some shelves or something," Robert said one afternoon when Casewell was loitering around the store. "Say, maybe you could come over and fix that old handrail on the front porch."

"Robert, I'll be glad to do that," Casewell said.

Robert brightened and moved toward the cash register.

"At no cost." Casewell held up a hand to stop his friend. "Don't worry, Robert. I've saved most all I've made over the years—never had much to spend it on except strings for the mandolin. Every time I took a notion to get me some fancy new woodworking tool, I reminded myself that I could make do with what I have. I've got no worries."

"Don't you?" It was Delilah coming from the storeroom. "Seems to me the town gossips have your worries lined up for you."

"Guess they've saved me the trouble." Casewell chuckled. "Life is full of challenges, no matter what I do. Seems to me, having a good woman to stand beside me will make things easier. Folks will talk. Eventually something else will come along that's more interesting." He shrugged. "And eventually folks will need a new milking stool, or maybe the steps will fall off the back stoop, or someone will want a fancy mantel for their fireplace. And then they'll forget that I married a woman who's no more sinful than they are, and they'll come round and hire me. Then they'll complain about what I charge, but they'll pay it because it's not a penny too much."

Delilah smiled and patted Casewell on the shoulder. "Right you are." She turned to Robert. "If we had any doubts he was really and truly in love, that speech there would put them to rest. Only a man in love can look on the bright side like that."

26

CASEWELL AND ROBERT CONTINUED to lead church services. The presbytery promised to send them a new pastor as soon as one was available, but so far there didn't seem to be many candidates vying for a small rural church with little money and strong opinions.

So Robert led the singing and read the Scriptures, and Casewell got up and talked about what he'd been reading in the Bible, and they both prayed. On this Sunday, Casewell asked if there were any prayer requests. He got the usual—Marion Cornwell's feet hurt so bad she could hardly walk, the first of the season's sniffles and coughs had struck, and someone's great-aunt had passed the night before. And then Cathy Stott rose to her feet, her son Travis on her hip. The red-faced child scrubbed his ear with one chubby fist.

"I got a complaint," she announced.

Casewell was taken aback. He'd never had a complaint during prayers before.

"All right," he said at last. "We can take that before the Lord, too."

"That woman what was supposed to of healed Travis of his ear trouble didn't do the job."

Casewell looked confused and glanced at Robert, who shrugged.

"Her," Cathy said, pointing to where Perla sat in the third pew from the front. "She give Travis a holy kiss that was supposed to cure him, and it didn't take. Just look at him." She waved a hand at her son who, Casewell suspected, was quiet only because he was too worn-out to cry anymore.

Perla's eyes widened and she shook her head. "I didn't heal anyone," she whispered.

"Durn right," Cathy said. "Now I want somebody to do something about it."

Casewell spread his hands wide. "Cathy, I don't know what anyone can do—"

"Either get her to do it right or run her on out of here. We don't need the likes of her around if she ain't at least good for healing folks."

Several people in the congregation began to look uncomfortable, and there was a soft rustling and shifting like chickens sensing a varmint outside the henhouse. Even Mom shifted uneasily in her seat next to Perla, who just looked stunned.

Travis chose that moment to find his second wind. He began to squall and his mother rolled her eyes heavenward.

"Day and night, night and day. This is what I've got to live with. Somebody better do something, or I'm gonna give him to the fairies."

Mom stood and stepped across the aisle, holding out her arms for the disconsolate child. Cathy gave him up only too gladly.

"Right. Take him on over there and have her fix him up."

She nodded at Perla. "If'n you can't do it, just take him with you when you shake the dust of this town off your feet."

Mom sat and began to cuddle and rock the little boy, who continued to rub at his ear. His cries kept on, but they seemed almost habitual, like it was just what he was used to. Sadie crept closer and patted the little boy's leg.

Casewell took a step closer to the mother. "Cathy, you've got to understand, there's nothing Perla or any of the rest of us can do right now. Maybe we can take up a collection and see if we can get him to a city doctor. But in the meantime I'd appreciate it if you'd stop talking like that about Perla. She's going to marry me, and she'll be staying right here."

Cathy heaved a sigh and flopped down in her pew. "Fine. But seems to me the least you'uns can do is keep him for a while and give me a rest. If you ain't gonna heal him, then take him on home and see how you like that howling all the time. As for a wedding, I reckon I'll believe that when I see it."

Casewell stiffened. "What do you mean by that?"

"You marrying the town tart has been the word going around for a time now. Seems to me if you was gonna marry her, you'd have done it by now." She slanted a sly look at Perla. "Only one reason to marry a woman like that, and if'n you don't hurry, everybody will soon see what's what."

Casewell felt his cheeks flush hot. He tried to control the red creeping up his neck, but the harder he tried the hotter he felt. He took two steps backward until he was once again standing near the pulpit. "Any other prayer requests?" There weren't any.

Robert closed the service with a short prayer. When he dismissed everyone, the whole congregation seemed to lunge for the door as one body. Casewell imagined if someone were on the roof looking down at the front stoop, it would look like a string of soap bubbles rushing down a creek. In minutes the church was empty except for Perla, Sadie, and his mother, still holding little Travis. She wore an astonished look.

"Guess we're babysitting this afternoon." Casewell tried to sound light, but he was as uncomfortable as he'd ever been in his life.

"I'll be happy to tend to him." Perla glanced around. "But for heaven's sake don't let anyone see me with him. Who knows what they'll think I've done to him this time?"

"Poor little thing." Emily stroked Travis's hair. He gave a shuddering sigh. "I think his ears have bothered him almost every day of his short life. Cathy does need a break. We should be ashamed that we haven't offered to do this before." She snuggled the boy against her shoulder. "Come on, little one. We'll pray over your ears all afternoon."

Sadie patted the boy again, and they all headed to Emily's for Sunday dinner.

Travis was better than they expected that afternoon. Casewell suspected he was used to life with sore ears and had learned to sleep and eat in spite of them. After dinner the little boy sagged against Perla's shoulder. She took him to her room and put him on the bed for a nap. Sadie, who had recently begun to resist napping, lay down beside him with one chubby little hand on his arm. Soon both children were sleeping, and Perla slipped out to see if Emily needed help clearing up.

Emily had already finished in the kitchen and sat on the porch with Casewell, who didn't seem much inclined to talk.

Perla sat next to him on the porch swing. They drifted to and fro in silence.

"I think we should get married as soon as Reverend Jones from over at the Methodist church is available to marry us," Casewell said without preamble.

"Do you?" Perla kept her voice light.

"Yes. I didn't realize how people were . . . doubting my intentions." He took Perla's hand in his. "And I don't want to give you a chance to get cold feet." He squeezed her hand.

Mom stood and offered to check on the children. Perla waved her back into her chair. "They're fine. I just left them and I'd like you to be part of any plans we make."

She sat again and looked out across the fields. "Perla, I suppose you know I struggle with knowing your . . . situation. And your marrying my son, considering that. I've been praying about it, though, and the Lord has reminded me of one or two second chances He's offered me over the years." She turned warm eyes on Perla. "All in all, I do believe I'll be mighty proud to call you daughter."

She turned and looked at Casewell. "But, son, I think I ought to point out that you've skipped an important step in this whole process."

Casewell looked bewildered. He thought all they needed to do was pick a date and stand up in front of a preacher. "I'm not sure what you mean," he said slowly.

"Seems to me you need to give Perla a promise ring."

Casewell cringed. Everything had happened so quickly, he hadn't given a moment's thought to a ring. Not that he could afford much, but maybe he could take Perla to the city and find something. While he was racking his brain for a way out of his dilemma, his mother leaned over from her rocker, took his hand, and pressed something into the palm. He looked down to find a sparkling ring.

"Your father gave it to me on our twenty-fifth anniversary," his mother explained. "I hardly ever wore it. I worried I'd spoil it somehow. I know it would please him no end to see it on Perla's hand."

Casewell turned to Perla. Tears streaked her cheeks. He knelt down from the swing and took her hand. "Will you marry me just as soon as I can run the preacher to ground?"

Perla laughed out loud and fell into his arms.

"So I'll give the preacher a call, then?" he asked. "Is next Sunday too soon?"

"Son, don't be silly," his mother said. "It can wait a few more days. Perla needs a little bit of time to get ready for her wedding."

Perla laughed again. "I've been getting ready for a long time. Waiting even one more day seems too long." She turned toward Casewell, and the look of love in her eyes brought tears to his. He realized he couldn't wait to make this woman his bride.

As the adults were talking over plans, Sadie stepped out onto the porch. She held a jar of grape juice with both hands. The lid was off and some of the juice had spilled down the front of her dress.

"Oh, Sadie, were you thirsty? Sweetie, you should have let me get that." Perla rushed to the child and took the jar from her. As she lifted it, she wrinkled her nose and raised the jar for a closer smell.

"This has fermented. Sadie, did you drink this?"

"No, Mama, it's medicine."

Perla looked confused. "Medicine? For what?"

"For Travis. He needed medicine for his ears, so I got some."

Perla's eyebrows shot up, and she rushed into the bedroom, Casewell and Emily close on her heels. Travis still lay on the bed, awake but peaceful in spite of the juice-stained sheets bunched up around him. It looked like something horrific had taken place, but Travis actually smiled and laughed a bit. He held his arms out to be picked up, and Perla lifted him. As she did, she noticed something in his right ear. She started to tug it out.

"No, Mama, that keeps the medicine in," Sadie said.

Casewell lifted Sadie into his arms. "Did you put grape juice in Travis's ears?"

"At church we drink the juice because it's from Jesus," said Sadie. "It wouldn't stay in his ears, so I stopped them up."

Emily checked both ears as Travis rested happily in Perla's arms. "She's plugged them up with some cotton batting from my quilt supplies. I guess there's some juice up in there, too."

"Will it hurt him? Shouldn't we pull it out?" Perla sounded alarmed.

"I can't see how it would hurt him," Mom said. "Might be like having water in your ears, but that could be a nice change for the poor little thing."

"He seems happy," Casewell said. "Maybe we should leave it alone. Maybe it is medicine."

"We'd better get him cleaned up, if nothing else," Perla said. "He smells like he's been on a two-week drunk."

An hour later Travis, washed and wrapped in one of Casewell's old shirts while his own things dried on the clothesline, remained happy. Perla finally removed the batting from his ears, and although he shook his head a little, he didn't cry.

"Could he really be cured?" Perla wondered.

"I hope so." Emily settled him on the floor, where he could play with some blocks Casewell had fashioned.

"Well, if he is, I'm going home before his mother comes back. I don't want anyone to think I did it. Goodness knows what they'd expect of me after that."

"Guess performing miracles runs in the family," Casewell said with a wink. "Ma, I'll run Perla and Sadie back over to the Thorntons'. Should I fetch Cathy on my way back?"

"Yes, please. I'm fair worn-out with all of this business. His clothes are almost dry, so I should have him ready to go home by the time you get back."

By evening Travis was returned to his mother's arms. Emily told Cathy that if she continued to have trouble with Travis's ears, she should put a little rubbing alcohol on some cotton batting and stuff it into the sore ear. Cathy looked skeptical, but she was pleased that her son seemed happier than he had in a long time. She took the bit of cotton Emily gave her and offered grudging thanks. Casewell took the pair home and resisted the temptation to tell Cathy he and Perla had set a date. That news would get around soon enough.

❦

The news did spread. Delilah invited everyone who stopped by the store. Casewell made sure the Talbot sisters and Frank knew about the wedding, and Emily shared with her friends. But the news was not met with enthusiasm. Casewell and Emily were at the store chatting with Delilah when Liza and Angie stopped by for a sack of flour.

"Emily, what can we do to help with the wedding?" Angie asked.

"I could use some help with the food. Perla tried to tell me she'd make everything, but of course I put my foot down and told her she couldn't cook for her own wedding."

"Oh, yes." Liza clapped her hands. "I'll make those little pink and green mints. How many do you think you'll need?"

Emily glanced at her son, then Delilah, who jumped in. "Well, we were just talking about that. Seems like maybe we won't have much of a crowd."

"Why? Isn't the whole town invited?" Angie asked.

"Of course, of course." Delilah hesitated. "But I don't think they'll come. Seems maybe there's still some hard feelings about Perla already having a child. And then all that business with the food this summer . . . People are funny." She shrugged her shoulders.

"I had hard feelings," Emily whispered. She twisted her mouth a little to one side and took Casewell's hand. "I've liked Perla from the day I met her, but to have her marry my son . . . Well, I've had a good long talk with the Lord, and He's helped me see past my own shortcomings. What I'm saying, though, is I can understand how some folks might feel funny about coming to the wedding."

"People have been fools since the beginning of time," said Angie. "There's not one of us without sin—not one. I just wish Jesus were here to ask those old fools which sinless one of them wants to cast the first stone."

Liza nodded her head one time hard. "We'll just have a nice wedding without them. I guess the four of us—and Casewell, of course—love Perla and Sadie enough for the rest of the world."

Emily and Delilah smiled. Fine then, they'd put on a wedding for themselves.

In spite of Perla's protests, Delilah quickly took over as chief planner of the wedding feast. She and Robert would provide a ham and biscuits. Liza would make her mints and a batch of divinity. Angie would supply an array of pickled items, from cucumbers to watermelon rind. Emily, with her chickens thriving again, would supply chicken-salad and egg-salad sandwiches. They would work together to bake a wedding cake.

"With a little bride and groom perched on top," Liza said.

"We don't have one." Delilah sighed. "And it's much too late to order one. We'll have to do without."

Liza grinned and reached into the pocket of her skirt. She pulled up some crackling tissue paper and handed it to Perla. "I thought I'd be getting married once upon a time," she said.

Unfurling the paper, Perla gasped when she saw the figurine. The groom wore a suit, black and shiny, and the bride had a bit of netting stuck to her head. They weren't entirely in fashion, but they would top the cake nicely.

As it turned out, Reverend Jones was available a week from Saturday. Casewell announced his wedding date in church that Sunday, but he didn't notice the downcast eyes or the shuffling feet. All he could see was Perla and Sadie, his girls.

Casewell had his only suit cleaned and pressed. Perla decided that she would make do with her pale-yellow dress for the wedding. But Emily had other plans. She invited Perla over for lunch—just the two of them.

Perla arrived with a lemon pound cake in hand. She just couldn't bring herself to leave all the cooking up to someone else.

"You shouldn't have gone to all that trouble," Emily said. "I'll have to get Casewell over here to help me eat this."

"It was no trouble." Perla felt shy now that Emily was about to become her mother-in-law.

Emily put the cake on the counter and turned back to Perla, running her hands down over her company apron, which was perfectly pressed and spotless. "Perla, I wanted to say something to you."

Perla thought she'd better go ahead and sit down, so she slid into a kitchen chair. The table was set for two, with a platter of sandwiches and a pot of soup that smelled wonderful—like rosemary.

Emily slid into her seat, as well. "I've wronged you," she said and folded her hands against the edge of the table. "I was against you marrying Casewell, and I'm sorry. I had a hard time accepting that you had a child out of wedlock."

Perla could see the older woman's knuckles whiten as she squeezed her hands together.

"The Lord reminded me that I have sins of my own. He also reminded me that it's not my job to judge other people." She looked up and met Perla's eyes. "There's more than enough judging that goes on around here. I'm sorry I took it upon myself to judge you too sinful for my son. There's not one of us too sinful for God's own Son. How could I think mine's better?" She cleared her throat and sat up a little straighter. "What I want to tell you is that I'm proud you're marrying Casewell, and I'm pleased more than I can say that I'm about to become a grandmother."

Perla smiled and placed a hand over Emily's, massaging just a little to ease the tension there. She found that she felt much more relaxed than when she'd first come in. "Sadie is blessed to gain such a father and a grandmother all in one day. Thank you for asking me over, and thank you for, well, for telling me how you feel."

"There." Emily released her hands and sat back. "Now we can eat and start getting to know each other as mother and daughter."

After they finished eating, Emily led Sadie into the bedroom she had shared with John. "I have something to show you," she said.

Laid out on the rose-carved bed was a dress. Perla gasped when she saw it.

"Is this your wedding dress?"

"It is. John said I looked like an angel coming down the aisle toward him. He wasn't given to compliments, so I always held that one dear."

The dress was simple but lovely. Emily explained that in wartime it had been hard to find much finery, but she had been gifted with bits and pieces from the women in her family, and together they had made this lovely gown. It was ankle length, with lace peeping out from the hem, and had a high frilled neck. A lace veil clung to a small cap. Emily caressed the veil. "My grandmother's lace," she said. "Maybe one day Sadie will wear it."

"Are you saying you want me to wear this?" Perla asked.

"Only if you'd like to. You probably already have something to wear, but I wanted to offer."

Perla swallowed hard and slid a hand over the softness of the dress. Tears blurred her vision. "I'd be honored to wear this."

"Then that's settled," Emily said. "Try it on and we'll see if it needs taking in."

The dress did need a few adjustments, but nothing Emily's quick needle couldn't handle. In short order Perla had a dress, a feast, an adorable little flower girl, and best of all, a groom.

When Perla got home, she told Delilah all about the dress, but her aunt seemed distracted. Finally Perla asked if something was wrong.

"We had a visitor while you were out." Delilah cut her eyes toward the ceiling.

Perla felt a cold knot form in the pit of her stomach. "Yes? Who was it?"

"It was Cathy with Travis. He was caterwauling again."

Perla felt the knot loosen. Why would Delilah hesitate to tell her about Cathy?

"She insisted that you'd cured him once before and wanted you to do it again. I told her you'd done no such thing, and you weren't home, anyway." Delilah sighed and rolled her eyes. "I asked her if she'd used rubbing alcohol in the child's ears like we told her to, and she said she didn't want old wives' tales. She wanted the real thing.

"I guess Sadie heard that poor young'un carrying on, and before I knew what she was doing, she'd fetched out that jar of juice. Cathy set Travis down on the hearth rug there, and Sadie got at him quicker than anything. She had a piece of old rag soaked in juice stuffed in that boy's ear just like that." Delilah snapped her fingers. "And wouldn't you know, Travis stopped crying."

Perla smiled a little at that. "Well, good. He must have remembered it felt better last time Sadie did that. Of course, plain grape juice probably wouldn't work so well as alcohol, but maybe it was soothing all the same."

Delilah looked at the ceiling again. "It might be she used the fermented jar again."

"Didn't you dump that out?"

"Now, Perla, lots of folks let a jar or two of juice turn. Sadie was right. It's good medicine."

Perla stared at her aunt, and then a smile began to spread across her face. "Well, now. I guess maybe it is." She laughed. "What in the world did Cathy do?"

"She took the jar with her when she left."

Perla began to laugh in earnest. "Oh my. I hope Travis gets some for his ears."

"Even if he doesn't, I think it might put Cathy in a better frame of mind to tolerate all that crying." Now Delilah was laughing, too.

"The Lord works in mysterious ways," Perla said.

27

DELILAH AND EMILY ROSE EARLY the day of the wedding to direct Casewell, Robert, George, and Steve in decorating the church. They sent the men out to cut armloads of the prettiest autumn leaves and any flowers they could find. While everything had been dead and dusty just two months earlier, nature seemed intent on making up for lost time with an exceptionally lush and colorful autumn that had lasted well into November. Delilah raided the sewing section of the store for lengths of ribbon and lace to tie bunches of leaves to the pews. Mason jars and vases filled with autumn flowers sat on every available surface. Wreaths with leaves, apples, grapes, and rose hips graced the front doors of the church.

All was ready when Casewell went home to change and then arrive an hour early to pace and fret. He wanted to go to the Thorntons' house and watch Perla's every move. He couldn't bear the thought of her slipping away from him again. Robert arrived about the time Casewell was debating driving by the Thorntons' to be sure Perla was really there.

"A mite early, aren't you?"

"I had nothing else to do." Casewell clasped his hands behind his back and paced between the two front doors of the church. "Shouldn't the women be here by now? Shouldn't someone be here by now?" He looked at his watch. "It's not more than twenty-five minutes until the wedding."

Robert grinned. "Women take their own sweet time most days. I've found they tend to fiddle around even more on wedding days." The smile slipped a little. "As for everyone else, I'm not sure there will be all that many. Seems like some folks are still a little shy of Perla."

"What are you talking about?"

"Not everyone thinks Perla is the best choice for you, Casewell." Robert held up a hand as Casewell began to protest. "I'm not suggesting they're a bit right. But people are funny, and some of them might stay home today. Of course, those are the ones that aren't worth having here."

Delilah and Emily finally arrived with Perla, not long after Frank escorted the Talbot sisters into the church. Frank looked like he was ready to attend his own wedding, dapper in a suit with his white hair slicked back. Angie and Liza wore matching plum-colored, high-necked dresses with lace overlays, lace gloves, and old-fashioned hats with short veils. Angie grumped about wearing matching clothes, something she never cared for among twins. But when Robert bowed low to the ground and said she'd never looked prettier, she smiled, rapped him on the shoulder, and accused him of being a flatterer and a scoundrel.

A handful of other folks from the church were also there, milling around, but it looked like the prediction of a small gathering would come true. Emily leaned over to Delilah and whispered that she was a little bit relieved, seeing as how they had only enough food for those they counted on.

❧

Perla waited for Casewell to disappear inside before she slipped out of the backseat of the car with Sadie, who looked less like an angel than an impish sprite. Her reddish curls had been tamed early that morning, but they were already beginning to escape and fly about her head.

Inside the church, Mavis Sanders, already the church's primary piano player though only in her early teens, struck up a passable rendition of the wedding march. Perla moved toward the church door closest to her and took a deep breath. But before she could send Sadie down the aisle, she heard the purr of a car coming up the mountain. Or perhaps it was the sound of two cars.

Those still outside turned to see who the latecomer was as a parade of cars began to fill the gravel lot and spill over onto the grass. Perla gaped as people began pouring out of the cars, Cathy in the lead and carrying Travis.

"Hey, there," Cathy called out. "We've come to see the marrying." She stepped up to Perla and made a face that might have been her attempt at a smile. "That child there," she said, pointing at Sadie with her chin, "has a heart of gold and showed more kindness to my little 'un than anyone else. I reckon anyone who raises a child up like that is better than some. Seems like the least we can do is come on out and see that this child gets a mama and a daddy." She looked at the ground, then raised her eyes to meet Perla's. "I guess I'm right proud to have you marry into our church."

Cathy moved on inside, and a stream of people, most of

whom Perla had helped feed over the long dry summer, walked by her nodding, shaking her hand, and even giving her hugs. When the last person stepped inside the church, it was standing room only.

There was a moment's quiet; then Mavis started playing again. Delilah sent Sadie down the aisle and then gave Perla a little tug toward the door. Perla shot her a wild look. "It'll be fine," hissed Delilah. "I'm going to walk down that aisle, and you'd better be right behind me. Trust me, I'll come back and get you if you aren't."

Twenty minutes later the crowd began spilling out both doors, ready to celebrate.

"What in the world are we going to do?" Casewell heard his mother ask Delilah. "We can never feed this many."

"We'll feed them until the food is gone. I can't see what else there is to do. I guess I could get some stuff in tins from down at the store, but that doesn't seem right."

Mom tried to smile and shoved her son away. "Guess we should have let Perla cook after all."

Delilah laughed. "You know, the Lord has provided before. Who's to say He won't do it again?"

Casewell didn't care if anyone ate—he was married and that was all that mattered.

Perla watched in stunned amazement as the crowd found their way to Robert and Delilah's house for the reception, where guests crammed into every nook and cranny. The dining room, which could seat twelve, became a buffet, with the chairs pulled out from the table and arranged around the house in the living room, on the porch, and even under a tree in the front yard. Delilah, Emily, and the Talbot sisters set out what food they had. Emily shook her head and allowed as how it wouldn't go far.

And then the guests began to add their bounty to the feast. Cathy had plates of deviled eggs, as did several other ladies. Perla counted six apple pies and several loaves of light bread with fresh butter and jars of preserves. There was a haunch of venison, braised rabbit, and fried chicken piled high on platters. Bowls of vegetables sat next to cakes of cornbread. Fudge found its place beside bowls of freshly cracked walnuts. And the food just kept coming.

Cathy edged up next to Emily and handed Travis over to be cuddled. "We figured you might not be expecting the lot of us, so we decided to pitch in." She smiled at Travis, who was resting his head on Emily's shoulder. "He likes you'uns." She scuffed a foot and tucked her hands behind her back. "I'm grateful for the cure Sadie done showed me. And I'm sorry for any trouble I caused."

"No trouble," Emily said. She rested her cheek on Travis's curly brown hair. "No trouble at all."

"It's a miracle," Casewell said. He tucked Perla snug against his side as everyone he'd ever known and a few he had yet to meet paraded through the house with full plates and ready words of congratulation.

"The food?" asked Perla.

"No. That you're my wife. I wasn't sure it would happen."

"Neither was I." Perla gave her husband an impish grin,

and he smiled back down at her as if they were the only two people in the overcrowded house. "I think Sadie is the star this evening," she added as their daughter pranced by with several children following in her wake.

"Sadie is a blessing better than any of us deserves," Casewell said.

Then he leaned over and kissed his wife, not caring who was watching.

Acknowledgments

HOW MANY PEOPLE DOES IT TAKE to write a book? How many people do I know? I wish I could personally thank every person who has touched my life because, in some way, each of them has contributed to my writing. There are a few, however, I'd like to thank specifically.

My parents, Larry and Nancy Loudin, who each passed on their love-of-words gene so that I got a double dose. My great-aunt Bess who taught me all about God, sometimes with words. Grandma Burla who taught me you don't have to be a blood relation to love someone a bushel and a peck and a hug around the neck. And my brothers, David and Daniel Loudin, who gave me SO much fodder for my stories.

And then there's my agent, Wendy Lawton, who loved my book just as it was. My editors, David and Sarah Long, as well as Sharon Asmus, who were generous in their praise and delicate in their suggestions for improvement. And all the folks at Bethany House who walked me through this publication process. Thank goodness you know what you're doing, 'cause I'm still figuring this out.

Thanks to the women of Christian fiction who have walked this road with me—sometimes briefly and sometimes mile after plodding (plotting?) mile. Laura Frantz, Heather Gilbert, Yvonne Lehman, Jennifer Major, Cindy Sproles, Ann Tatlock, and all of the Blue Ridge Writers.

Then there are the friends who don't necessarily write, but who gather around me to pray, support, and love on me. Meg Barbour, Christy Bennett, Jeannie Burns, Madeline Dillingham, Suzi Gibbs, Lisa McCallister, Carla McLendon, Jessie Ogle, Judy Ross, Rhonda Turpin, Buffy White, and Joan Wilson.

Penultimate thanks (isn't that the *best* word?) go to the man who has been there every step of the way. Thanks for being patient—mostly—with the hours of writing, rewriting, social media, conferences, and so on. I literally couldn't have done this without my husband, Jim Thomas, cheering me on. God knew what He was doing that night He rained out a football game.

Finally, ultimate thanks go to God. I don't know why He made me a writer, but He did, and I know His plan is perfect. I thank Him for the gift of words and for the patient endurance to write them.

Sarah Loudin Thomas is a fund-raiser for Black Mountain Home for Children, Youth and Families. She has published free-lance writing for *Now & Then* magazine as well as the Asheville *Citizen-Times* and the *Journey Christian Newspaper*. Her poetry has appeared in *Now & Then*, *Appalachian Heritage*, and the *Pisgah Review*. She holds a bachelor's degree in English from Coastal Carolina University. She and her husband reside in Asheville, North Carolina. Learn more at www.SarahLoudinThomas.com.

Reader Discussion Questions

1. When Perla shared Sadie's parentage with Casewell, he judged her. In what ways do you judge other people? Have you ever kept information to yourself because you didn't want to be judged?
2. John, Emily, and Casewell each deal with John's cancer diagnosis differently. How have you handled difficult information in your life?
3. John assumes people are praying for him but doubts that it will have any effect. What effect do you think prayer has in people's lives?
4. Perla says that things always work out—not necessarily the way we expect—but they work out. Do you agree with that statement? Why or why not?
5. People tried to explain Perla's gift away by calling it witchcraft. How do we try to explain away the miraculous? Have you ever witnessed something you couldn't explain?
6. Perla talks about people's tendency to place labels on one another. How have you labeled others? How have you been labeled?

7. The community came together to help one another during the drought. How have you seen people come together in times of need?
8. Casewell is called upon to preach a sermon at church. If you had to preach a sermon, what topic would you choose? Why?
9. Casewell thinks he needs a lesson in wooing Perla. In your opinion, what's the best way to show someone you care about them?
10. Perla feels unworthy of love—have you ever felt unworthy? What do you think makes people worth loving?
11. Although Emily has been kind to Perla, she has qualms when it comes to her son marrying a "scarlet woman." Have you ever caught yourself having double standards?
12. Ultimately, just about everyone in the novel needed to be forgiven. Who do you need to ask for forgiveness? Who do you need to forgive? What stands in your way?

More Fiction From Bethany House

When voyageur Pierre Durant is reunited with his childhood friend Angelique, they must both decide where their loyalties lie. Caught in the midst of the fight for British-occupied Mackinac Island, will they do their duty to their country, their families, or their hearts?

Captured by Love by Jody Hedlund
jodyhedlund.com

A powerful retelling of the story of Esther! In 1944, blond-haired and blue-eyed Jewess Hadassah Benjamin will do all she can to save her people—even if she cannot save herself.

For Such a Time by Kate Breslin
katebreslin.com

With her job on the line and her heart all a-muddle, aspiring actress Ellis Eton discovers what might be her role of a lifetime....

Love Comes Calling by Siri Mitchell
sirimitchell.com

BETHANYHOUSE

Stay up-to-date on your favorite books and authors with our free e-newsletters. Sign up today at bethanyhouse.com.

Find us on Facebook. facebook.com/bethanyhousepublishers

Free exclusive resources for your book group! bethanyhouse.com/anopenbook

You May Also Enjoy

Working side by side at a rural medical practice in 1935 Alaska, will nurse Gwyn Hillerman and Dr. Jeremiah Vaughan find hope or heartbreak?

All Things Hidden by Tracie Peterson and Kimberley Woodhouse
traciepeterson.com
kimberleywoodhouse.com

United in a quest to cure tuberculosis, can physician Trevor McDonough and statistician Kate Livingston overcome past secrets and current threats to find hope for a future together?

With Every Breath by Elizabeth Camden
elizabethcamden.com

When an abandoned child brings Nick Lovelace and Anne Tillerton together, is Nick prepared to risk his future plans for an unexpected chance at love?

Caught in the Middle by Regina Jennings
reginajennings.com